Last Call, *Cairo*

A NOVEL

Julie Tulba

OTHER BOOKS BY JULIE TULBA

The Tears of Yesteryear
The Auschwitz Photograph
(originally published as *The Dead Are Resting*)
Red Clay Ashes

To my one and only Nanny Lum- best baker,
pen pal, doll dressmaker-
And BEST beloved grandmother.
Always my number one fan.

AUTHOR'S DISCLAIMER:

This is a complete work of fiction. Names, characters, places, and incidents either are the product of the author's imagination or are used fictitiously, and any resemblance to actual persons, living or dead, business establishments, events, or locales is entirely coincidental.

Note: The symbol used for section breaks is called "The Eye of Horus." It's an ancient Egyptian symbol that represents healing, protection, and well-being.

"Never say goodbye because goodbye means going away and going away means forgetting."
-*Peter and Wendy* by J.M. Barrie

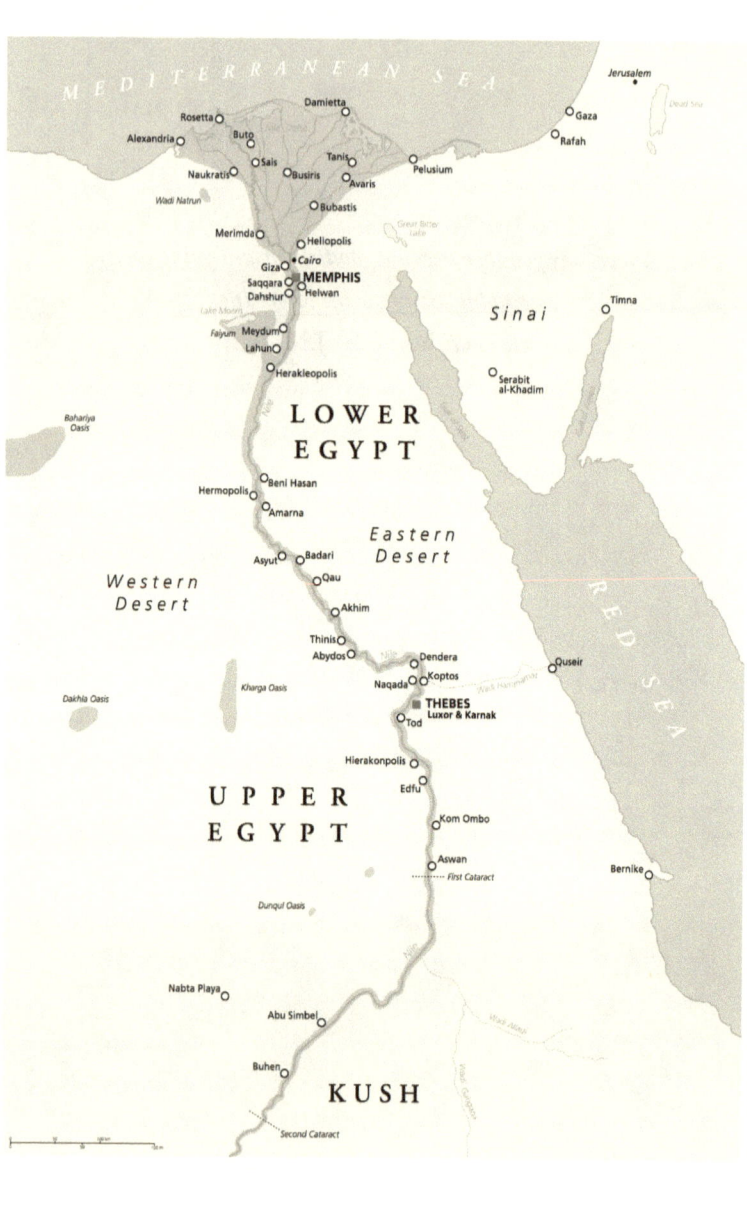

MEDITERRANEAN SEA

Jerusalem

Rosetta ○   Damietta ○
Alexandria ○   Buto ○   Tanis ○   Gaza ○
              Sais ○   Busiris ○   Rafah ○
    Naukratis ○   Avaris ○
                    ○ Busiris ○ Pelusium
Wadi Natrun

              ○ Bubastis
  Merimda ○   ○ Heliopolis
          Giza ○ ● Cairo
      Saqqara ○ ■ MEMPHIS
      Dahshur ○ ○ Helwan
                                        Sinai   Timna ○
Faiyum ○ Meydum
Lake Moeris   ○ Lahun
          ○ Herakleopolis
                                        ○ Serabit
                                          al-Khadim

Bahariya
Oasis   **LOWER**
                 EGYPT

              ○ Beni Hasan
  Hermopolis ○
          ○ Amarna   *Eastern*
                              Desert

Western   Asyut ○ ○ Badari
Desert   ○ Qau

                    ○ Akhim
          Thinis ○
          Abydos ○   ○ Dendera
                    Naqada ○○ Koptos   ○ Quseir
Dakhla Oasis   Kharga Oasis   ■ **THEBES**
                          ○   Luxor & Karnak
                          ○ Tod
                                                        RED SEA
              Hierakonpolis ○
                      Edfu ○

    UPPER
    EGYPT   ○ Kom Ombo

                      ○ Aswan
Dunqul Oasis   ·········· *First Cataract*
                                                Bernike ○

  Nabta Playa ○
          ○ Abu Simbel

          ○ Buhen
              KUSH

          ·········· *Second Cataract*

PROLOGUE

"So, I guess we're the lonely 'three' of the tour?" the young man jovially asked as he pulled a chair from the table. The two older women, who hadn't been talking to each other at all, looked up in surprise. Judging by the looks on their faces, the man wasn't sure what had surprised them more- the fact that he'd had the audacity to sit down uninvited (and yet the table they occupied contained the sole remaining empty chair) or that he was a man (although now upon closer inspection of their faces he deemed them both far too old to have been part of the bra burning contingent of the 70s).

"I'm not lonely," said the slightly younger looking woman of the two in a stern and somewhat unwelcoming tone. She spoke in a rather peculiar accent, one the young man couldn't place.

"I don't know her," the other woman replied and the man could immediately place an English accent. Well, that explains the frigid air, he thought. But he was just happy they had both heard him over the loud and blaring music that the belly dancer was, as his *yiayia* would say, "doing her thing to." He would never say this out loud, at least not in front of the suffragette contingent as he would dub the two elderly ladies, but he was surprised by how rather rotund the dancer was. Granted, this wasn't Arabia and yet he had still pictured any Egyptian belly dancer to look like Disney's Princess Jasmine, not someone whose belly protruded over her sheer and gauzy scarlet red pants legs.

"Well, mind if I join you?" he said now, realizing it was much more of a polite afterthought considering he was already seated, doing his best to tuck his very long legs uncomfortably at his sides lest they accidentally brush up against one of the women and set off an international incident.

"Seeing as how you're already seated, I think you can forgo the asking part," the woman with the peculiar accent said. She still wasn't smiling but the man could already feel a slight thawing of temperatures. Pure irony considering the oppressive Cairo heat. It was almost eight o'clock at night and the temperature was still above 90 degrees. No one in their group had wanted to sit indoors even though the restaurant's air-conditioning was at its max. Every time a waiter came and went through the automatic doors, a fresh arctic blast would waft their way, for all of a few seconds. Then the stagnant hot air would return just as quickly.

But it was worth it, all three of them were thinking at that very moment. For in front of them, set against the backdrop of beautiful illuminating floodlights, sat the Great Pyramid, and my God, if that wasn't a sight you would always remember. Air-conditioning and sweating through one's clothes be damned. A more than 4,000-year-old structure sat there before their very eyes. But this was the Mena House after all. A hotel in operation for more than 100 years whose sublime location made tourists lust for it- it was situated next to the pyramids and a royal hunting lodge before that. There wasn't a tourist in all of Egypt who wouldn't want to stay here if given the chance.

"I'm Jimmy," the man said, extending his hand first to the British woman, and then the younger one.

"Eleanor," the British woman said, taking his hand in hers.

When Jimmy turned to proffer his hand towards the other woman, she regarded it almost quizzically. As if when earlier he thought she acted like she was from another time, a time where women, even if they were what, 70, 80 years old, didn't shake men's hands even if it was almost 2000. But then rather reluctantly, she finally accepted.

"Lux."

"So, first time to Egypt for you ladies?" Jimmy said, not sure why he so desperately wanted to win over women who could have been his *yiayia's* age.

"I'd say you're being rather rude, asking so many questions," Eleanor said, "but then you are a Yank after all, the rudest, most impertinent of bunches if I ever saw any."

And here Jimmy had thought the Brit would be the easier of the two to fold. But then she smiled, a deep warm smile which instantly reassured him that what she had said moments earlier was all in jest.

"I was actually here during the war, working."

At Jimmy's questioning look she added, "The Second World War. I was a companion to a countess."

"Have you ever been back?" Lux asked.

"No, I haven't stepped foot here in more than 50 years," Eleanor replied, her tone slightly catching, making Jimmy feel there was more to her history, her connection to this place than she was willing to share right now.

"And you, our inquisitive young traveler?" Eleanor posed to Jimmy. "Are you one of these young people on, what are they calling it now, 'gap year'? Traveling 'round the world?"

"I'm actually almost 30," he replied, chuckling that Eleanor thought he was ten years younger than he really was. "My *yiayia*, um, my grandmother I mean, she recently died. She was born in Greece but she fled here, fled to Egypt during the war with an aunt. Her parents, brother, sisters, grandparents, aunts, uncles, cousins, they had all been deported to the camps. None of them survived. But Egypt saved her. She had always wanted to come back here, come back to the land that had taken her in but she never got the chance. She made me promise on her deathbed that I would. And so," he said almost nervously, his voice now catching, thinking of his tiny little *yiayia* just about to cross over, asking that of him. "But no, I've never really been much of anywhere before. Egypt, well, it's all a bit much."

It was clearly not the type of response she had been expecting. But recovering quickly and unruffled she said warmly, "What a beautiful thing," then placed her impeccably manicured hand on top of his before turning to Lux and saying, "And you my dear?"

"I feel as though this has always been home, but it's not. I've never been here before now," she began, not looking at either of them. Rather, her eyes were entranced by the glistening silhouette of the Great Pyramid before them. She was quiet for a few moments before continuing. "But I feel so inextricably tied to his place."

Jimmy and Eleanor exchanged a quick bemused look between them, each perhaps thinking was Lux a now aged hippie that had once traversed the infamous Hippie Trail in Asia during the '60s.

A table of secrets, multiple lifetimes of heartache and regret between them, these three very different strangers would have no idea on how much the next 10 days would change them.

"I read that if you drink the water of the Nile, you'll always come back," Jimmy said, raising his glass of water.

"Whether or not you want to," Eleanor said half-jokingly, clinking her glass with Jimmy's.

"The moment you come here," Lux began, "she leaves her indelible mark on you, no matter how hard you try to erase it," her tone now catching, tears brimming in the deep blue pools of her eyes as she continued gazing at the Great Pyramid, which eerily enough was almost reflected back in them. "*Qui aquam nili bibit rursus bibet.*"

PART I
ALEXANDRA

CHAPTER 1

Would she even know him if she were to find him again? Their time together all those many years ago in the land of pharaohs and a thousand suns had been fleeting and brief. Their romance doomed and short-lived from the start. But of course, that was all before the war, the war that was to end all wars and that had come at a cost of millions of lives. More than five years had passed since the armistice had been signed at Compiègne forest in northern France on the eleventh day of the eleventh month on the eleventh hour but it might as well have been yesterday for how raw and fresh the scars of it all still felt. Would she be the coward she was then, choosing family and commitment over her heart? Of course not. She was going to Egypt, determined to win back the piece of her she had far too easily turned her back on, not even considering the possibility that perhaps he was no longer even alive.

Mediterranean crossing –
Marseille, France to Alexandria, Egypt
February 1922

"First time traveling to Egypt?"

Alexandra whirled around at the sound of a voice behind her, so lost had she been in her thoughts as she gazed out at the crashing waves of the sapphire sea that she hadn't heard the woman's approaching steps.

"First time traveling to Egypt?" the young man asked but not before Alexandra heaved the contents of her almost empty stomach out into the Mediterranean once more. And then he was there smoothing the tendrils of hair back from her clammy face and rubbing his palm onto the small of her back in a soothing circular motion until the nausea had subsided.

Alexandra was lost for a moment then, hearing the woman's question, almost as if both her body and mind had been transported back all those years ago to another time and place. The woman was looking at her quizzically, undoubtedly wondering if Alexandra was perhaps not right in the head since she had still not spoken. She was much older than she was, Alexandra observed, in her 60s perhaps, English too from the accent she had detected. But what had given Alexandra the most pause was the woman's hair- it was cut in a bob fashion, entirely de rigueur for Alexandra's generation but something else entirely for a woman who had lived more than half a century earlier. Had Alexandra's mother seen it she would have been scandalized and by default dubbed her "that" kind of woman.

"Um, no," Alexandra recovered. "I was here once many years ago, before the war." A pause then before politely asking, "And you?"

"I live here," the older woman replied, rather brusquely Alexandra thought to herself. But the older woman didn't offer any additional information as to herself. Instead she asked, "Traveling with Cook?"

It took a moment for Alexandra to realize that she was referring to Thomas Cook & Son, the estimable travel outfitter that had been guiding the tourist masses up and down the Nile for decades now.

"Yes, as a matter of fact," Alexandra politely answered.

"You 'Cookies' are ruining the country for us," the older woman said, her tone oozing with antipathy over each and every tourist who'd had the nerve to book a tour with Thomas Cook & Son.

"And why's that?" Alexandra asked, more bemused than irritated over the older woman's irrational outburst.

"Flooding both Cairo and the Valley, bedecked in your pith helmets and ignorance of the world. Guest houses erected at sites millennia old, completely ruining the landscapes, all so 'Cookies' can have some shade and a cup of tea. As if that's what Hatshepsut had wanted when she built her monastery."

"And yet, you yourself are an outsider, are you not?" Alexandra asked. "The colonial face that many an average Egyptian wants gone from their land, the colonial oppressor?"

The woman's face grew red then and before Alexandra could offer an apology for what she knew had been rudeness on her part or receive an additional rebuke (she wasn't sure which was more fitting), she stormed off.

1913

"I'm Alexander," the man said, extending his hand towards Alexandra's.

"Alexandra," she replied, and they both laughed then, for what were the odds that two people with the same name would find themselves traveling together to a city of the same name too.

"Feeling better?" he asked.

"Much," she replied, warmth flooding her cheeks that this stranger had seen her at such a mortifying time. "Thank you for your assistance earlier," she said, still looking down at her hands which were encased in their immaculate white gloves, too embarrassed to meet his gaze now.

"Even the toughest of men don't always escape the wrath that is sea sickness," he said, undoubtedly trying to make her laugh or at least smile. "Nothing to be embarrassed about."

Alexandra looked up then, acutely taking in his image. He was older than her, mid-20s perhaps? His hair was dark and thick, what her mother would have called unruly. His eyes reminded her of a rich, luscious chocolate bar for how brown and creamy they appeared. But it was his hands that gave her pause. They were browned but reddened, dotted with calluses and scars. A working man's hands, she thought. And yet here he was traveling in first class.

"Alexandra!" Alexandra turned, startled at the sound of her mother's shrill voice calling her name.

The common question that seemed to be asked over and over on the sailing from Marseille to Alexandria was if it was one's first time traveling to Egypt. Excluding the ornery older woman from earlier, everyone else Alexandra had met so far had been kind. She was particularly fond of the young American couple who were on their honeymoon. Fond and slightly jealous of too.

As she heard every imaginable Egypt question being asked- Would Nefertiti's tomb ever be found?... Was Khartoum worth visiting?...Which hotel was better to stay at in Cairo, Shepheard's, which was right in the thick of Cairo's upper echelon or Mena House, which afforded guests a bird's eye view of the pyramids, although one supposed one could still go there for afternoon tea or a game of golf-

Alexandra retreated in her mind to memories of eight years earlier as she looked at the empty table in the corner of the dining room.

"May I join you?"

Alexandra looked up, surprised to see Alexander standing there, outfitted in formal evening wear. His hands aside, he looked every bit the gentleman. They had been seated in a corner table, her mother requesting it from the ship's dining room steward, so catty she was that she had taken an immense disliking to most of the women on board the ship that were of a similar age and station.

Her mother looked like she was going to say something, a hard 'no' judging by the way she had pursed her lips but before she could do so, her father stood up and said "of course," extending his hand towards Alexander's as he said "William Garis," who shook it and said, "Alexander Clarkson," and sat down.

Jack had stayed seated, not saying anything but looking a tad sullen over the arrival of this interloper.

Jack Cavanaugh was the son of one of Philadelphia's most prominent families, on par with that of Alexandra's. Alexandra's father was an esteemed physician, catering to the medical needs of Philadelphia's high society, while Jack's father was president of the Pennsylvania Railroad. It had been decided long ago that one day Jack and Alexandra would marry, thus joining together two of the city's richest and most prestigious families. Alexandra was nearly 18, she knew that an engagement would be coming soon if her mother had her way. It was she, after all, who had insisted Jack accompany them on their trip to Egypt. Her father had balked at the idea, saying that it wasn't proper, what with Jack not being family yet and without his parents, how would it look. But Emily Garis had insisted and what Emily wanted, Emily got. Jack was indifferent to it all- to what they would be seeing and experiencing. Jack only cared about money and his possessions and in his mind, Alexandra was his. A possession.

Alexandra caught Alexander studying her then from across the table, appraising her in her black, rhinestone embroidered, tulle satin gown with its high empire-style waist, and her grandmother's pearls that graced her neck. He smiled at her then, giving Alexandra the gumption to smile back until she caught her mother's icy stare.

"So, what brings you to Egypt?" her father asked Alexander. "The pursuit of travel, exploration of someplace new?"

"I actually live here. I'm currently serving as the director of the Nubian Archaeological Survey."

"How extraordinary," her father said, a look passing across his face just then as if saying he wished he was 30 years younger.

"Well, it's not always as glamorous as it sounds," Alexander replied laughingly. "And my beginnings were much humbler."

"And they would be?" her mother said, contempt oozing from her tone.

"I grew up in New York, on the Lower East Side. Your very own Tower of Babel if you will. My father was an Irish immigrant, my mother German. He worked as a shoe cobbler."

Her mother harrumphed at this.

Ignoring Emily's rudeness, her father continued. "And how on earth did you end up here in Egypt of all places? A far cry from the likes of New York."

"I earned a scholarship to Harvard." This got her mother's attention, Alexandra thought. "My parents had wanted me to study law, become a lawyer. But I took a class on ancient Greek and I fell in love with it and instead decided to study the classics."

"But Egypt? How did you end up here?" her father's curiosity still not sated. Her mother's attention now waning.

"I met by chance Mr. George Reisner, an American archeologist who also came from humble beginnings, so I think he took a shine to me. Anyhow, he was directing an expedition in Egypt around Quift and

invited me to join it. It was being financed by Phoebe Hearst."

"You know Phoebe Hearst?" her mother exclaimed, her attention piqued once more.

"I only met her once, briefly," Alexander added lest he be accused of being forward. "But we found some remarkable things including the stela of Prince Wepemnofret."

"Stela?" Alexandra asked, unsure of what could be so remarkable about something she didn't even know the purpose of, or how to pronounce it.

Turning to her and regarding Alexandra as if she were his pupil he said, "It's a sort of monument in the ancient world. In ancient Egypt they were used as tombstones, sometimes for religious usage, and even to mark boundaries."

"And this Prince Wepemnofret was someone of importance?" Alexandra asked.

"The greatest," her father cut in, excitement running through his voice. "His father was Khufu."

Alexander smiled at Alexandra then, clearly bemused by her father's enthusiasm for ancient Egypt.

"I had always dreamt about becoming an archaeologist, working at sites in the Holy Land-"

Her mother interrupted to say, "Yes, because digging in the dirt is befitting a gentleman."

Alexandra was mortified, shocked her mother was behaving so horribly towards her father in public, in front of a complete stranger. Her eyes locked with Alexander's then, his letting her know she needn't worry, that he didn't consider how her mother was behaving to be any reflection on her.

"Alas, it is a lot of time in the dirt or sand," Alexander joked, no doubt wanting to lighten the tension that had manifested at their corner table just then, which made her father laugh. Alexandra quickly joined in, her mother and Jack abstaining.

"*Although he was just a lowly shoe cobbler, born in a sod house in Galway, for some reason he had always loved ancient Egypt. Was obsessed with it. And from when I was a little boy, he would tell my brothers and sisters and me the story of when he saw Cleopatra's Needle unveiled in Central Park.*"

"*You don't say!*" Alexandra's father interrupted excitedly. "*I was there for it too! 1881 if I remember.*"

Alexander smiled then, a small, almost obliging one at her father as he continued.

"*It wasn't until I was older did he tell me the part of how he had lost his job by going, by not showing up to work that day. But he always said he never would have changed a thing. He said it was the closet he'd ever get to Egypt and there was no way he would have missed it.*"

"*A most beautiful tale, my boy,*" her father said genuinely. "*Your father sounds like he was a wonderful man.*"

Another snort from her mother at this.

Ignoring her, he added, "*It was his untimely passing too, when I was 14 that made me decide to change my studies. Make it to Egypt, see the ancient world.*"

"*How impressive, from the streets of New York to the deserts of Egypt. And all with humble street urchin beginnings.*"

"*Really, Emily!*" Alexandra's father exclaimed, clearly mortified.

Ignoring her mother, Alexander turned his attention to Alexandra and asked, "*Are you an Egyptologist too, like your father?*"

"*Why do you think we named her Alexandra?*" her father said jokingly, which made them all laugh, save for her mother.

"*We actually honeymooned here in '91. Such an incredible visit.*" Alexandra waited for her mother to add some hurtful comment to her father's words but she remained noticeably quiet.

"*I hope to study the Classics at Bryn Mawr,*" Alexandra answered. "*They don't have a degree in archaeology but I've been told they have a couple of classes in ancient Egyptian.*"

"A proper young lady does not go to university," her mother said emphatically, her shrill, hurtful voice suddenly making itself quite known again.

Alexandra was about to say something but the look her father gave her stopped her cold. "There's time enough for that," he said calmly but not before downing a generous swig from his wine glass.

And Jack Cavanaugh, the intended betrothed, remained sullenly quiet throughout the entire exchange.

1922

As the car drove through the streets of Cairo, meandering its way past ornate buildings, structures that looked like replicas one would see on the continent, the Baroque-style churches of Rome, the Haussmannian facades of Paris, it was made complete with perfectly placed palm trees. A reminder to any visitor that they were indeed in a Mediterranean climate and not the unfriendly and inhospitable (at least during the winter months) climes of northern Europe or Philadelphia. Alexandra remembered then what Alexander had said all those years before- It's what the Western traveler wanted to see. Comforts and sights of home in a far off, exotic land.

She had read that during the war, Cairo was very much the ghost town, one devoid of 'Cookies' at least and yet filled up in other ways, namely by the British Army and its colonial soldiers, ANZACS they were called. Shepheard's, where Alexandra stayed with her parents when they had visited in '14, even served as British HQ in the Near East during the war. Ladies and their evening gown finery had been replaced by men and boys in khaki.

The sandy streets were filled with locals going about their day-street vendors selling sugarcane as flies swarmed around them, women who had long since mastered the art of balancing stacks of baskets on their heads as they made their way past emaciated donkeys, and oxen who were undoubtedly worked to the bone as they dragged their overloaded carts along, and herds of bleating goats, each one, Alexandra thought, trying to make its voice heard over the cacophony of noises around them. A powerful reminder of how Cairo had not changed in more than a thousand years.

When the car pulled up in front of Shepheard's, the door was immediately opened by a regal looking colored man whose skin was black as the night. Nubians, she remembered they were called, an ancient people that hailed from southern Egypt and Sudan. Their onyx-colored skin startled her just as much as it had the first time seeing it.

She felt keenly aware that she was on display as she walked up the flight of eight steps, trailing behind her parents and Jack.

Alexandra knew she was no doubt the subject of curiosity from the men and women who sat in rattan chairs on the terrace, idling away the hours while gossiping about what this person did and where or musing about a current event, thousands of miles away. She even felt the pair of stone sphinxes that flanked the top of the steps, wondering who she was and why she was here. Although since the last time she was here, the world had drastically changed- American women finally having gotten the right to vote with greater numbers of them entering the workforce and of course, an entire generation of boys lost on the scorched earth of Belgium and France- and yet some things never seemed to change, namely that of a young woman unaccompanied and unchaperoned in a foreign land when she was clearly of means.

The Entrance Hall was still breathtaking with its Arabian looking arches and its domed ceiling of colored glass.

"Entirely too garish. Who designed it, Alva Belmont?"

Alexandra smiled, remembering her mother's horror upon entering the hotel and seeing the ostentatious displays of wealth and gaucheness in each of the design details (a redesign since their last visit in '91). Although they had been social acquaintances at best, Emily Garis had never cared for the infamous and indomitable Alva, formerly Vanderbilt, the husband through which she had accrued both her fortune and her tactlessness.

1913

"Care to steal away with me?" a voice said from behind the chair that Alexandra was sitting in.

She craned her neck and looked up to see Alexander standing there. Looking quite handsome in a white linen suit, she thought to herself, when she saw what she thought was a pelican, moseying behind him.

"And go where?" she asked, playing along.

"Explore Old Cairo with me. Well, I'll be your tour guide as I know it quite well and there are few corners of it that I haven't yet uncovered," he said dashingly.

"You're serious." Alexandra wasn't sure if she meant this as a question or a statement.

"Dead. So what do you say?"

She paused then to consider his offer. They had been in Cairo for almost three days and she had yet to see anything beyond the confines of Kamal Pasha Street, one of the city's main thoroughfares and onto which the hotel faced. She had gone on a hurried walk when she knew her mother was otherwise engaged and her father was sending a telegram back home to his practice and Jack was, well, she hadn't known where nor did she care. But she longed to see more than this fabricated, insular world she found herself in. Her father promised they would visit the Great Pyramid soon but when would that be, as she found herself passing hours reading books she had borrowed from the hotel's library. But her mother was napping now, no doubt spent from that morning's gossip session she had participated in on the terrace with a gaggle of matronly American women she had become besotted with. And her father and Jack were off visiting an acquaintance of her father's from university, an Englishman who lived in Egypt.

"I can't be too long," she told him.

He looked at her then, studying her so long and intently that she blushed from his gaze. "How old are you, Alexandra?"

"Seventeen. Why?"

"I had already been on my own for two years by then," he said neither boasting nor harshly but rather as just a fact. A fact of life that she knew she was entirely ignorant of.

"I'm not a child."

"I never said you were. You're just a product of your station."

CHAPTER 2

From the first time she had visited, Alexandra had loved Old Cairo. She didn't see what her mother saw when she gazed upon its "filthy streets" or its "crumbling pavements and shoddily constructed buildings"; rather, she saw the past before her very eyes.

She felt confident as she hailed a horse and carriage on the street and in Arabic, asked to be taken to Khan el-Khalili, Cairo's most famous bazaar and souk whose origins dated all the way back to the 14th century.

"What do you smell, Alexandra?"

Was it a test, she wondered? Would he think her dumb if she said the wrong thing, gave the wrong answer? But his eyes were warm, she noted, as if they were encouraging her to solely rely on her senses and nothing else just then.

"Butter," she said. "Other spices, pungent ones I can't recognize, like something out of Scheherazade. Smoke… leather."

"Very good," he said as if he were the teacher and she his student. Walking over to a stall that was a myriad of colors, looking almost like a rainbow, he pointed to a yellow, almost golden powder and said, "This is turmeric. It has many medicinal qualities; Eastern doctors have long used it to treat patients." Then, reaching into the barrel, he picked up a cup and filled it with what appeared to be miniature seeds. Holding it out towards

her he said, "Smell it, even taste it if you want. It won't hurt you."

"Oh, it stings," she exclaimed, shrinking back from the strong-smelling seeds. "What is it?"

"Cumin."

"Merhaba, welcome. Can Mademoiselle be tempted by any Arabian spices? Cumin perhaps?"

Alexandra looked up to see an elderly Egyptian in a dark green galabeya, his thinning gray hair covered by the customary ammama, looking at her, no doubt hoping to make a sale.

"No, shukran," Alexandra said politely, shaking her head demurely at the merchant as she kept walking deeper into the bazaar.

"One could get lost in here," Alexandra said in wonder as she looked around at the never-ending maze of stalls before her.

"It's possible, but always use Bab al-Futuh as your landmark." Then taking her hand in his, he started leading them until they were outside.

His touch thrilled her, for never had Jack taken her hand in his other than the obligatory waltz they had danced together on numerous occasions.

He stopped then in front of a massive gate with some of the most beautiful stonework Alexandra had ever seen.

"Bab al-Futuh. It's one of the three remaining gates in the city wall of Old Cairo. If you can believe it, this was rebuilt and dates from the late 11th century. It's known as the door of conquests."

"It's beautiful," she said as she gazed up at its intricate details. "Some of it almost looks-"

"Byzantine," they said at the same time, making both of them smile.

"Yes, I thought so too the first time I saw it. If we ever lose each other, always come back here."

Alexandra pulled up short at the sight of the gate, expelling the breath she had been holding upon her approach. He wasn't there like she had imagined him to be all these weeks and months after she had decided to return. They hadn't just lost each other that day, they had been lost to each other for nearly a decade. Was she really that naïve to think it would be different? That he would suddenly be standing there after all this time, waiting for her to return?

To her mother it had been an abomination, especially considering its frequency, but both Alexandra and her father had loved the adhan, the call to worship for the Muslim people. She had especially loved the first one of the day, at times even throwing on her robe and opening her room's window to hear it better as she watched the rising morning sun, a practice that would have horrified Emily Garis had she known what her daughter was doing. Embracing such a heathen ritual.

To Alexandra, the call to worship had been calming, a ritual so foreign to her and yet one that soon become a source of comfort upon hearing it, seeing the native men praying to their God as they kneeled down upon their prayer rugs.

But it was the Citadel she had loved most of all. Just as he had earlier in the bazaar, Alexander had also taken her hand as he guided them over the upper esplanade to the striking overlook which provided a picturesque view of the city, one that didn't include the Cairo of new but rather one of old, one where you could see the vastness of the entire city before you, replete with its mosques of all ages and sizes while minarets gracefully dotted the landscape. It was a view that had long stayed with her, just as the scents of jasmine and peppermint had too.

1913

"You need to stop this infatuation with the boy, Alexandra."

Alexandra was surprised by the sharpness of her father's tone, something she would have expected from her mother but not him.

"I don't know what you're talking about."

"I know you've been going off, traipsing around Cairo with him."

"I'm not doing anything improper, Daddy."

"A girl of 17 going off alone with a strange man in a foreign country and whose background we know nothing about is the very definition of improper. Word will get back to your mother eventually, Alexandra, and I know you don't want that either. And besides, it's not fair to Jack."

He had spoken the part about Jack as almost an afterthought, Alexandra thought, knowing he cared for him as a prospective son-in-law perhaps even less than she did as a future husband. Incurring her mother's wrath however, was the very last thing Alexandra wanted. But ever since that day when Alexander had taken her into Old Cairo, she had snuck out on three other occasions with him. He had shown her a side of Cairo she knew she never would have seen in a Baedeker's guidebook or accompanied by her parents.

"I've fallen in love with him, Daddy." She hadn't said this out loud to anyone, not even Alexander, but she had. She loved his warmth and kindness; she loved the way he looked at her as if she were a Botticelli painting; but most of all she loved the way that he saw her as her own individual person, not just Alexandra Garis, only child of William Garis, one of Philadelphia's wealthiest and most prestigious families with a dowry to match.

Her father drew in a sharp breath then, taken aback over what Alexandra had just said.

"You don't know him, my girl. It's easy to say you're in love when you're just a child."

"A child who's old enough to be married, provided he's the "right" sort of gentleman. Is that it?" she interjected, hurling her words back at him. "And besides, you knew Mother your entire lives before marrying and I'd hardly call your marriage one based on love." Alexandra regretted saying it the moment it came out of her mouth when she saw her father's pained expression. She knew she had hurt him. She also knew his failed marriage, his inner misery over the last nearly 20 years pained him daily, that Alexandra was the only remotely wonderful thing to come of it. But a man like William Garis didn't divorce. It simply wasn't done.

But all he said was, "There are all sorts of mistakes one can make. No two are the same and most can never be undone."

18 December 1891

I fear there are no words in the English language worthy of capturing the emotion one feels upon seeing the Great Pyramid of Giza for the first time. To stand before a structure that was built thousands of years before the birth of Christ and which still stands to this day is perhaps the most awe-inspiring feeling I have ever felt.

I journeyed before dawn with our dragoman which I have learned is both a tour guide and fixer. The latter I find slightly bemusing since he is a fellow of barely Emily's height and yet his bark seems far worse than any bite he might bestow upon you, perhaps even more venomous than the infamous tarantulas I have heard so much about. But Tariq was there to meet our ship as it arrived in Alexandria and of course saw us safely on our journey onto Cairo. He's also a genuine marvel at getting rid of those irksome beggars, both child and adult who put out their dirtied hands at every chance they get asking for 'baksheesh' which I have learned is the word for a tip. I am glad my sister is not traveling with us for she would have surely depleted her entire inheritance by now with the trip barely having begun, such is her too generous of a heart for those less fortunate?

I am glad to have come alone for Emily would have undoubtedly spoiled the experience for me what with her incessant complaining and sour disposition. The feeling I felt at the top of Cheops, seeing the sun rising on this ancient land, is one I shall never forget for as long as I draw breath.

W. Garis

1913

"Come with me," Alexander implored from the other side of the massive statue of Hatshepsut, one of ancient Egypt's few female pharaohs. "There's nothing more magical than seeing the pyramids against the night sky and the stars."

"You know I can't," Alexandra said, slightly annoyed he would even suggest such a thing.

"Pretend you're sick and just say you don't want to be disturbed that evening. You can, you just won't."

She wasn't sure how he had known to turn up at the Egyptian Museum that afternoon, since Alexandra hadn't told him she would be visiting with her father and Jack, the latter seeming even more bored and disinterested than usual. Her mother naturally feigned off going saying she had no desire in visiting a museum filled with dusty antiquities, so she remained behind at Shepheard's where as custom, she was holding court on the terrace. But there he had been, casually admiring a small glass-enclosed case that held a statue of a seated man and woman. Rahotep and Nofret she had read on the case's placard. The woman, Alexandra thought, was quite beautiful in her white robe, black painted hair and colorful necklace. Alexandra wondered what it would be like to have hers cut that short, in Egyptian pharaonic style.

"My father knows we've been out together," she quietly said. "He's none too happy about it. Although I don't think he'll tell Mother. I don't think he wants to ruin the trip." She said this last part more to herself than to him.

"You're nearly 18, Alexandra. You-"

"Alexandra," her father called to her from further down the gallery. "Come along now, we're going upstairs."

Alexandra worriedly looked back at Alexander only to see that he had already gone, his retreating figure traveling in the opposite direction of her father and Jack, his boater hat back atop his head.

Alexandra drew in a sharp intake of breath upon seeing the approaching Great Pyramid. The last remaining wonder of the ancient world still standing tall against the backdrop of the modern world. She had borne witness to the rise and fall of countless empires, conquering armies, and yet here she was, still bedazzling all those who stood before her.

Alexandra was always amazed at the stark difference between Giza and Cairo, even though the capital was only mere miles away from the pyramids. But where Cairo was loud and chaotic, pulsating with the frenetic pace of life and modernity, Giza remained firmly rooted in the past, a willing captive of its five and a half millennia of history.

"I can see why you prefer it at night," Alexandra said as she looked up in amazement at the perfect framing of Cheops against the silky, moonlit black sky.

"Come on," he said, grabbing her hand and pulling her towards the Great Pyramid.

"Wait," she protested. "I can't climb it, I'll fall!"

"I'll never let anything happen to you," he said and Alexandra knew he wasn't just saying this, that he genuinely meant it.

And then atop the Great Pyramid of Cheops with nary a soul around, he kissed her. Her very first kiss, for even Jack had only ever given her a perfunctory kiss on the cheek at his mother's behest. But his kiss was long and hard and soon she found herself opening her mouth, his probing tongue gently meeting hers. And she had never wanted that sweet and delicious moment to end.

CHAPTER 3

1922

"Excuse me, but you wouldn't happen to know a young American by the name of Alexander Clarkson, would you?"

Alexandra had come to the Mena House for afternoon tea. Originally built as a hunting lodge by Khedive Ismail for the opening of the Suez Canal in 1869 to receive Empress Eugenie and other dignitaries who had attended the event, it shortly after became a hotel and soon one of Egypt's most popular, due to its nearness to the pyramids and the unparalleled views it afforded visitors.

"Where do you stay when you're in Cairo? If not at Shepheard's?"

"The Mena House, always the Mena. Waking up each morning and seeing the pyramids right there, it's the best reminder of how far I've come from the likes of Orchard Street. And how proud my father would be of me, living the dream he never had the chance to."

Alexandra remembered the first time she had seen the hotel, thinking how drastically different in appearance it was from Shepheard's, a hotel clearly envisioned as the Ritz of Arabia. But the Mena House was different, what with its oriental exterior with its long, low, white façade, its flat roofs, and its verandahs of dark mashrabiya, a beautiful Islamic architectural element that Alexandra had loved from the moment she saw it. Nothing like she had ever seen. It had only recently reopened in the last couple of years, having been requisitioned by Australian troops during the war. But much to the delight of its faithful flock, it had rid itself of its uncouth and rough and tumble temporary guests and returned to serving its genteel and decidedly better behaved guests.

But just like Shepheard's, the Mena House's terraces were equally popular, especially for the daily tea-hour which is why she had come then. But so far, after asking numerous staff, none of them remembered or knew of an American man in his late 30s with brown colored hair and a tiny scar under his left eye who was an archaeologist.

"Excuse me my dear, I couldn't help but overhear you earlier inquiring about your Yank friend or paramour perhaps?"

Alexandra turned to see a tiny, elderly woman, British judging by her accent, standing there in a black gown that looked straight out of the Victorian era. And yet she knew what a paramour was, Alexandra thought to herself, smiling.

"Yes," she replied, thinking how on earth would this spinster possibly know Alexander.

"May I?" she asked Alexandra, pointing to the empty chair from across her.

"Of course," she answered.

Taking a seat as she proceeded to smooth out a non-existent wrinkle on her taffeta gown, she began. "You see, back in 1920 I journeyed here. I had lost my two sons in the war and my husband not shortly after from the Spanish Flu. We had traveled a lot before the war, even visiting Constantinople and the Holy Land if you can imagine. Anyhow, there was a Yank on board. Well, there were many Yanks onboard but this one stood out."

"Why was that?" Alexandra asked, not remembering anything remarkable about Alexander's appearance that would differentiate him from others.

"Well, for starters he walked with a limp. I attributed this to a war injury like so many poor boys of his generation. And he also had the saddest eyes I've ever seen in a man. Like he had suffered the most painful loss."

That described just about anyone who had fought in the war, Alexandra thought. Or vacant eyes that showed nothing, like Jack. "But his name was Alexander?" Alexandra asked excitedly.

"Well, you see my dear, that's the thing. I can't remember. But the one day I did ask him why he appeared so sad," she said as she took a massive bite of a watercress sandwich she had plucked from Alexandra's tea stand.

"And?" Alexandra asked, waiting with baited breath while inwardly wondering if this woman was just having her on.

"He told me that a long time ago, he had lost the love of his life here in Egypt, that is even though he had only known her a short time. And that she had chosen her family over him."

1913

He was sailing up the Nile on a dahabiya, this much she knew. She wasn't sure where he would have gotten the money to have rented the Egyptian-style yacht all to himself, but perhaps her father was right. How much did she really know of Mr. Alexander Clarkson after all? Besides his very humble beginnings and his father's penchant for ancient Egypt. But surely if he did have money, that would be a very good thing indeed. Wouldn't it?

Alexandra knew her parents had sailed on a dahabiya when they had visited for their honeymoon. Her father had reserved one per his personal inclinations to all things in life- complete privacy and utter independence with no set program or pre-arranged schedule. Her mother, being the exact opposite of her father in every way, the oil to his water, had detested it, everything from being surrounded by nothing but "those brown people," the solitariness, and most of all, having no social pursuits of any kind for multiple weeks. In fact, part of her condition upon returning to Egypt was that they journey up the Nile on a Thomas Cook cruise, not a dahabiya even though Alexandra, like her father, would have loved it.

It was at Saqqara, home to what was believed to be the world's oldest complete stone building complex known in history, that Alexandra first thought she saw him but she hadn't been certain for it had been at a distance. And then at Dendera Temple, she thought it was perhaps him again but like before, her spotting of him had been from afar. And the man never gave any indication, either in the form of a bow of the head or tip of the hat, that he knew her. Alexandra fast believed she was becoming like the wife in Charlotte Perkins Gilman's short story, The Yellow Wallpaper, her mental state clearly deteriorating if she was seeing Alexander Clarkson everywhere she went.

But then the following afternoon, while lounging on the Nile Terrace of the Winter Palace, gazing out at the timeless beauty of the Nile, its azure waters framed by picturesque palm trees, just like the scenes in the paintings that hung at Shepheard's, watching an endless cascade of traditional boats float past, feluccas her father had said they were called, wooden gull-winged lateen sail boats that had been used since antiquity, a man stopped directly below from the street and tipped his hat. And she knew it was him. She looked around to see if her mother had noticed but too engrossed was she in a letter she was writing. But when Alexandra looked around again, he was gone.

"Mother, if you'll excuse me, I need to use the W.C.," Alexandra said, standing up.

"Do hurry back," she said without looking up. "Your father and Jack will be back any moment. We'll have tea then."

Hurrying off, she rushed into the inside, only to wait a moment before dashing down the hotel's sweeping front stairs to the street. She looked *around almost frantically until a hand shot out, grabbing her by the wrist and pulling her into a crevice behind the staircase.*

"You were at Saqqara and Dendera, weren't you-"

But he cut off her off, planting his mouth firmly on hers and kissing her with all the passion and frenzy of two young people in love.

She kissed him hungrily back, desperately wanting more. But he stopped then and stepped back from her.

"You better go, or you mother will think Bedouins have taken you," he said, his breath as ragged as hers. The fire in his eyes showing just how much he wanted her.

"But when will I-"

But he gently placed a finger on her lips to silence her. "You'll see me again. I'll never be far."

I'll never be far. Alexandra could hear those words as clearly in her head as if they had just been spoken yesterday.

As she sat on the Winter Palace's terrace, where she had been enjoying a cup of now cold hibiscus tea, the sun setting on the ancient city of Thebes across the river, the afterglow of which would soon be illuminating the not so far away desert sands, Alexandra felt calmly at peace here. Perhaps she would be the twentieth-century version of Lady Duff-Gordon, the British woman who had turned her back on her husband and children in England to move to Egypt where she became known as the Sitt el Kebeer, the Great Lady, by the Egyptian peasants who knew her. Egypt had a way of capturing one entirely and never letting go. But Alexandra hadn't wanted to think the alternative, which was if she didn't find him, what life did she have to return to?

1913

It was while traveling on a donkey that Alexandra desperately wished she had been born a man. They had risen early that day to start their trek to the Valley of the Kings, burial site of almost all the pharaohs of the 18th, 19th, and 20th dynasties. It was also one of the most important archaeological sites today, every archaeologist and their wealthy benefactor (or benefactress in some cases) wanting to be the person credited with making that decade's most impressive discovery and of course, getting all the riches and notoriety that came with it.

It seemed like they had been riding forever although Alexandra knew in reality that it hadn't been that long. They first happened upon the Temple of Kurna which was small and unimpressive save for its façade of lotus pillars, but this at least offered her the excuse to get off the scrawny and emaciated donkey she had been riding.

They then arrived at the desert, which had greatly surprised her with its dull color and rocky plateaus. She had just assumed she would see nothing but vast stretches of golden sand dunes.

"Any moment now," her father said to her, the anticipation and excitement he felt so clearly visible on his face. She knew much had to do with the fact that her mother had chosen to stay onboard the Prince Abbas, holding court all day in her usual spot in the promenade lounge, save for when there was luncheon.

"But why bury one's king in such a barren and desolate place?" Alexandra called out to her father, his donkey having taken on a faster gait, perhaps sensing his master's excitement which had carried over to him.

Gently pulling on the reins, for her father was just as gentle with animals as he was with his patients, he said, "To stave off grave robbers. All pharaohs were buried with the most extravagant of riches and so by burying their kings in a remote valley in such deep shafts, potential robbers wouldn't have the faintest idea on where to even begin looking. Or so they thought. Many tombs still ended up being cleared out in antiquity."

Alexandra was intrigued by the idea of there being an afterlife, a thought she would not share with her staunchly Christian mother who decried anything not Presbyterian as being "entirely heathen." She liked the belief that there was more than just this one life you were given at birth. And that one would need things to take with them into the afterlife. But she still found the Valley to be an emotionally cold and uninviting place. She wondered if there was such a thing as loneliness in the afterlife as Jack helped her off her donkey.

"May I offer you a personal guided tour?" The three of them turned to see Alexander standing there before them, hat in hand. Where on earth had he come from, she wondered? She hadn't seen him once on the ride as they dutifully followed along the dragoman her father had hired to take them and yet here he was.

Before any of them could speak, he continued, "I've worked here before. I helped in the discovery of 55."

At Alexandra and Jack's blank looks he added, "All of the tombs have been assigned a sequential number in the order of their discovery."

Her father appeared as if he wanted to say no and decline Alexander's kind offer. But surprising her he said, "That would be lovely." William Garis was a man who staunchly conformed to the dictates of society because of the world he had been born into and what that same world expected of him, except where Egyptology was concerned, apparently.

1913

While she never would have admitted it to anyone, least of all Alexander Clarkson, for then what would he think of her, Alexandra wasn't entirely sure if she'd make a good Egyptologist. Although the tombs were awash in glowing light, electricity having been previously installed so that visitors to the tombs could see every incredible detail, she couldn't believe the number of steps they had taken as they descended into the deep underground of the Valley of the Kings. She tried imagining what it must have been like for the first person in modern times to have come here when they first discovered the tombs, only supported by perhaps a candle or lantern as they descended into utter darkness, not knowing what awaited them. But Alexandra supposed that for people like Giovanni Belzoni, or the Great Belzoni as he was called due to his immense stature (he stood at 6 feet 7 inches), the man responsible for the clearing of sand from the entrance of the great temple at Abu Simbel as well as the discovery of the tomb of Seti I, excitement, not fear pulsed through their veins when it came to matters of the unknown.

"Are you okay, Alexandra?" Alexander asked her, a look of concern appearing on his face.

Her father looked sharply at Alexander then, no doubt peeved over the younger man's disregard for manners by addressing her by her first name. And in front of Jack no less, as if they were the soon-to-be betrothed. But he remained silent.

"Yes, thank you," she replied. "I was just thinking how different an experience it would be to come down here without-"

"Any light," he said, finishing her sentence. As if they knew exactly what the other was saying.

"And yet I don't think I've ever seen anything more beautiful," Alexandra said, her words trailing off as she gazed in wonder at the artwork that covered every inch of the tomb.

From floor to ceiling, images depicting a vast array of scenes- the deceased offering a sacrifice to a god, snakes, gods, weapons, and scorpions- all believed to protect the tomb and keep evil spirits away, the deceased completing a deed or achievement- along with row after row of hieroglyphics.

But it was the vibrant colors that astounded her the most.

"Extraordinary, isn't it?" Alexander asked her, as if reading her thoughts.

"But how is it so that everything is so pristine?" she asked. "Like it was just painted yesterday and not thousands of years ago."

"Being so deep down, they've been protected from the air all this time, Nature's best form of preservation," he said, his eyes bright with passion for down here he was clearly in his glory and what, love? Love towards her? Dare she hope?

The moment was broken when her father came towards her and guided her away towards a particular cartouche on the wall.

"Houses of eternity," Alexander said later on after they had emerged from the tomb. "What the ancient Egyptians referred to the tombs as."

"I think I like that more," Alexandra answered. "I much prefer that to the whole "final resting place" that we have. It doesn't seem grand enough."

"A luncheon has been arranged for us at 17," her father said, once more inserting himself in conversation between her and Alexander. "Would you join us?"

So there in the entrance of 17, the tomb of Seti I, they feasted on cold roasted chicken, veal galantine, ham sandwiches, pickled eggs, cheese, and bread, beneath the inscription which said "specifically reserved for visitors who wish to lunch." While she was glad for the electric light, she found this inscription rather appalling for it completely ruined the ambiance of this house of eternity. As she took a bite of her veal galantine, an extremely dark Nubian man dressed in a white galabeya refilled her glass of lemonade as the other worker almost stood to attention.

"Are you well enough to travel on, my dear?" her father asked her, a look of concern crossing his face as he took in her matted hair, her cheeks visibly pink

from both the intensity of the sun as well as the day's rising temperatures.

"Of course," she cheerily affirmed. "I haven't come all this way only to miss the temple built by one of ancient Egypt's most formidable ladies. I am a suffragette after all."

"By all means, don't let your mother hear that," her father replied, half joking, but also half serious. Her mother detested the suffragist movement and detested anytime their "foolish antics" became a topic of conversation at social events.

"Then you have something in common with Hatshepsut," Alexander said. But seeing her blank look, he started to say something until her father cut in-

"My dear girl, have you remembered nothing of the bedtime stories I told you as a child?" William Garis said, mockingly stern.

Turning to Alexander she added, "While other little girls were treated to stories about princesses in storybook castles, I was regaled with stories about ancient Egypt to dream about."

"I can't think of a better childhood," he said to her father but looking at her as he did.

"So what exactly do I have in common with this 'Hatshepsut' since I know I hardly look the part of an Egyptian," Alexandra joked as she executed a near flawless curtsy in her white linen finery whose hem had become as brown as the sand they traversed upon.

"She was a woman ahead of her time," Alexander answered.

"A visionary leader of her people," her father chimed in.

"A gal who just wanted to be treated like one of the men," Alexander added, a twinkle in his eyes as he said this.

"Ah, hence the suffragette part," Alexandra replied.

"She was truly one of Egypt's greatest pharaohs," her father said. "One of the kingdom's most prolific builders and one who brought great wealth and artistry here as well."

"It's a good thing she never crossed paths with Mrs. Dodge then,"

referring of course to one of America's most prominent members of the anti-suffrage movement. "She would have undoubtedly not approved of a female pharaoh," to which her father and Alexander both laughed, Jack not participating for he appeared far too engrossed with trying to buff a mark off his shoe.

"Will we see any of the buildings she commissioned?" Alexandra asked, her interest having been piqued remembering her father's words about the female pharaoh being one of ancient Egypt's most ardent builders.

"We're headed to Deir el-Bahari next," Alexander casually said, as if he had been part of this expedition all along, as if he naturally belonged here. Alexandra looked to her father to see if he would say anything, politely decline Alexander's offer, say that they were fine proceeding with their dragoman but he didn't. Egyptology was winning out again, she thought, inwardly smirking. While her father was extremely knowledgeable on ancient Egypt, she knew his level of knowledge paled in comparison to that of someone like Alexander, both with his education and on-site experience.

"Her piece de resistance," her father said, "to herself. You'll see."

And so, she did. She stopped short, pulling on the reins of her donkey so she could truly admire the majestic sight before her. Although she still had countless ancient temples to visit, Alexandra could tell this one was different. Whereas in the Valley of the Kings, there was no way of knowing the immense treasures and grandeur and thousands of years of history that lay beneath you, beneath the very earth one walked upon, here you immediately saw the sheer majesty of the setting-a massive structure that almost looked like an amphitheater backed by a towering vertical cliff face. There couldn't possibly be anything like this she believed as she gazed up at the temple with its many perfectly symmetrical

colonnades and terraces one above the other set against the rock with flights of step between them.

Imagine if women ruled the world, she thought. But here at one time, in a land far away from the one she had grown up in and lived, a woman actually did.

And now American women have the right to vote, Alexandra thought to herself as she gazed across the banks of the Nile to where Deir el-Bahari stood, fondly remembering that near perfect day from all those years before. Sadly recalling what no longer was.

CHAPTER 4

1922

"Oh, my dear, you simply must come!"

Alexandra politely smiled at the young British woman Eliza whose lively manner seemed in stark contrast to that of her new husband's and yet they seemed genuinely in love and happy. Although she was bedecked in the latest fashions, her neck and ears adorned with expensive looking pieces of jewelry along with a monstrous sapphire ring on her right hand, Alexandra had detected a roughness to the younger woman's words, an upbringing she was clearly trying to hide. And when she was introduced to Eliza's husband, a Sir Robert Greaves, Alexandra had understood why.

She had been startled at first when Sir Robert approached the table she and Eliza were sitting at. Her back had been to him and so she hadn't noticed the limp he had nor the cloth that covered his right hand where she could see the end of a jagged scar peering out from under it. Alexandra had estimated him to be around her age, perhaps a few years younger. But the outward physical wounds he bore were an all-too common sight of men of his generation. It was only when his hands shook as he clutched his teacup, the china nosily rattling against the saucer as he attempted to place it back on the table, that she suddenly was reminded of Jack.

But Eliza had gently and wordlessly taken the cup and saucer from her husband's shaking hands and placed it back on the table, still talking as she did so, not in the least ruffled from the stares and whispers of the other diners on the Winter Garden's terrace.

"It will be scores of fun! And you'll meet some people too, there's even some eligible young men, wouldn't you say, my dear?"

Sir Robert had smiled wanly at his wife and simply nodded his head in agreement as his way of answering. Alexandra had yet to hear him utter a word; he seemed to speak more through his eyes than anything else.

Although normally Alexandra couldn't be bothered with someone like Eliza- a young, silly chatterbox whose world revolved solely around the latest fashions and gossip- her interest had piqued when she discovered that the Greaveses had moved here nearly two years ago and were well acquainted with the English-speaking residents of Luxor. Well, Eliza was. If there was ever the chance to learn if Alexander had been in Egypt or still was, it would be through Eliza and her circle of contacts. And if meant dusting off her rather faded social skills and graces and donning a frock that Eliza Greaves would no doubt consider out of fashion, then so be it. For the first time in a long time Alexandra felt a faint glimmer of hope become lit within her.

"I'll be there," she said. And fervently hoped he would be too.

1913

Alexandra had always considered her parents to be like oil and water; they just didn't mix well together. But it was in Egypt of all places, a land that her mother abhorred, that Alexandra discovered they had one thing in common after all- their shared disdain of the native Egyptian people.

And she had been taken aback to see this other side of her father, one that seemed in stark contrast to a man whose life's work had been to help people. Well, she reasoned, people of the right sort and station as her mother would say.

There had been the many almost cruel comments about the natives' dress, how their language sounded like nothing more than "childish jibberish," and how they seemed like an altogether "heathen lot" and were it not for the likes of the educated American and European tourists, their country's most important treasures would be completely gone, reduced to nothing more than printed words on a page like when one talked about the Hanging Gardens of Babylon.

"So you're saying the Egyptian people, the very same people who are not just the rightful but actual descendants of ancient Egypt, don't have a right to their country's own treasures? That it's completely fine for Western museums to carry out the modern version of pillaging by taking out of the country every artifact of value and prestige they find all to better line their pockets and enhance their reputation?"

A hushed silence fell over the terrace of the Old Cataract hotel then. Alexandra was shocked to have heard such vitriol coming from Alexander. It was a side of him she hadn't been privy to before and one that also exhibited his hardscrabble upbringing, something which she knew he was careful to keep hidden. They had arrived in Assouan earlier that morning and came to the famous Thomas Cook hotel to partake in afternoon tea on the terrace which overlooked the magnificent Elephantine Island. As he had done since they had begun their journey sailing up the Nile, Alexander had been already been seated here at the Old Cataract's terrace. Alexandra knew her father had grown weary of Alexander, by his always "appearing," by his daughter's growing attraction with the ill-suited young man. But ever the polite gentleman, he of course had invited him to join their group which along with Alexandra and her parents had also consisted of a widowed American woman and her dour niece and two rather elderly British spinster sisters. *Emily Garis had been less than enthused with their choice of afternoon tea companions.*

"My dear boy," her father began lightly. The breeze that had been gently flowing only moments earlier had vanished just as the countless ancient treasures Alexander had been referring to in his outburst. "That's not at all what I meant."

"Isn't it?" Alexander replied, a challenge in his tone which, as Alexandra looked about the terrace, was still loud enough for people to be staring at them. Her mother looked positively mortified, a reaction she was not accustomed to.

"Oh, and I suppose all the work you're doing here is benefiting the natives? Didn't you say you worked on a dig financed by Phoebe Hearst of all people?" to which everyone at the table politely laughed considering the immense wealth of the Hearst family. That is, save for Alexandra and her mother.

"I had, yes," Alexander answered as his jaw clenched. "But I soon saw the error of my ways, that I-"

But he was cut off by one of the British sisters who said, "If it weren't for the white man, all ancient treasures in these ancient lands would be completely destroyed."

"Dust to history," her sister affirmed with a downward shake of her head, the immense giblet on her neck jiggling as she spoke.

"And besides," the widow began. "If they're not black-market thieves selling their country's ancient history to the highest bidder, then they're entirely blasé about what's right there before them. Who was it, Belzany-"

"Belzoni, aunt," the shy, meek niece cut in. "Giovanni Belzoni," the girl continued in what sounded to Alexandra to be the most exquisite Italian accent.

"Heavens, child," the aunt replied, clearly irritated over her niece's audacity in correcting her and in public too. "As if I care a fig about some *illiterate Italian giant." Belzoni was famous for having been immensely tall, six feet seven inches. But before he began a long and illustrious career as an explorer and pioneer archaeologist of Egyptian antiquities, he had worked in a traveling circus too. "My point in referencing Signor Belzoni was that it was he who saved the bust of Ramses II and also cleared the sand at Abu Simbel. All these treasures right before these people's noses and they didn't care. It is all the same throughout the uncivilized, non-Christian world. It is our job to save both their souls and their antiquities."*

Alexandra glanced at Alexander and saw nothing but anger and disgust on his face. But then the Harvard educated Alexander came back a moment later, his visage once more that of a perfect gentleman and he said, "If you'll excuse me, I have an appointment in town I can't be late for. Thank you again for letting me join your party." And with that he was gone. And before he was even fully out of earshot, their table erupted in a flurry of gossip over this arrogant upstart with her mother delivering the final blow-

"No wonder he's so fond of the natives. After all, he's still just one of them at the end of the day, isn't he?"

CHAPTER 5

1913

"Do you think there will be war?"

Silence then as they both stared out at the flowing waters of the Nile, its color almost incandescent against the setting sun. There would be so many things Alexandra would miss about Egypt when she went home, but its ethereal sunsets might just top them all, the sky ablaze in the most striking fiery orange colored hue. Well, that and the man she had fallen in love with.

Kom Ombo was a place that had utterly bewitched her from the moment the steamer had rounded a wide bend of the Nile and there before them on the right-hand bank at the river's edge had stood its magnificent ruins. Her father had told her that the temple had been dedicated to not one but two deities, Sobek and Horus. Although she was well acquainted with Horus, god of war and the sky, married to the goddess Hathor, Sobek had been someone new. A crocodile god and bringer of doom to the unwary. He had told Alexandra that Sobek's prominence at Kom Ombo was no accident, that where the river bends around, there is a large island in the Nile and an associated series of sandbanks and that in times past, a favorite spot for crocodiles to laze about. As crocodiles have long been considered one of Africa's most dangerous animals, the ancient Egyptians knew that the crocodile was to be feared, worshipped, and appeased and so a temple was built in its honor. Alexandra had even remembered her father telling her that he met a couple of gentlemen who had come to Egypt for the sole purpose of hunting them, a most exotic and coveted of prizes.

He still hadn't responded so Alexandra thought that perhaps he hadn't heard her but then said almost cryptically, his eyes never once breaking from the water, "I think it's inevitable. For with a new century comes change- a new world order is upon us- those who will fight to achieve it and those who will fight to their last breath to maintain the old."

"You sound like a socialist with that kind of talk," she said jokingly. "Make sure you don't let my parents hear you or they'll think you're secretly a worshipper of Trotsky."

"Come with me, Alexandra," he said suddenly, turning to her to take her hands in his. "Come to Nubia with me. We'll get married and start a life here, together. I know you love Egypt as much as I do. I know it runs through your blood now."

Alexandra's heart seemed to stop at his words, a feeling of immense lightheadedness washing over her. Had he just asked her to marry him? Had she heard him correctly? And then he was kissing her, tentatively at first, perhaps sensing her shock, but then more passionately when he felt her mouth responding to his.

"I think it's time we return to the ship now," a voice said from behind them.

Both Alexander and Alexandra's heads whipped around to see her father towering before them, anger at both of them, but disappointment and hurt at Alexandra. How long had he been there. Had he heard Alexander asking her to run away with him? And then the kiss they had exchanged. With their ship docked at Kom Ombo for the night, Alexandra had snuck off, returning to the temple, knowing Alexander would be there, waiting for her. She had chanced it after hearing her father say he was going to lie down, that he wasn't feeling well after their morning visit to the Greco-Roman temple.

"Sir, I apologize, I didn't mean anything untoward-"

"I think it's time we parted ways," her father cut him off coldly. "Once and for all."

And with that, he roughly grabbed Alexandra's arm, and led her back towards the ship, and she not daring to look back, not even once.

1913

"I'm dying."

Alexandra's father hadn't said a word to her all evening- stone silence as they returned to the ship then completely ignoring her at dinner, rather gaily carrying on with her mother who was in an unusually cheerful mood, no doubt excited that their time in Egypt was almost at an end and that she would be returning to Philadelphia before too long- until now. Until those two heartbreaking words.

He had asked her to come up on deck with him after dinner, even asking Jack to accompany Emily back to their stateroom.

"But I don't understand," she had protested, her mind racing, her mouth all of a sudden bone dry, her heart beating rapidly in a nervous fashion. "You don't look sick at all!"

"It's cancer, I'm told. The specialist who I've seen gives me till the end of the year."

And then it dawned on her, why they were here, why her mother had consented to returning to a place she had absolutely loathed. It was all for her father, his last dying wish. And one that even Emily Garis, blackest of hearts, had granted.

"Why didn't you tell me sooner?" she demanded, her eyes now brimming with tears, her throat catching. "Why have you kept it from me?"

"I was going to wait until we had returned. I didn't want it hanging over you, marring things. I wanted you to experience Egypt as I had all those years ago. See it in its utterly spectacular and unbridled glory."

"But what changed? Why tell me now?"

"Because I can see how serious you are with that boy, Alexandra. And I don't want to lose you, have you run off with him one day and never see you again." So he had heard Alexander earlier, she thought. And now was using it to play his last hand.

"But Father, I would never do that." She was going to add, *"especially not now"* but knew that was understood. Or why else would he have dropped this on her?

"No, I don't think you would either. But I also can't give my blessing."

"Your blessing?" she asked, not understanding.

"My permission for you to marry him should he do the decent thing, the gentlemanly thing, and ask. I could never allow it."

"So you'll ensure I'm married off to someone I don't love and who doesn't love me back?" she cried out, a gamut of emotions engulfing her like a rising wave.

"You come home and forget about the boy. I'll make sure you attend Bryn Mawr in the fall."

"But what about Mother?" And then of course there was the matter of Jack. But she didn't dare ask this, not now.

"You leave her to me. A man should after all be permitted another dying wish if he so pleases." He said this to be funny but neither of them smiled nor laughed, for in their religion and culture, death was finite, the final journey but one in which there were no stunning frescoes and gifts adorning it all, unlike in ancient Egypt. Death was simply the end and life was no more.

As Alexander stood on the deck of the dahabiya, he saw a group of pelicans floating on the water. He took this as a good sign since in many cultures, Egypt among them, the pelican is considered to be a symbol of prosperity and good fortune. She would come. She loved him as he loved her with all his heart. She would come so they could be together, forever. Together as one.

But even as he waited, the sun growing lower and lower in the sky until it was that time of the day where it was ablaze in color, a landscape no words could do justice to, he never thought she wouldn't come. Until he heard the sound of a native boy calling out "sahib" waving a note in his hand as he ran towards the dahabiya.

And even as he snatched the note from the urchin's hands, one of which remained outstretched to which he hurriedly tossed a couple of piastres into, did he think the note would say anything other than "I'm late, but I'll still be there. Soon, we'll be together." Until he read the words she had written-

I'm sorry but I can't go with you. Please forgive me.
Alexandra Garis

The blood draining from his face, he didn't even turn around when he heard the dahabiya's captain behind him say, "Sir?"

In a broken voice, all he said was, "South, to Abu Simbel."

CHAPTER 6

Philadelphia, Pennsylvania
1921

"The Cavanaughs will be coming to dinner tomorrow night. I expect you to shine."

Alexandra put down the book she was reading, *This Side of Paradise* by F. Scott Fitzgerald, a debut work by an up and coming new author about 'carefree American youth,' a concept so foreign to her now after having moved back home and living under the iron first of her dour mother once more.

"And by 'shine' you mean don't espouse my thoughts on the ideals of Lenin and Trotsky at dinner?"

Her mother gave Alexandra a withering glare in response.

"Jack is coming too." This said in almost tortuous delight.

It was Alexandra now who shot back a dark look at her mother. Jack Cavanaugh, a name she had not heard in quite some time, one that she had been immune to during her studies at Bryn Mawr. But she had graduated nearly five years ago and then of course there had been the war. Long before Wilson had changed his tune, going against the isolationist ticket that had won him reelection in '16 and sending America's boys to the battlefields of Europe, it had been understood that she and Jack would marry. But the war had changed all that, changed Jack like so many other young men. Injured at the front in the Meuse-Argonne Offensive, two bullet wounds to his leg and shoulder, his physical injuries had healed but he seemed to still be there in that wild and mountainous strip of woodland in northeastern France. Shellshock was the name given to what returning soldiers like Jack had- staring into nothingness, completely unaware of what was transpiring around them or screaming their heads off in abject terror, drowning from the sound of imaginary artillery fire, the smells of rotting bodies, gunpowder, rats, dampness, human waste permeating every breath they drew in. And Alexandra thought that she had been saved from a fate worse than death.

"He's a living corpse!" Alexandra half-shouted, a bit too unkindly she knew and yet it was the truth. "You can't possibly expect me to marry someone like that. I'll be his nursemaid, not his wife."

"Nonetheless, it's been talked about since you were children that the Garis and Cavanaugh families would one day be united in marriage and that day has come." Emily Garis' tone was equally unkind and without any trace of maternal love or affectation. "The foolishness that was your father's lark for you to get your degree is over and done with. It's time now for you to do your duty to this family. Mrs. Cavanaugh has assured me that the doctors have said that the injuries Jack sustained in the war would not preclude his being able to have children," her mother added, slightly blanching at the mention of this. True ladies did not ever discuss what went on behind the closed doors of a husband and wife.

"If he even knows how to use it," Alexandra cried out, throwing her book down on the floor and storming from the room, knowing how utterly scandalized her mother would be from the mere mention of male anatomy.

It was that night, after enduring an hours long one-sided conversation with Jack, who had said nothing to her, who only exhibited any sense of being alive when his hands violently shook when holding the glass goblet of wine or his attempts to cut his lamb, the sound of the fork clattering loudly against the china plate, a scene which caused his parents to look alarmed and her mother to be casually indifferent, that Alexandra decided she needed to leave. Leave home, leave Philadelphia, leave her whole life behind before she was forever sealed to a fate she could never escape from.

She knew she would have to go as far away as possible to escape her mother's thumb. But where? Just then a sudden gust of wind came through the open window, causing some curios on her armoire to fall over. Getting up from her bed, she went to the window to close it and then turned to her armoire to right the fallen object. It was only then that she noticed what had fallen over- small ceramic statues of Horus and Sobek.

Egypt. She would go to Egypt to find him. She would right the mistake she never should have made all those years before.

Alexandra had never been one to shy away from a challenge, a headstrong trait of hers that went all the way back to childhood. The school bully at Agnes Irwin (who was rather ironically named Agnes Ipswich) had said to the other girls in their class that Alexandra couldn't possibly climb to the top of the massive oak tree that stood in the front yard of the school. Well, she had, rather impressively, until she was almost to the bottom and her scratchy wool uniform had snagged on one of the tree's branches, thus cutting off her mobility and ruining any chance she had of not being caught by the headmistress, who had been gleefully relayed of this by Agnes Ipswich herself. But as she walked into the Greaves' drawing room, all eyes settled on Alexandra and at that very moment she almost wished she were eight again and about to receive a dressing down from Headmistress Clayton.

But no, that simply wouldn't do as she advanced further into the room, multiple sets of eyes still upon her, sizing her up with looks of not only curiosity but also as if she were their prey. But not one of them was him.

"Alexandra!" Eliza exclaimed rather loudly as she hurried over to her. "You came, how marvelous!" Then crying out over to her shoulder she said to Sir Robert, "Look darling, Alexandra came. Didn't I tell you she would?" Sir Robert didn't say anything, just wanly nodded his head in acquiescence from his chair at the far side of the room.

The rest of the evening was a blur for Alexandra. She was introduced to a slew of people- those that were wintering in Assouan and others like the Greaveses who lived here permanently, some Americans, many British, a few French. But none of them knew of a man named Alexander Clarkson or an American archaeologist who fit his description.

"Oh my dear, you mustn't give up," Eliza said consolingly to Alexandra, who had given up on being social almost an hour ago, as she patted her gloved arm with hers.

"I don't think he's here. I don't even know if he's still alive. This has been a fool's errand," Alexandra glumly replied, feeling it was time she took her leave, anxious to be rid of all the couples and good cheer around her.

"Well, you haven't traversed the whole of Upper Egypt, now have you?" Eliza said, her tone one of almost sage wisdom now.

"What do you mean?" Alexandra asked, not understanding.

"Didn't you say that all those years ago he asked you to run away with him. Run away to Abu Simbel, the once kingdom of Nubia, all the way to Khartoum even."

Alexandra remained silent, the enormity of what Eliza was saying slowly sinking in.

Then in almost a gleeful whisper she asked, "What if the reason that you've not found him yet is because you've not gotten there yourself?"

"Yes," Alexandra said, sitting up straighter, feeling a surge of energy she hadn't had since that night in her bedroom all those months ago in Philadelphia. "I've simply not found him yet," Alexandra said, this time louder.

"Good. It's settled then," Eliza replied. "We'll hire a *dahabiya* and start our journey. Just because Assouan is the end of the journey for Thomas Cook cruises does not mean it's the end of the journey for you and Alexander."

"We?" asked Alexandra, rather incredulously.

"Why yes," Eliza said, a twinkle in her green eyes. "I do love Robert with all my heart but he knows I need a good adventure now and then. And besides, a young woman cannot go sailing up the Nile unchaperoned."

"But I'm a spinster," Alexandra protested. "And older than you!"

"Yes, but I'm a proper married woman whose husband is an earl."

"But are you sure?" Alexandra asked.

"Most."

CHAPTER 7

1922

The *dahabiya* Sir Robert had hired was magnificent. Although it lacked the more modern amenities found on a steamship like the Sudan (for instance, a well-equipped hair dressing salon), it more than made up for it in other ways like knowing that it was just them on board. Well, them, the dragoman, the ship's captain (the *rais*), steersman, eight crewmen, and a cook, along with a kitchen boy who Alexandra had surmised to be the rais' son, judging by the way he both yelled and patted the boy's head affectionately. Eliza had even surprised her by covering her eyes with her hands upon approaching the *Zinat al-Nil* and saying, "Okay, now" only for Alexandra to see the American flag flying alongside the Union Jack, along with a third that was adorned with a crocodile- Sobek. It was custom for every *dahabiya* to fly the national flag of the party aboard but Eliza had ensured that this journey was **her** journey. Her journey in search of her lost love. She was touched in a way she hadn't imagined possible from someone so entirely different from her, that she had just met.

Alexandra felt a sereneness as the *Zinat al-Nil* glided effortlessly upon the Nile's waters. It was something she hadn't felt in years, not since before the war, since her father's death. How he so would have loved this she thought, as she gazed out at the unrivalled splendor of the landscape that was still the same after thousands of years. The small Arab shepherdess with her one flock of sheep she guided towards the irrigation canal for a precious drink; the boats they passed by that were laden with sugar cane, a crop of immense height, nearly six feet; the hedges of cotton plants whose tufts seemed stuck to the decrepit brown pods; the lone village post that bore the word "poste" along with a flag that was embellished with a crescent and star.

She thought with a pang of sadness then how her father's last time in Egypt was robbed by the banality of sailing up the Nile on the *Arabia*, surrounded by travelers who were content to catch just a glimpse of ancient Egypt, caring nary a thought about its lush landscape and immense history. Cook steamers made their presence on the river known with the black smoke of their chimneys. They told Egypt that a modern dawn had arrived on its shores for good, whether or not she wanted it to. But a *dahabiya* treated Egypt's past as gently and sacred as it did its landscape when sailing up the river. Whereas the steam ship behaved like a colonial occupier upon foreign shores, taking all that it wanted willy-nilly, the *dahabiya* was a polite guest, one you would always want to return.

"Alexandra!"

Alexandra turned to see Eliza running towards her like she was a schoolgirl of eight, pure excitement spreading across her face. Eliza Greaves, Alexandra had concluded, did nothing at a slow or half pace, but rather everything came at a gauntlet's sprint.

"The dragoman tells me we'll be at Abu Simbel by sunset! Robert said it's the most magnificent place he's ever been."

"You mean you've never been here before?" Alexandra asked, somewhat surprised.

"No, Robert doesn't like to leave Assouan. Ever. He was at Abu Simbel. Before," saying the last word rather solemnly. As with all young people their age, no further clarification was needed as to what she meant.

Alexandra knew that the love Eliza had for her husband was genuine and for this she was glad, and yet a small part of her, one that she would never voice to the other woman, found it strange that this vivacious young woman whose infectious personality would bring a smile to the gravest of faces, was content to live a life in a far off country, so far from home, so removed from family and friends. And it wasn't even that they lived in Cairo where the social scene was at least more on par with that of London's.

"Well, then I'm doubly glad to be sharing it with you," Alexandra cheerily replied, looping her arm through the younger woman's.

Abu Simbel, the great temple that the pharaoh Ramses II had built as a place for the ancient Egyptians to worship him as a god following his death. But Alexandra also remembered her father saying that Ramses had also built it as an imposing message to any unwelcome visitors traveling on the Nile- that the Pharaoh is all mighty and is the owner of everything past this point, so always show respect and defer to his supreme authority. But as the *Zinat al-Nil* rounded a bend, it was then that she saw them, the four colossal figures that made up the Abu Simbel temple, four giant statues of Ramses himself.

There were two on each side of the doorway although one of them had lost its head, which was laid at its feet. But the other three, Alexandra thought, were the most exquisite sculptures she had ever seen. All in perfect size and harmony with each other, their eyes exuding an almost calming and peaceful look to them. But it was the sand that captivated her the most. Although most of the temple was indeed visible, when she closed her eyes she could just imagine how it must have looked to Giovanni Belzoni when he first came here in the early 19th century, the first Westerner to do so, and had found the entry blocked by deep sand, a blankness of desert sand with such a myriad of treasures buried underneath it. How extraordinary it must have been, knowing you were the first person to discover such an ancient site, knowing your name would be forever remembered by history.

Staring up at them, she turned so that her back was to them and she could have the same view as they did. Alexandra realized with a start that the four statues weren't just looking down the river but what lay beyond the point of the river that wasn't visible from where they rested, standing guard to the might and authority of Ramses the god, the words of her father about the temple serving as an imposing message to outsiders, ringing true.

As she and Eliza passed through the doorway, dutifully following behind their dragoman who was hurriedly saying about the temple's design- "each side of the corridor balustrade was covered with chains of captives, Syrians on the right, Ethiopians on the left" and "inside there are eight Osiride pillars, their faces near perfect," Alexandra found herself stopping, remembering her father just then-

"Baedeker had described it as such an enormous space which would even contain Notre Dame."

He had said those words to Alexandra when they had passed through the great Pylon, the gateway to the inner part of the temple, and into the immense great hall of Karnak. She remembered her father calling it "the great wilderness" for how immense a space it was and how nearly dark it was too. Although Alexandra had thought of her father constantly since arriving in Egypt, it was only now, while walking through Abu Simbel's inner space, that she felt him. But it didn't matter, for here she had felt his presence, felt him there with her even though they hadn't come here together all those years before. And perhaps, it was his way of telling her she had been right to come here, to keep traveling up the Nile, that Alexander was indeed still alive.

"I dare say," Eliza began. "That we have no right to consider ourselves the so-called 'superior' people when you stop and think what geniuses those ancient Egyptians were with their building designs and whatnot."

She was of course referring to what their dragoman had told them about the temple's sacrarium- twice a year in the early morning hours, sunlight comes through to reach the four statues thus illuminating the four statues that for the 363 other days of the year, sit in the temple's rock in a perpetual blackness, more than 200 feet from the principal entrance of the temple. That on February 21 and October 21 each year, sunlight enters smoothly on Ramses's face and soon spreads to become a ray of light illuminating the four statues' faces inside the sacrarium Alexandra had been quite disappointed to learn she had missed witnessing this phenomenon by mere weeks.

"I mean, we look down on the *fellaheen,* and yet most are probably smarter than your average toff. My own mum gave birth to 11 kids, left school when she was 10, and I feel is still smarter and craftier than any number of female relatives of Robert's."

This was debatable, not that she would say this out loud to Eliza and offend the young woman, but Alexandra knew what Eliza was saying had merit. When the ancient Egyptians built such incredible buildings, practiced remarkable astronomical feats, their people were still behaving like utter barbarians and would be for hundreds of years to come.

"I think I liked Nefertari's temple the most though," Alexandra said, speaking her thoughts out loud rather on purpose.

"Well, of course you do," Eliza answered, smirking. "It was a 'temple of love' after all."

"Not quite," Alexandra said, laughing. Although Ramses, like all pharaohs, had had multiple wives, Nefertari had been his favorite, his beloved one. And so the smaller of the two temples at Abu Simbel had been built to honor her- dedicated to the goddess Hathor, the cow goddess who was among the most famous goddesses worshiped in ancient Egypt and who was personified by Nerfertari. "I like that he considered them to be equals." The statues of Nefertari were the same height as those of the statues of Ramses that were on his temple. And just like at Ramses's temple, at Nefertari's their children were depicted around their feet. They were a unit of one, Alexandra thought. Man had not been superior in ancient Egypt, just look at Ramses's love for his beloved wife, look at the gumption of Hatshepsut, becoming one of the Egyptian kingdom's most popular pharaohs, never mind the fact that she had been born a woman.

"Well, I think it's simply all marvelous," Eliza replied. "If me mum and brothers and sisters could see me now."

Father too, Alexandra thought to herself pensively.

They had eaten a delicious picnic lunch that the *dahabiya's* cook prepared. It had been set up on top of the temple by the kitchen boy, no small feat considering the exertion it required of Eliza and Alexandra to climb such an arduous and unwieldly distance (climbing sand was quite laborious) but thankfully the dragoman and a crewman were there to assist, offering their arms to the women and at more than one time, nearly dragging them upwards. But it had been worth it- imagine, picnicking on top of an ancient Egyptian temple that was nearly 100 feet tall! She had always been fascinated by the idea of flying, remembering fondly as a little girl when her father told her that history had just been made when the Wright brothers successfully piloted the first powered flight, or during the war and reading about the famous fighter aces, the "Knights of the Sky" that the newspapers had dubbed them. Alexandra had spent hours, no days, gazing out onto the waters of the Nile but it was a view that she would never tire of, a craving to see it that could never be sated. It had a calming element to it that no modern medicine could compete with.

Qui aquam nili bibit rursus bibet- he who drinks of the Nile returns. Alexandra, a classical studies major, had many great loves when it came to the ancient Greeks and Romans, but Herodotus might just have been her favorite. While many scholars debated if Herodotus had ever actually come to Egypt, Alexandra believed he had. For without seeing the Nile for oneself, how could anyone adequately convey its beauty to others?

Egypt is the gift of the Nile.

Eliza had retired to the *Zinat al-Nil* to nap but Alexandra decided to stay on shore, preferring to read a copy of J.M. Barrie's *Peter and Wendy* under a lush palm tree that stood at the river's edge as it offered the loveliest of breezes. She and William Garis hadn't had much in common when it came to literature, Alexandra much preferring the popular novels of the day whereas her father gravitated towards Dickens and Sir Arthur Conan Doyle, that is when he wasn't drowning in the latest medical study. However, they both had adored the story of the lost boy who didn't want to grow up. Alexandra had loved its whimsical and fairytale elements but she thought her father perhaps envied Peter, envied a life free of responsibilities and societal dictates, a life where you were the sole architect of how it was to be constructed.

"It is not in doing what you like, but in liking what you do that is the secret of happiness."

Alexandra wasn't sure how long she had been dozing but when she awoke, she was startled to see a felucca, a traditional sailing boat popular with the natives, moored next to the *Zinat al-Nil.* And turning on her head ever so slightly, more startled to see a man dressed in white linen, sitting at an easel, his back to her. She rose then, trying her best to remedy her now horribly wrinkled frock.

As she approached the man, she could see that he was painting a watercolor scene. He was quite good, she thought, as she saw the Nile so beautifully depicted on the canvas.

"Hello," she said softly, not wanting to startle him or cause a paint stroke to go awry.

Whirling around, "Oh, hello there." The man was American she could hear, early 30s perhaps. "Apologies, I would have introduced myself when I arrived but you appeared to be having the most delicious slumber."

Alexandra blushed over the idea that this stranger had seen her sleeping. Was delicious a polite way of saying she had been drooling? Her cheeks reddened at the thought.

"Your paintings are quite lovely," she said to him. "May I?" she asked, indicating the leather-bound portfolio that rested at his feet.

"Of course," he said, returning his attention to the easel.

She lowered herself to the ground, making sure to arrange herself in a ladylike position, Emily Garis' rules of decorum and etiquette forever drilled into her, and started to leaf through the canvas sheets.

"Oh, apologies. I'm Joseph, Joseph Locke." He said this still painting, no hand was offered.

Following suit, Alexandra said, "Alexandra Garis."

Returning her attention to the portfolio she added, "Your work is incredible, such attention to detail," in sheer awe of such remarkable talent, envious of those like this Joseph Locke who could replicate what they saw so effortlessly. "You truly make ancient Egypt come alive before one's eyes."

"Where's this?" she asked, pointing to the canvas sheet that in charcoal roughly depicted a water scene that was empty save for what appeared to be the tips of ruins above the waterline. And then she gasped when she noticed the initials in the lower right-hand corner. AC.

"Did you draw this?" she asked, her heart pounding, desperately trying to collect her thoughts and make sense of the initials. It must be a coincidence. Alexander hadn't been an artist she told herself, and yet looking down at the roughly drawn charcoal sketch she could tell it was not the work of Joseph or someone of a similar talent.

"Oh that," he said, not looking up from the canvas. "That's Philae. No, I didn't draw that. Nothing really to draw as you can see, the whole island, temple ruins and all, got submerged after the dam was built. And only two months of the year can you even see anything other than the tower over the gateway on the temple to Isis. Otherwise, you have to imagine it all."

"Yes," Alexandra said, impatience building in her tone. "But who drew this?"

He looked at her oddly, like he hadn't understood what she asked. "My friend. Alexander."

And then it felt as if time had stopped, her heart seemed to momentarily stop beating before it started thumping loudly in her chest, so loudly she could hear it since there were no other sounds around them. Even the Nile seemed to pause; the banks of the river and the sky above it, normally replete with signs of life, were eerily silent.

"What's Alexander's last name?"

"Clarkson."

Alexandra took a moment to pause then. It can't be, she told herself. It can't possibly be this easy, this fortuitous. Kismet didn't exist for people like her, people who had their whole lives dictated to them before they were even born. Kismet was for those who took chances in life, gambled on what they wanted, dared to risk it all.

"Is he here?" Alexandra asked, her throat suddenly parched, on the verge of being unable to speak.

"Oh no. It's just me I'm afraid. Alexander had to return to Luxor."

But was it actually him? Alexander Clarkson was a fairly common name. And never once had she seen him draw anything, nor had he mentioned it was a talent or passion of his either.

"He's American?" she asked.

Joseph regarded her quizzically again, undoubtedly confused by this stranger's interest in his friend who wasn't even there.

"Yes," he said, cautiously. "Do you know him?"

"Well, that's the thing. I did know an Alexander Clarkson once. I met him here in Egypt in fact, before the war that is. But we parted and I never knew what happened to him. He was an archaeologist."

"Oh yes, that's him," he said cheerily returning to his easel, his momentary suspicion of Alexander's prying nature now cast aside. "We met in the war, in the trenches in fact. After the war, he returned to Egypt, to 'home' he called it and I went back to the States. We exchanged some letters, I told him how I couldn't rid myself of the nightmares, that I felt that I was back in the trenches and took to the bottle. My wife kicked me out of the house, said I was scaring the little ones. It was probably for the best, she didn't look at me the same, never touched me again after I returned home. I know my injuries frightened her."

Alexandra studied the other man. Unlike Sir Robert, who no doubt appeared to some a walking corpse, Joseph looked fine. Healthy in fact. But then she thought of Jack and the shell shock state he was in all those years after the last shots had been fired.

"And you came here," she asked.

"Yes, Alexander sent me the money too. One of the best. This is his boat," he said, nodding his head towards the felucca. "He knows I need to move around, put new memories into my head, stuff out the bad ones. So every month I go sailing, sometimes up the Nile, sometimes down it."

"Did you study as an artist?"

"Oh no. I was a school teacher. Taught high school mathematics and science, namely chemistry. But I had always liked to draw. In the trenches, I kept a little tiny sketchbook with me. After I got injured, Jerry had thrown a grenade into our trench, I woke up and it was gone. Before I was sent home, Alexander came to see me and gave it to me. He had found it in the mud and cleaned it off as best as he could. But when we got to Luxor, to his house, he showed me the oil paints and charcoal he had gotten me and told me that these would help me to find myself again." He paused then, and Alexandra could see tears brimming in the man's eyes. "He's the best friend I could ever have."

CHAPTER 8

Later that night, Alexandra invited Joseph to have dinner with them on the *Zinat al-Nil*. When she told Eliza that she had 'found' Alexander, that he was alive and here in Egypt, the woman had jumped out of her chair where they were sitting in the drawing room and thrown her arms around Alexandra in pure joy.

As they were lingering over cool glasses of lemonade, their plates long since emptied of what cook had prepared for dinner, Alexandra asked the one thing that had been plaguing her since that afternoon.

"Does Alexander ever talk of me?"

Joseph looked stricken then, his face revealing the answer that Alexandra knew to be true.

"In the trenches once, after a particularly bad night, Jerry had been shelling us for days it seemed, there had been a pause and he spoke about a woman he had met long ago in a far-off land he called it. How he had fallen madly in love with her and yet in the end had broken his heart. The way he spoke, it almost sounded as if it were a fairy tale but now I know it to be true. That it was you."

Me, Alexandra mouthed silently at the same time that Joseph said the word 'you.'

"Do you think he will even want to see me?" she asked, another nagging thought entering her mind, her feelings of jubilation and excitement over having found Alexander now replaced by fears of doubt and uncertainty.

Joseph looked at her squarely then and said, "As Geoffrey Chaucer once wrote in *The Canterbury Tales,* "nothing ventured, nothing gained."

It was Joseph who had sent word in Assouan onto Alexander in Luxor that he would be returning from his sailing venture early and could he please meet him on the terrace of the Winter Palace for a long overdue catchup (Joseph had been away for nearly three months by now). The former teacher of course would not be there; he in fact would be sailing back up river to the ancient kingdom of Nubia and sketching those ancient sites of importance and to some degree, lesser notoriety since the "Cookies" so rarely ventured off the Nile's much too beaten path.

Alexandra and Eliza still had another month's use of the *dahabiya* at their disposal and Eliza said "there was no bloody way she was going to miss out on witnessing the most exciting and romantic event of the century." They would have to hurry if they were to make it to Luxor on the prescribed date that Joseph had written in his letter. Sir Robert had appeared indifferent upon their return to Assouan and hearing their new travel plans, just saying "it seems like a good adventure" (a romantic he was not).

Alexandra hadn't thought of the possibility of what would happen if Alexander wasn't happy to see her; that what if upon sight of her, he left the terrace or worse, shouted at her and said she was a horrible person for doing what she did. Before saying goodbye to Joseph, she had asked him if he thought Alexander still loved her, would be willing to give her, them, another chance. He knew Alexander much more deeply than she ever did, especially after all these years apart, and a great war interspersed between them as well.

At this Joseph had looked out onto the Nile from where they stood on the deck of the *Zinat al-Nil* and said nothing. But after a pause he spoke. "The war changed me in the worst of ways. Although it would be easy to say the war was what ended my marriage, it was I, my inner demons that lay root to the evil that spread throughout and destroyed it. Alexander is a steady sort of man, one who seems has always had his head on straight. But I know in some ways he also keeps his thoughts and emotions inside him and know that can be just as deadly as the nightmares that make me call out in the night. You knew him before the war, before we saw the true horrors of war and the horrible extent of what man was capable of doing to his fellow man. But as my favorite 14th century English poet once said-

"Nothing ventured, nothing gained," Alexandra answered.

"Indeed. And I'm not much of a religious man but one verse from the Bible got me through many a dark and harrowing night in France-

"For we are powerless before this great multitude who are coming against us; nor do we know what to do, but our eyes are on you."

"I'm impressed," Alexandra said.

"Second Book of Chronicles, Chapter 20, Verse 12." A pause then before continuing on. "Son of a preacher man. Literally," he added, his eyes twinkling even against the black sky. "Best of luck my dear girl. And I hope to see you again soon." And with that he was gone in the darkened night.

Mahshallah, what God pleases, silently whispering the timeless Arabic phrase to herself. She wasn't a God-fearing woman, but for once she hoped God would touch her heart.

Alexandra approached the Winter Palace, its striking yellow stuccoed façade replete with ornate balconies and balustrades easily visible even amongst the chaos of the Luxor streets that at all hours of the day seemed to be bursting with mule trains, souvenir shops, tour buses and more. Her heart was pounding with each approaching step she took, the anxiety and flutter of butterflies only increasing in size. She climbed the front entrance's staircase slowly, each step requiring an infinite amount of both energy, for her legs seemed to hang heavy on her person as if she was dead weight, but mental concentration too. The latter was so that her inner worst thoughts and paranoia didn't consume her, didn't let her listen to the ever quiet voice in her head that was telling her to run far away from here, go back to Philadelphia, go back to anywhere but here, to not allow herself to have her heart broken again. But no, she was at the top now, a smartly attired native adorned in a fez holding open the door for her.

Stepping through, it was as if she had passed into another world for inside the opulent Palace's interior was a calming oasis, the chaos and noise and smells of what lay just on the other side of those doors long forgotten. Inside, with its high ceilings and marble floors covered with beautiful silken rugs, its art nouveau ironworks flanking the main staircase in an ascending fashion, one would almost think they were back in Europe somewhere- London or Paris, or perhaps even the Amalfi Coast.

She kept walking until she was out on the terrace and it was only then that she drew up short. Although his back was to her, she would know that tall figure with the lush mane of dark hair anywhere. And as if she had beckoned him in a silent language that only they knew, he slightly turned then so that he was facing her. He smiled politely at her until she saw the recognition of her in his eyes and his face immediately turned white. He didn't move, just stared at her in shock. Seeing that he wouldn't come to her, she started to walk towards him, each step laboriously taken, every inch she moved feeling as if she was attempting it in quicksand. And then she was before him, her face and body now having grown equally slack, seeing him here, in person. They both stared at each other, equal parts disbelief and amazement.

It was he who finally spoke. "Is it really you or am I dreaming again? If it's the latter I'll gladly take it over the nightmares that haunt me each night, that I'm back in the trenches awaiting orders to go 'over the top.' If I am dying right now, then this is the memory I want to have," he said, tears pooling at the side of his dark brown eyes, his hand starting to tremble ever so slightly.

"It's me," Alexandra rushed to say, taking his now trembling hand within her gloved one. "I'm really here." And then not sure if she should say it or not she added, "Your Alexandra." At least she hoped she still was.

Looking around and seeing they had become the subject of unbridled curiosity, he now took her hand firmly in his, leading her down the terrace's steps and into the garden where he kissed her with as much passion and fervor as a nearly 10-year absence would warrant.

"So should my dear friend Joseph's new name be Cupid for orchestrating such a scheme?" Alexander asked. They were at his house now, a charming cottage-like building that had the loveliest of gardens in the back, as so many Egyptian houses did, utterly plain and nondescript in the front but then stunning oases in the rear. She realized how improper this was, she, an unmarried woman, alone at a man's house but propriety be damned. The war had changed everything, not just the lengths of a woman's dress and the doing away of corsets. The end of the war had brought about not just the long fought for right to vote for women but also the realization and understanding that for once, a woman needn't be defined by who her father or husband was. That a woman could be someone outside the home, have a real job and support herself. And that a woman could fall in love with whom she wanted, not what a pedigree chart proscribed. And if she wanted to wile away the hours with that same gentleman, unmarried or gasp, not even betrothed, then so be it.

"Yes, but only if we can call Eliza Aphrodite," Alexandra replied, thinking of both their friends who had been instrumental in orchestrating all this and who she could not hold any dearer to her then. Two complete strangers that had completely altered her life's path.

"Tell me why you left," Alexander said, his voice quiet but tinged in pain. "Why you didn't come that day."

"My father."

"I know that," he cut in, his tone now slightly impatient. "But you seemed so sure of us, of everything."

"No, you don't know," she said, her hooded eyes thousands of miles away from that tiny little Egyptian garden they found themselves nestled in. "He was dying."

She told him the whole story then, beginning with her father's confession to her all those years ago the night they had snuck off to visit Kom Ombo Temple and had been discovered by him, his fighting with her mother to ensure she attended college to fulfill her lifelong dream. And how he was dead by the end of summer and her heart had never been the same, until now.

"I couldn't do that to him," she said, her voice now catching in her throat. "I know I broke your heart but I couldn't break a dying man's. I couldn't have him go to his grave feeling that I had abandoned him, chosen a stranger over my own father."

Alexander remained quiet. Alexandra wasn't entirely sure if telling him the truth, the whole story behind her actions, had lessened the pain she had caused or just added to it.

"Can you ever forgive me?" she asked him as a small child would ask a parent after breaking a teacup.

"There's nothing to forgive my love," Alexander answered, placing a feather light kiss upon her forehead as he continued stroking the top of her hand with his thumb. "If I could go back in time and have just one more day with my father, I would seize it in a heartbeat."

"Never say goodbye because goodbye means going away and going away means forgetting."

"That's lovely. Did you come up with that?" he asked her.

"No, it's from a book my father read me as a young child. *Peter and Wendy.* And you know something? They were his very last words to me." And with that she cried, soft almost hushed sobs until she was all cried out, the front of Alexander's shirt thoroughly damp, nearly soaked through. He hadn't said anything during this, hadn't told her to stop her crying, that she wasn't a child anymore, that it was God's will. He had just let her be.

Philadelphia, Pennsylvania
July 1913

"You must be strong now, my dear girl," her father said, taking her hand within his own limp, pallid one. He had been bedridden for weeks now, Doctor Morris saying it was only a matter of time. He had insisted that Giles, his valet, prop him up against the bevy of pillows that adorned the ornate brass bed even though she could see that such an undertaking had depleted what remaining pitiful ounces of strength he still had left. But he had overrode everyone's raised voices and objections, saying that he was going to die and leave God's earth in the manner that he wanted to and if that included sitting up in his bed so he could say proper goodbyes to his loved ones, then so be it.

Alexandra had been at his side as he said goodbye to cousins, dear family friends including the Cavanaughs, her mother's sisters and their families. And then he had asked for everyone to leave the room as he wanted to speak to his daughter in private. Her mother flashed her a peeved expression but acquiesced to her husband. While Emily Garis hadn't become a doting and caring wife anew in the months since they had returned from Egypt, she had curtailed both her bitter disposition towards life and protestations on her daughter's behavior. For this Alexandra was grateful, grateful that her father's last months on earth with his wife had been if not pleasant, then at least amicable.

"Come September, you'll be a college student. And I couldn't be prouder," his voice straining to speak. "From the day you were born, you have been my pride and joy. You have always deserved the best and that includes a college education. It's the 20th century now, you can be and have anything you want in life. The world's order is changing and that includes that of a woman. Always remember that."

Alexandra just stared at him as she continued to hold his hand, tears pooling in her eyes. Her dear father, her best friend, her only ally in this house and he was leaving her. Forever.

"I can't say goodbye, Father. I can't," her voice broke now, sobs escaping her.

And then perhaps with the last bit of strength he would ever muster, he drew her forward into his now emaciated arms-

"Never say goodbye because goodbye means going away and going away means forgetting."

CHAPTER 9

1922

They were married in a small ceremony with Eliza and Sir Robert and of course Joseph serving as both witnesses and guests. To some, their union was perhaps rushed, what with only having known each other a few short weeks all those years ago, but if her father's rapid succumbing to death and the war had taught people their age anything, it was that life was entirely too short to continue to squander it. When one finds happiness, one is to seize it and never let go.

It was only on their wedding night, in a suite at the Winter Palace, did Alexandra learn of the horrors that Alexander had experienced during the war. He hadn't been shell-shocked as Jack had been, unable to function at the barest minimum, or Joseph, who had turned to drink in order to battle his inner demons. No, he had seemed quite normal. Sad, pensive looks when he thought she wasn't looking. She knew the horrors and ravages of war were scenes one could never fully purge from one's memory, forever etched in time whether they were wanted or not. But on their wedding night, only after they had both fallen into a deep slumber, spent from the hours it seemed they had spent making love, was Alexandra startled awake by the sounds of horrible screams and horrified they were coming from Alexander, who lay on his back violently thrashing his body, his eyes open but clearly not there in the present with her, but thousands of miles away back in France.

When Alexandra had come to him naked on the bed she had noticed a small, brightly colored scar on his lower right abdomen but didn't ask about it. It was only when she was running her hands over his back did she feel more scars and asked him to turn so that she could see. His back was covered with the most horrific of scars, ones of varying sizes and angry looking hues of red and pink.

"Do they disgust you?" he asked, his voice tinged with sadness. "I am not the man I was all those years ago."

"Of course not," she said, quick to reassure him. And then as if to further cement both her love and devotion to the man he was now, she covered every inch of his scarred back with feathery light kisses.

"My darling, please wake up," Alexandra cooed to him, trying to gently wake him from his nightmares while all the while dodging his thrashing arms.

But he kept screaming until she whispered the word 'Kom Ombo' into his ear. And as if it were the miracle tonic he needed to calm him, he stopped.

"Alexandra?" he asked almost whimpering. "Are you here?"

"Yes, I'm here. It's me. We're here together. Just us two," she cooed to him as she drew him to her, comforting him as a mother would comfort her small child. "You're okay, we're here in Egypt, in Luxor at the Winter Palace. And soon we'll be embarking on our honeymoon cruise up the Nile, all the way to Abu Simbel, just like we always dreamt about."

She talked of ancient Egypt then- of the Creation Story of Ra, of Isis who was 'Mother of the Gods' and who cared for her fellow deities as she did for human beings, and also of the great love affair between Ramses II and his favorite wife, Nefertari. It was those soothing words that finally allowed him to return to sleep and not wake till morning. It was a ritual Alexandra would soon discover that she would need to perform on an almost nightly basis.

Unlike when she and Eliza had careened up the Nile on the *Zinat al-Nil*, Alexandra and Alexander's honeymoon sailing was taken at a languid pace, one in which Alexandra reveled. They stopped at a plethora of places, some she was familiar with due to their history and global fame and others where Alexander regaled her with their histories.

Alexandra remembered from before that it was the Great Temple they would see first, its massive façade looming more than one hundred feet into the air, the four enormous seated statues of Ramses that flanked the entrance, daring those that passed by to defy him, whether in this life or the next.

"Of the seven different sites in Nubia that Ramses ordered shrines built during his reign, do you know why he chose here for the greatest, most majestic one?" Alexander asked, as though he were the professor and she his student.

"It's beautiful location of course," Alexandra quickly answered, confident in her answer.

"Consider where we are, my dear," he said, taking her hand and guiding her to the top of the Great Temple that they had climbed just a short bit ago. "I know that looking out as we are at this very moment, it's easy to see nothing but sheer beauty- the verdant oasis, the desert sands just beyond, the calm Nile waters that could soothe even the fussiest of babies- but here, this particular spot is just north of the river's second cataract- a stretch of splintered rocks and monstrous and often deadly whitewater rapids. Ramses choose Abu Simbel's location on purpose; the strategic location was just as much a warning to his enemies and all those that sought to challenge Egypt's power and might as its design."

Alexandra thought about this for a moment but then, not wanting her honeymoon trip to turn into an academic colloquium, turned to him and said, "And yet Ramses was still a great romantic, perhaps the greatest," smiling while batting her eyelashes at him in the most coquettish fashion she could muster.

He regarded her almost quizzically. Alexandra wasn't sure if he was annoyed at her for interrupting his impromptu lecture or simply taken aback over this sudden impish behavior she was exhibiting. But then he did the most decidedly wonderful thing ever- he threw back his head and laughed and then she joined in with him.

"Have there been a lot of women in your life?"

Alexander's eyes had been closed. Following their picnic repast that the ship's cook's kitchen boy had laid out in a shady spot near to the Temple of Nefertari, Alexander had said a nap was in order while Alexandra decided to try her hand at sketching, although she'd also decided not too long after that she wasn't very good at it. But they shot open at her question.

"Where the dickens did that come from?" he asked, his tone cautiously polite but also suspect.

"I just meant you're a man of the world-"

"And in your mother's world, that's a polite way of saying 'man of the streets'."

Ignoring him, she continued. "You're older than me and you're still a..." She trailed off, suddenly feeling childish and somewhat embarrassed.

"Yes?" he prodded, clearly unsure of where she was going.

"A man!" she said, saying these words as if someone had just fired a gun.

"Well, yes, I thought this was universal knowledge," he said jokingly.

But seeing his barbs were not enough to mollify her or change the subject he said, "I was all of these things one week ago, one month ago, and nearly ten years ago when we first met. Why are they mattering now?"

"Ramses had scores of women in his life, but it was always said that his heart belonged only to Nefertari." And then because she was too embarrassed to continue, she turned away from him so he couldn't see her and added almost in a whisper, "I just hope that I'll always be your Nefertari."

Silence then. Only the sounds of birds could be heard but if you stayed really still and concentrated, one could also make out the flowing rhythm of the Nile. Not being able to take it anymore, she flounced around to see him smiling broadly at her until he rushed to take her in his arms and kissed her more passionately than she could have ever imagined was possible.

"While I'm hardly the Ramses type," he began, "you will always be my Nefertari. You and no one else."

"You are," she whispered into his ear as she playfully nibbled at it with her tongue. "That and more."

Two days later they began the long journey down the Nile, back to Luxor, back to home. Alexandra had stationed herself on the deck of their *dahabiya* so that she could stare at the retreating temples of Abu Simbel until they were no more.

At the final glimpse of the Great Temple, one of the four seated giant statues of Ramses just visible, she thought of her father. She liked to think that he would be happy for her now, that even though it had meant leaving behind her mother and that life forever, she would have a lifetime of happiness. She would have the life she deserved, not the life set out for her by societal dictates and familial obligations. And she undoubtedly knew he would have been pea green with envy over the incredible honeymoon trip she'd had.

It was here at Abu Simbel, where Alexander had wanted her to go with him all those years before when she had just been a girl, did she realize that she, no, rather they, had finally come full circle.

CHAPTER 10

Luxor, Egypt
1924

In the initial years since they had married, Alexandra and Alexander had settled into a simple yet comfortable existence in Luxor. Simple in the sense that by Emily Garis' standards they might as well have been living in poverty (although certainly not by native standards)- long gone were the days of lavish fêtes and six different spoons at one's table setting (naturally each one serving its own purpose). And comfortable if for no other reason Alexandra and Alexander were so in love with each other, so deliriously happy to just be in the other's company. Each of their parents' marriages hadn't been easy ones- Alexandra's for lack of love, Alexander's for lack of money- but with them, it was as if they had taken what they had seen and emotionally endured growing up and made silent vows to themselves, that they would never be like that. If they had each other, that would always be enough.

They had also survived what had become known as 'Tutmania.' Although the discovery of the tomb of Tutankhamun, the boy king who had only been around eight years of age when he ascended the throne, had gripped the world with the creation of new fashions, hairstyles, films, books, and more, nowhere had this been felt more jarringly than in Luxor itself, the city directly on the other side of the river where the boy king's tomb had been finally found in the famed Valley of the Kings. Following the Armistice and the signing of the Treaty of Versailles, many in Egypt, both Western and native officials alike, had feared that the world would never be what it once was, that the pockmarked terrain of the Western Front was much too fresh in people's minds to consider a "grand tour" of the continent and subsequent foray into Egypt, as had been done by thousands of travelers in yesteryear, that Egypt would now become a destination only frequented by the intrepid traveler, the not-always welcomed oriental sort. But then the boy king's tomb had been found and the rest was history. Everyone- American, British, German, French- adult, child- they all wanted their own taste of Tutmania, anything that would allow them to forget for a time all that they had endured during the war- hunger, bombing raids, inflation, loss of loved ones, loss of an entire generation of young boys who would never get the chance to become men. And so the world gladly ate it all up- hawkers selling every imaginable supposed relic of the boy king himself.

But what had made it so remarkable was the fact that the tomb itself had remained hidden for more than 3,000 years after Tutankhamun's death and burial. Although the tombs for most of the pharaohs had been plundered by graverobbers in ancient times, the boy king's had not; this was attributed solely to the debris that had hidden it for most of its existence. Therefore, it was not plundered to the same degree as other tombs had been. And so it became the first largely intact royal burial site from ancient Egypt, making it one of the most famous archaeological discoveries of all time. A discovery that could be credited to one man who had been searching for it for more than 25 years, a Mister Howard Carter.

After being introduced to Carter, Alexandra wasn't entirely sure what to make of him. Although he had been agreeable enough the first time she'd met him, not to mention clearly knowledgeable after having lived in Egypt for so long by then (she remembered Alexander telling her he had first come to Egypt in what was it, 1891? '92?), she couldn't help but shake the feeling that all Carter was truly after was fame, money, and glory, for both himself and of course his benefactor, the 5th Earl of Carnarvon. She didn't tell Alexander this for he would undoubtedly have called her a snob, but she much preferred the company of Lord Carnarvon and his daughter, the delightful Lady Evelyn, to Carter's.

Subsequent interactions with the middle-aged, self-taught archaeologist left Alexandra finding Carter awkward to be around, especially, she observed, when the British man was around those of a much higher social rank, as well as abrasive in his bearing. Although she and Alexander rarely quarreled, they had one night, and over Carter's personal character of all things.

"Why must you always stick up for the man?" Alexandra yelled, her usually placid temper getting the best of her now. "It's simply maddening!"

"Because he's not the money hungry charlatan you make him out to be," Alexander calmly replied, his serenity almost mocking her.

"You're always saying ancient Egyptian antiquities must be for the good of today's Egyptian people, and yet Carter's helping to ensure they're taken away from her. Helping his already wealthy benefactor get even richer." Alexandra felt a pang of remorse at saying this since she genuinely liked Lord Carnarvon. And he reminded her so much of her father, his and Lady Evelyn's father-daughter relationship almost mirroring the one she had shared with her own father.

"He cares more for the Egyptian people than any white man I've ever known. I told you about the Saqqara Affair, didn't I?"

It had happened ages ago, back up north at Saqqara. Apparently there had been a violent scuffle between a group of ill-behaving French tourists and some of the Egyptian monument sentries there.

Forever loyal to his men, not the French equivalent of 'Cookies', Carter had defended the actions the sentries and refused to apologize to either French government officials or his superiors at the antiquities service. He resigned from his post and returned to Luxor where he would spend the next few years working as an artist.

Alexander had her beat; he knew it and she knew it. There were few white people in the world who would take the side of a dark-skinned person over one of their own. And then it hit her, like a bolt of lightning. He saw a bit of himself in Carter. Sure, Alexander had actually gone to university, one of America's most prestigious and elite, but he still came from humble beginnings- the child of immigrants, a childhood growing up in a dark and dank tenement on New York's Lower East Side, using his wits to survive on the streets, to make something of himself. But both men had been ambitious enough, hungry enough to want more than the lot they had been born into, to do what they truly loved in life. And for both men, that was to publicize the glory of ancient Egypt.

Alexandra would have never dared say this to anyone, let alone Alexander but she was bored. Although she adored living in Egypt, she was not playing the role of Emily Garis here. She had no immense house to maintain, no retinue of servants, no dinner parties to plan, no social calls to be made (although she did correspond regularly with Eliza who she now considered to be a dear friend and was delighted to hear that she was expecting her first child). And the topic of children only added to Alexandra's inquietude, her feeling that something was off, that why hadn't she conceived by now. Twice her monthly bleeding had been late and each time she had thought, this must be it, that she and Alexander were going to finally have the baby they both so wanted. But then the monthly bleeding would start, taunting her as a schoolyard bully would taunt those he teased, saying, "I fooled you," all the while snickering at his folly.

Alexander was of course oblivious to it all- so happy and immersed was he in his work. While Carter had gotten the global notoriety and fame from having found the tomb of a pharaoh, Alexander had spent the year and a half working at Deir-el-Medinn, which during ancient times had once been home to many artisans and other laborers who had been involved in the digging and decoration of the pharaohs' tombs in the Valley of the Kings over a period of 400 years. It was located on the West Bank of the Nile, across from Luxor.

He was working on a team that was headed by Bernard Bruyère, a dedicated and fastidious French Egyptologist who had been in Egypt since long before the war. His area of passion had always been in the lives of the ordinary people of ancient Egypt. When Alexander had first told her about his newest dig project, she had been confused.

"But what can you and Bruyère and the others stand to gain from such work?' she had asked him. "I mean it seems better suited for the local archaeologists," by which they both knew she was referring to native Egyptians.

He had looked at her then, saying nothing until he rose from his chair and cooly said before leaving the room, "Sometimes you really are your mother's daughter."

She had regretted her words as soon as she said them, but also being the type of stubborn person that she was, she didn't go after him, asking for his forgiveness, telling him she knew better than to utter such ignorant drivel. Wasn't that why they were here, after all? Living here, not just wintering here but then returning to their Western homes.

He didn't speak to her the rest of the night, coming to bed long after she had. But the following morning she was surprised to enter the small dining room and find him still there. Usually he was across the river before sunrise. "Prepare a bag for the day," he had told her. "I want you to come with me today."

And so that day and in the days after, she had gone with him to Deir-el-Medinn and had been utterly entranced by the site. She had never loved Egypt more than the first time she had seen the sun set there- the sun going behind the steep cliffs towering over Deir-el-Medinn as if it were playing a game of peek-a-boo. Alexandra had never seen such a breathtaking sight and here in Egypt, she had already seen so many. But this one was different- this wasn't tied to royalty that were buried in tombs laden with hundreds of pounds of gold.

"It's tedious and frustrating, our names will never grace the *New York Times* or be uttered at famous balls during the Season in London, there's no guarantee of even eventual success, and yet I can't think of anything more meaningful," Alexander said to her one night as they enjoyed a gin and tonic in their garden out back, the stifling hot air of the afternoon finally starting to dissipate. "But our work will eventually become one of the most thoroughly documented accounts of community life in the ancient world- and I don't mean just here in Egypt, or even nearby Mesopotamia- Asia, Europe, the Americas. It's going to matter, Alexandra. There's never been anything like it."

"I was speaking with Jaroslav earlier today," she said. Jaroslav Černý, a noted Czech Egyptologist was also on the team and Alexandra found him to be brilliant. "I mentioned how at Bryn Mawr I had studied hieratic writing and he asked if I would be interested in assisting him with the decipherings found on the ostraca." These were fragments from pieces of pottery and shards of limestone that had been unearthed at Deir-el-Medinn, fragments that through the hieratics told the story of the lives of the everyday Egyptians. "I told him I would speak with you about it."

"You don't need my permission," Alexander said, downing the rest of his G & T in one fell swoop, not looking at her. And then, "I'm not your keeper."

"No, I didn't mean it like that. But I don't want to push in, it's your work, it's your dig site," she said, coming to stand before him.

"I know you're restless here," he said so softly she strained to hear. "I fear the allure of being with me, the dream you had of a life together with me is starting to wear off or perhaps already has."

"Is that what you think?" she asked, gently taking his glass from his hand and then settling onto his lap, wrapping her arms around his neck. "Not at all my dear," she said, lightly kissing him on the lips. "I never wanted the role of a woman like my mother, and so I got an education. I'm living in one of the most fascinating parts of the world and feel like I'm just going to rot, not being challenged intellectually at all."

He didn't say anything. Alexandra could see that her words, as honest as they were, had perhaps hurt him a bit. "Only I would be lucky enough to procure a wife proficient in the cursive form of hieroglyphs," he said, as he rained light kisses down upon the nape of her neck. "Puts me to shame as I am entirely ignorant on such letterings."

"So you don't mind if I tell him yes?" she asked, a thrill of excitement building within her.

"All I want, my dear, is for you to be happy. Nothing else matters."

But something else did matter, quite a lot it seemed. Although the modern era had come to Luxor in the form of automobiles, electricity, and running water, basic medical care at the dig sites was lacking or in many cases, nonexistent. When Alexandra had remarked on this to Alexander, he said that it was no different than what he had experienced during his childhood, growing up on the Lower East Side, when diseases such as dysentery and typhus ran rampant and clean drinking water was considered a luxury out of reach for the newly arrived immigrants. Alexander rarely showed emotion, that is besides being loving and affectionate with her. But his usually warm and inviting eyes, the color of toffee she had thought from the first time she had gazed into them, were hard and steely then, devoid of warmth. He added, "And the cruelest part is that my childhood wasn't even that long ago. And yet if it weren't for the Jacob Riises of the world, so many children in New York, Boston, Philadelphia, Chicago, they'd still be living like this, with as fleeting a chance at truly surviving life as the swimmer escaping from the mouth of the crocodile." He walked away from her then, his mind no longer with her in 1924 Egypt but 30 years before to a crowded urban slum across the ocean.

"What if I were to open a makeshift dispensary?" Alexandra asked her husband later that evening as they were sitting outside in their garden, their nightly ritual of G & T's long since drunk, now just listening to the concert being performed by the omnipresent cicadas.

"What?" Alexander asked incredulously, turning to look at her as Alexandra continued gazing up at the near perfect night sky replete with stars. "But you're not a doctor, not even a nurse; you have no medical training or background of any kind."

Alexandra knew he hadn't said this to be mean or to hurt her, he was merely speaking the truth. And yet had he forgotten that her father had been a doctor? That she had grown up around medical talk and as a little girl, when struggling with her ancient Greek and Latin, had often snuck into her father's library to look at the anatomy books.

She was hardly a dunce and had even gotten high marks in a physiology class she had taken at Bryn Mawr, a class she had not dared mention to her mother for how scandalous a subject it was for a young woman to be studying.

"My background was having a prominent physician for a father," she retorted, mentally reminding herself that he wasn't picking a fight with her so nor should she with him. "I'm not saying I'm adept at removing cancerous growth from the esophagus or performing reconstructive surgery on a shattered jaw," she paused, not knowing why she had brought up the cancer that had taken her father, "but I can set a broken arm, provide the right tonic for an upset stomach, and then of course there's the always bothersome cobra and scorpion bites." Alexandra had said the last two things rather jokingly but in truth, both plagues (what she considered them to be) horribly frightened her. Bites from each brought a quick and yet also painful death. Her worst fear was being bit by one and being alone when it happened, and thus dying alone. She had never dared mention this fear to Alexander, not with what he had gone through in the trenches.

"You're serious," he said, not as a question but a statement.

"Yes. It's not just you and the other archaeologists I want to help. It's the Egyptian workmen too. There's nobody for them when they fall ill or have an accident. Tell me, how many deaths at the dig sites do you think could have been prevented if there was someone present to take care of them?"

Alexandra could tell he was contemplating her words. Although she knew her father had harbored racial prejudices against the native Egyptians, he hadn't been like that back home in Philadelphia, with the city's poor, well, the poor white immigrants. William Garis had always referred to the downtrodden, the bereft, the orphans as Alexandra's "fellow man." He had told her once that, "you may live in opulent splendor, wear the finest clothes, have the best of everything afforded to you, but you never forget God's other children."

"Where are we going, Father?" Alexandra asked, excitement bursting inside her. She had hoped he was taking her to Bassett's. Her mother rarely let her eat ice cream, not even allowing Alexandra to have any when cook prepared it as a dessert course for her mother's dinners. She claimed Alexandra looked like she had a tendency to "appear fat.". But butterscotch was Alexandra's absolute favorite flavor and Bassett's made the best. It was located inside Reading Terminal Market, in a part of the city that was awash with cars, horse drawn carriages, noise, soot, dirt, and rough looking people Emily Garis would avoid. The first time she had gone there with her father, Alexandra had been mystified by all the wondrous things before her- stalls selling every sort of food and other edible good imaginable- fruits and vegetables, sweets, fish, meat, cheese, and of course, Bassett's. Although some of the people had frightened her- people whose skin was much darker than hers, speaking in strange languages whose words almost sounded as though they were made up, smells that seemed like they belonged thousands of miles away back across the ocean in the Old Country. Holding tight to her father's hand, she had stared back at the sights before her in sheer amazement. How different this was from the stuffy drawing rooms she typically sat in when her mother took her along to pay social calls.

"Are we going to Bassett's?" she asked him eagerly, entirely oblivious to the fact that he had taken his medical bag with them.

"You're 10 now, Alexandra. It's time for you to see how the other half lives."

He didn't say anything more, and Alexandra didn't press him further. She didn't speak up when it was clearly evident that they weren't going to Bassett's for ice cream. Or when upon looking out the windows of their Ford Model T and no longer seeing the opulent mansions of North Broad Street but rather derelict buildings that newspapers called slum houses. Were they having to travel through this unsavory area to get to something else, Alexandra wondered, as she stared back at a girl her own age, who unlike her wore a threadbare dress, a tattered shawl, and, Alexandra realized with a start, wasn't wearing any shoes. The girl looked at Alexandra's agape mouth with expressionless eyes, eyes whose haunted nature made her seem less like a little girl but more like an old woman.

The Model T stopped then, her father parking it in front of a row of squat houses that were all connected. People stared at them as her father helped her out- a group of young boys who had been throwing a ball, a girl younger than her who had a baby on her small-framed hip and another child clutching at her skirts with a grubby hand. They just kept looking. The air smelled rancid- of unwashed bodies, rotting food, waste, and cooking smells Alexandra couldn't place. But her father merely took her arm in his and started walking them down the street, Berks Street the marker said. And then he stopped at a building where Alexandra read a sign that said "Free medical care for the needy and infirmed. All are welcome."

"Dr. Garis," a young, smiling woman said while opening the door. "How good of you to come. And I see you've brought help today," now smiling warmly at Alexandra, moving aside to let them pass.

"It's time for Alexandra to start seeing the world that exists beyond finishing schools and drawing rooms, Dr. Sikorski."

That afternoon, when Alexandra wasn't writing down what her father dictated to her from his examinations with the patients he saw- patients who had ranged in age from infants to the very old, presenting every sort of ailment and malady possible, symptoms ranging from a cough to a stomach ache, to boils that made Alexandra blanch at the sight, to even a broken arm on a small boy her father had her help him set- Alexandra learned two very interesting things. One, her father came to Dr. Sikorski's

clinic to volunteer his time at least once a month, sometimes more if her mother was away (this was something she wasn't privy to and her father said it was of the utmost importance that it remained that way), and two, that if Dr. Sikorski, a woman, could become a doctor, then she as a woman, granted, a young one for now, could be anything she wanted to be too.

Alexandra and her father had shared many secrets. But it was the times he took her to Dr. Sikorski's clinic that she cherished the most when looking back on the time she'd had with him. It was his way of showing, if not outright due to societal constraints, how much he valued not only her intelligence but also how much he wanted to share his life's work with her. For her to know about this other side of him, one that he had always had to keep hidden. "I may have been born into immense wealth and privilege," he had told her one time, "unlike Dr. Sikorski, who had two strikes against her- being the daughter of immigrants and a woman- but just like her, I became a doctor because I wanted to help all people, not just those that constitute the First Families of Philadelphia," referring to the families that had first settled the city and whose influence and fortunes succeeded them.

Alexandra told all of this to her husband, who nodded in understanding and at the end like so many times before simply said, "My most fervent wish in life is merely for you to be happy- happy here, with me, with us, with our life."

And later that night before drifting off, Alexander already asleep, Alexandra whispered into the dark room- "I know I've always made you proud, but now I hope even more so. I'll always love you, Father."

CHAPTER 11

1934

"How is it that you've never had a family?"

The old Alexandra would have stared at the woman aghast at such a question, not understanding how "proper society" had once deemed it inappropriate for a pregnant woman to appear in public but inquiring into procreation of such a pregnancy, and coming from a quasi-stranger (but one who her mother would have deemed "the right sort") was perfectly innocent. The new Alexandra had acquired a backbone, a rather ballsy one.

"Oh, I wasn't aware that it was anyone's business save for that of me and my husband if our nightly coupling was for sheer sport and pleasure or the act of procreation. Good day," Alexandra said to the woman whose face was as pink of that of the Egyptian Museum's facade, from where she had been seated at a table on the terrace of the Mena House. She spotted Alexander then, walking towards her, so she hurried over to him, before the woman could hurl a slew of indignations her way once she recovered from the emotional apoplexy Alexandra's words had caused.

"Who was that?" Alexander inquired, no doubt his curiosity piqued from the woman's outraged expression.

"A fellow countrywoman," Alexandra said, taking her husband's arm to lead him further away from the terrace. She had met the older

American woman the day before, a woman who made Alexandra immediately think of Emily Garis. She had been seated alone at the table next to Alexandra's on the terrace where Alexandra had gone for afternoon tea. Upon hearing Alexandra's clearly American accent, she had changed tables without being invited to do so. And Alexandra hadn't been able to shed the woman since, until now.

"She looked flustered, shocked even," he replied. "Were you spouting your once bandied about 'votes for women' talk?" he said jokingly, his playful innocent side so endearing to her, even after all these years.

"If a couple loves each other, why is that not enough? Why must the world place so much stock in having children? Starting a family? What if it's simply just not physically possible?" And with that last sentence, Alexandra's steely resolve and determination to not let Mrs. Stanley Moffet's meddlesome words dissolved and she started to cry.

"Oh my dear girl," Alexander said, taking her hand in his and hurriedly leading her away until they were in a more secluded area. Seated on a bench, he gently wiped at the tears on her face. "I thought it was as much," he softly said, "she reminded me entirely of-"

They spoke at the same time then, her saying "my mother" and he "your mother."

"I'm not condoning that sort of behavior, it's just women of that generation. And it's the one topic of inquiry that joins all classes together, poor like my mother had been, or rich like yours."

"I know it's a truly horrible thing to say, what with his horrible injuries and all, but I think of Sir Robert and Eliza, and how effortlessly she gets with child."

"The wonders of the male anatomy," Alexander sardonically smirked. "What can I do?"

"Take me away from here," she said, not even thinking of how her words could be misconstrued.

"Leave Egypt?" he asked, his turn now to be aghast.

For a fleeting moment she wanted to say yes- yes to no more worrying about deadly snakes and scorpions, to the unimaginable and unrelenting heat of the summer months, to bearing witness to the plight of the native Egyptians, but especially the children whose stomachs protruded from lack of food or succumbed to any number of the sicknesses and diseases that so easily wiped out entire families. But she couldn't, even without looking at his face; she could never say that. Egypt was home for without her father and he had been gone how many years by then, she no longer considered anywhere else but here, anywhere else not with Alexander, to be home.

"No, I just meant on a trip. Somewhere other than Egypt," and she saw the relief exude from his face.

"Absolutely, my love. Of course, you would never mean you wanted to leave here, you love it just as much as I do," he said. And then sounding incredibly business-like but also excited, he asked, "Anywhere in particular you'd like to go?"

"What about Venice? And the Orient Express? And Constantinople? And end with-"

And just like moments earlier when they had said the same exact thing, they both uttered the name Ur. For that is how in tune they were with each other, how much they were one.

1935

If there was one city in the world that so perfectly captured the essence of love, Alexandra decided it must be Venice. She and Alexander had arrived in *La Serenissima*, the 'serene,' the day before, and from the moment she had stepped out into the bright sunshine of the day from the Santa Lucia train station, Alexandra had drawn in a sharp breath, momentarily at a loss for words by its ethereal charm- the blue, shimmering water of the canal, the buildings that lined it that almost seemed as if they were floating on water.

When the gondolier, a young man who at first had shyly glanced at Alexandra when helping her into the gondola that Alexander had procured in his feeble attempts at Italian, had noticed her staring at the building directly adjacent to the train station, he had said, "*Chiesa di Santa Maria di Nazareth*," to which Alexandra had responded with an equally shy and timid, "*bellisima*" which brought forth a lovely smile that spread across his olive skin.

Alexander had laughed when Alexandra seated herself in the bow of the gondola but she didn't care. She leaned forward in her seat, her head anxiously darting left then right, then back left, then back right, taking in each of the Gothic styled palazzo and Baroque churches, one more ornate than the next.

"Our *pensione* isn't on the Grand Canal, is it?" Alexandra turned back in her seat to ask her husband.

"No, but I negotiated or at least attempted to have the fare include a ride up and down the Grand Canal. I'm not entirely sure if the amount of *lira* he asked for was a good deal," he said wryly.

"But isn't it worth it, my love?" Alexandra asked from over her shoulder, already having turned back around in her seat, imagining this is how John Smith and all the other famous explorers of history must have felt the first time they embarked on journeys of exploration in the New World.

"Oh, look, it's the Rialto Bridge," Alexandra called out in pure delight, looking up and marveling at its elegant façade as the gondola effortlessly glided underneath it.

"And we must not be too far from the Rialto Market either," Alexander replied, a bit dryly this time, a shade of ashen green passing across his handsome face. Alexandra had to agree that the fish smell, since the moment they had alighted from the train, had been somewhat overpowering.

"Ca' d'Oro," the gondolier called out. Alexandra turned back to face him and saw that he was indicating a stunning building on the left-hand side of the canal. As she studied its spiny white roofline and pink and white façade, she said to her husband, "Oro, isn't that gold?"

"You're the linguist of this family," Alexander responded back, smiling.

Turning around in her seat to face the gondolier she said, "Ca?" hoping it sounded like the question she wanted it to be and not as a statement.

The young Italian man looked at her, puzzled, perhaps wondering if she wasn't all right in the head until it dawned on him what she was asking and he bobbed his head up and down, almost eagerly and said, "Ca, casa."

"Oh, house," Alexandra said out loud, pleased at her ability to piece words together in a language other than ancient Egyptian or Arabic. "House of gold. How extraordinary."

After arriving at the unassuming and slightly austere Pensione Ferraro and being instructed in rapid-fire Italian by the stout *signora* on what Alexandra could only surmise to be house rules since one look at Alexander's befuddled face confirmed that he too hadn't understood a thing the signora had barked, she had been pleased to discover that their room did indeed overlook a canal complete with a footbridge and charming and brightly colored buildings.

"I could stay here forever," Alexandra said, gazing out the window whose shutters she had thrown wide open. Just then a passing gondolier floated beneath her window singing what, a love ballad?

"The first stop of many, my love," Alexander said planting a soft kiss on the nape of her neck. "Besides, I thought you were looking most forward to Constantinople?"

"I didn't expect to fall in love with it at first sight," she replied.

"I know the feeling," coming back to wrap his arms around her. "But that's how Egypt is for me."

"Perhaps Ur will steal your heart," she answered, basking in the warmth and comfort of his embrace.

"Cheat on ancient Egypt? Never!" he said in mock horror.

From Constantinople they planned to travel on to Ur, an ancient Sumerian city-state in Mesopotamia. When word had broken out that Leonard Wooley, a British archaeologist had discovered the burial site of what may have been Sumerian royals, Alexander had expressed interest in going there saying, "If we're that close," as if Constantinople was a mere two-hour train ride away from Baghdad. But Alexandra was up for the adventure. The truth was she was up for anything when it came to her husband. They may have had completely different childhoods but it was kismet that brought them together on the boat from Marseille to Alexandria all those years ago and kismet that reunited them once more on the banks of the Nile but it was also their shared love of the ancient world that forever connected them, in both body and soul.

"I'd buy you a palazzo if I could," Alexander said, suddenly, his lighthearted tone now changing to one of seriousness and almost sadness. They never spoke of her former life- of 11 course meals, of balls that lasted till dawn, of allowances solely reserved for the acquisition of new dresses- but she knew it bothered him that he would never be able to give her any of that. Not that she wanted it. She wanted him and nothing else. Even if their simple home back in

Luxor was nicer than the Pensione Ferraro, albeit with not as lovely a view.

"A palazzo would be nice," Alexandra began "but I'm in *La Serenissima* and I simply must explore or I will die," fainting onto the lumpy, narrow bed, her arm thrown across her forehead in a dramatic fashion.

"Perish the thought," Alexander said, pulling her up using his one strong hand, but not before passionately kissing her where afterwards she did legitimately feel faint in the knees. "Then explore we must."

Their four days in Venice went entirely too fast. They explored more churches than Emily Garis would have deemed appropriate, what with all their pagan symbols and ghoulish crucifixes scattered on every visible inch of space, Alexandra could just imagine her mother saying. She had been especially entranced by St. Mark's Basilica, namely because it looked like no other church she had ever seen before, with its bulbous domes and breathtaking Byzantine design, appearing more Oriental than Italian. When Alexander read from his Baedeker's how one of the mosaics in the lunettes on the western façade of the basilica told the description of St. Mark's relics from Alexandria to Venice, a feeling of unbridled warmth had crept across her, reminding her how much Egypt was always with her.

She had looked forward each afternoon to when she and Alexander would take an indulgent daily repast at Caffe Florian, Italy's oldest coffee house located in St. Mark's Square. Dining outside allowed them unparalleled views of both the basilica and the bell tower, *campanile* they called it. She reveled in the richness of the café's famous sweet hot chocolate but also its signature drink, the Florian coffee that was made with espresso, cream and chocolate.

Alexander always opted for the much simpler and less rich standard coffee. Although she had convinced him to try a glass of *limoncello* before they left, an especially tart lemon liqueur.

"I'll make an Italian out of you yet," Alexandra had joked, sitting back in her seat, studying her husband as he tentatively sipped his limoncello, an overwhelming feeling of love washing over her.

"Well, if a former deb can become an archaeologist's wife who prefers digging in the dirt and sand to stuffy drawing rooms and fancy soirees, then I suppose anything is possible," he said, his eyes glittering as he smiled across at her, but not before he threw back the remaining yellow liquid in his glass.

Arriving at Sirkeci Terminal in many ways made Alexandra feel like she was back in Egypt. The Tower of Babel from the myriad of foreign tongues being spoken, the many different ethnic costumes being worn by the dark-skinned natives, the minarets she spotted off in the distance that flanked the mosques. And then of course there were the smells- the smells of unwashed bodies, of foods cooking, fires burning, and the smell of potent spices whose aromas she could easily identify as those of cumin and sumac.

The Orient Express had been a marvel; Alexandra was in awe the entire journey by how they had boarded the train in Venice and now were standing in the once farthest eastern point of the Roman Empire, straddling the divide between east and west.

"It's called the 'Golden Horn'," Alexandra said to her husband as they gazed out at the body of water in front of them. "Nobody is entirely sure where the name comes from, well, the 'golden' part that is, but I want to believe that it refers to the rich yellow light that illuminates the water as the sun sets over the city. It's just like the

Gudin painting my father hung in his library."

"A romantic to her dying breath," Alexander said, gently squeezing her hand. "My own Elizabeth Barrett Browning. Shall we come back at some point to catch the sunset?"

"I thought you'd never ask, Robert."

Their accommodations at the Pera Palace were divine, a hotel that had been specifically built to receive passengers from the Orient Express. It was as lush and ostentatious as any of the hotels that graced Cairo's European quarters. But it was the city's ancient quarter, their walks along the very same cobblestoned hilly streets that the Byzantines and Ottomans and Crusaders once walked on that had left her enthralled, so captivated by all the wondrous history all around her.

"I feel that we should have done Venice last," Alexandra said, tentatively sipping from her delicate tulip-shaped glass. She had tried the famous Turkish coffee the day before and felt like she was drinking, or rather eating, coffee flavored sludge. Alexander, however, had taken to it with gusto, even going so far as to say that the Egyptians could learn a thing or two from their former overlords, back when Egypt had been a province of the Ottoman Empire. "I mean, one of the best mosques in all of Cairo is the Alabaster Mosque and that was modeled after the famous Blue Mosque here," he added, as if Alexandra was in opposition to his claim.

"Why do you say that?" he asked, eying her quizzically.

"I just mean being purveyors of the past, we should have - ," she trailed off, not entirely sure what she wanted to say.

"Recreate the past?" he smiled at her indulgently as he took another sip of his sludge. Yes, that's what she would be calling it as she noticed the dark, thick coffee grains from his cup momentarily staining his perfectly white teeth. "Traveled in chronological order?"

"You know what I mean, you rascal," she said, returning his equally indulgent smile with one of her own. "I mean, just consider how much of Constantinople is in Venice, let alone the rest of the continent," thinking then of the set of bronze statues of four horses that adorned the loggia of St. Mark's Basilica, plundered during the Crusades after the sacking and looting of Constantinople.

"No different from what's currently taking place back home," he said, his tone more serious now. "I'm hardly condoning the act of cultural plundering but the horses were taken in what, the 13th, 14th century? Egypt, the plundering was still being sanctioned in a way as recently as fifty, sixty years ago."

"I asked you this a long time ago. But do you think there will be another war?"

Alexander pondered her question, looking out onto the Golden Horn and the enormous sprawling city that lay before them, interspersed with so much of the blue of the sea.

"Yes."

She didn't press him to elaborate, knowing that he would in his own steady time. Knowing that the ghosts of the Western Front still haunted him, aware of how much the "mad man" of Europe, as the newspapers jokingly referred to Germany's leader, Adolf Hitler, chilled him so. Going so far as to say that he was a man not to be trusted and to not underestimate him.

"I remember a professor at Harvard once said 'to the victors belong the spoils.' I think Andrew Jackson was the one to say it. Anyhow, I think France believed its 'spoils' of the war to be in the form of the reparations it felt it was owed and given by the Treaty of Versailles." A pause then before adding, "But victors of what? Victors of a war that brought about the deaths of millions? Decimated an entire generation of young men, made more widows and orphans than one could ever imagine. A war that made all horrible conflicts of the past pale in comparison. There were no victors here," Alexander quietly said, a sad glint in his eyes. "Only the plantings of something even more horrible to come."

"If I close my eyes I can almost imagine we're standing in 'New Rome' and instead of it being the year 1935 it's December 27, 537."

"Rather a specific date you have in mind," Alexander jokingly said.

"You philistine, clearly you did not do the assigned Baedeker's reading," Alexandra answered, playfully swatting at his arm. "It's the date that Hagia Sofia was inaugurated by Emperor Justinian.

They were standing inside what had once been the symbol of the power of the Byzantine Empire, the Great Church of Hagia Sofia. Living in Egypt, Alexandra often found it nearly impossible to be impressed by 'the past' since what could ever come close to matching the sheer majesty of sites like Abu Simbel or the Great Pyramid of Giza, and yet here she was. So dazzled was she by the profoundness of it all she was for lack of a better word, speechless when they stepped inside and gazed up- its dome of monolithic dimensions, its breathtaking mosaics, and its marble pavement that ran throughout.

Seeing its rather austere façade, nothing could have remotely prepared Alexandra for the sight that awaited her after crossing over the threshold.

"Is it selfish of me to be glad that it's now a museum?" Alexandra discreetly whispered into Alexander's ear as they continued their touring of the interior.

"Come again?" Alexander asked, confusion sprouting across his face.

Alexandra just smiled in response, her previously crafted hypothesis ringing true- you can literally take the man out of ancient Egypt, but not figuratively.

"To think of all the history this one building has borne witness to," Alexandra said, breaking from her husband's hand to study a mosaic more closely. A Byzantine church, then a Catholic cathedral, a mosque, and now a museum.

"Solomon, I have surpassed thee!"

"Are you just making this up? Or reciting a line of a play that you've been secretly working om?"

"Legend has it that Emperor Justinian said those words after it was consecrated, that the building was a feat of such power," Alexandra replied, although not directly to him so intent was she on making out each of the delicately crafted mosaic tiles that comprised the most beautiful image.

"Have I lost my wife to the wonders of the Byzantine world?"

Alexandra whirled around to face him, his eyes twinkling with pure delight, his face mirroring the extreme happiness and joy she had not felt for such a long time now- meddlesome widows and spinsters long forgotten.

"Only if I were to ever lose you."

Before long, it was time to push on to Ur, into the heart of what was once Mesopotamia. For all the traveling her father had done, he had never made it this far east, this deep into the cradle of civilization. And for that, Alexandra felt a deep pang of both sadness and regret- the former over missing her long dead father, the latter on how cruel a world it was to have taken a man long before his time.

As they alighted from the Baghdad-Basra train at a stop fittingly called "Ur Junction," Alexandra couldn't help but think of how much this vast, desolate landscape reminded her of Deir el-Medina. Excavations had finished a couple of years before; Alexandra remembered Alexander telling her that as many as 1,850 burial sites had been uncovered during a 12-year excavation period, with 16 having been described as "royal tombs." Today, it was filled with everyone from the amateur, self-proclaimed archaeologist to the slightly more intrepid 'Cookies' who were indeed doing the 'Grand Tour' of Arabia, to people like her and Alexander, those who came alive by the past.

They had even met a most agreeable British woman, a popular novelist no less, whose husband had served as one of the assistants to Sir Charles Leonard Woolley, who had led the excavations. Alexandra hoped she would be able to get a copy of the woman's most recent published work, *Murder on the Orient Express,* on their return to Cairo in one of the British bookshops.

Alexandra supposed she was prejudiced against Ur from the start, having just come from as magnificent and culturally rich a place as Constantinople. But if there was one thing she could appreciate about any past civilization, it was one in which female rulers were given as much deference as male ones. Standing before the unlooted tomb of Queen Puabi, whose body was adorned with a golden headdress, a beaded top, and a belt made of gold and precious stones, she was considered by some to be the first female ruler in all of human history. Alexandra was in awe. The most lavish Mesopotamian tomb ever found belonged to a woman. And that was enough for Alexandra to be thoroughly impressed.

CHAPTER 12

Luxor
September 1935

"I never thought I'd say it, but I truly do miss winter, freezing fingers and all," Alexandra said to her husband as they were deciding on what could be saved, and what needed to go. Although the waters of the Nile had receded weeks ago, in its aftermath they were still dealing with the annual flooding. "One's personal treasures were never ruined as a result of too much snow," she said sadly, as she caressed the now water-logged and ruined remains of a stuffed camel children's toy.

"No, just fingers and toes," Alexander replied jokingly, no doubt wanting to lighten the mood after seeing what Alexandra had picked up. He gently took it from her and placed it in the rubbish pail. He had gotten her the object a decade ago after she had told him she was pregnant. But of course, there was no child to ever cherish the toy for that pregnancy and the two that followed had all ended early. "But yes, the flooding this year was the worst I've ever witnessed since living here."

The annual Flooding of the Nile was a natural cycle since ancient times, even being celebrated by the natives as an annual holiday for two weeks known as Wafaa El-Nil. Ancient Egyptian legend considered the rising waters as Isis's tears of sorrow for Osiris when he was killed by his brother Set. Although Alexandra normally enjoyed ancient poetic lore and of course recognized its importance and necessity for the country's farmers whose livelihood depended on it, the annual flooding was one poetic waxing she could do without. Work at dig sites was often halted and daily life in the ghastly hot temperatures of the summer was even more unbearable than usual.

"Well, I could do without *Akhet* altogether," Alexandra proffered, referring to the ancient Egyptian word for the flooding season.

"What, and just skip right to *Peret* and *Shemu*?" Alexander replied, referring to the other two seasons of planting and harvesting.

"Naturally," she replied, coming to face him to kiss him on the lips.

"I don't mind the waters, well, not the mess and bother of the aftermath," tossing what seemed to be the fourth ruined book into the bin. "It's the scorpions that I could do without."

Alexandra knew there was nothing her husband was afraid of, except scorpions. The annual flood waters meant instead of hiding under rocks or desert burrows, one would see them scampering on the city streets, lurking under stones and nestling in shoes and blankets. Four inches in length, six eyes to haunt you, a tail full of venom that was so toxic, the species had earned the name "death stalker." Alexander had once told her that he would gladly go back in time to the battlefields of France and take his chances in no-man's land than be bitten by a scorpion. Alexandra had countered that he stood better odds in no man's land since with its vast deserts, Egypt was home to 24 species of them, a true heaven for the frightening and deadly arthropods whose venom could kill humans in mere hours, or even less. But she knew he had come close to being bitten a couple of times before; she had too but she was much more afraid of venomous snakes and their frightening ability to lunge at you.

"Serket will protect you," she said, slightly alarmed now over how pale his skin had become over their talk of scorpions.

"I fear not even the goddess of healing venomous stings and bites would be able to protect me."

"Poppycock, stuff and nonsense," she said. If she had believed in the occult, Alexandra would have said it was almost as if Alexander had been foreshadowing his own death.

October 1935

"Alexander?" Alexandra called upon entering the darkened foyer of their house. She had just returned from afternoon tea and bridge at the Winter Palace. Eliza was visiting, sans Sir Robert and their six children who had remained behind in Assouan. Their visit had lasted for more than six hours and what, they would be seeing her again tonight for dinner. As she went from room to room, the house was eerily quiet, almost as if it were deserted. Their house girl and boy, an orphaned brother and sister pair named Farouk and Fatima respectively, had gone away two days earlier for their annual trip home to their native village after the flooding.

"Alexander," Alexandra called out again as she climbed the steps. When she had woken that morning, he had told her he didn't feel well and she had told him to stay in bed. He's probably just sleeping she told herself, trying to quell the uneasy feeling forming in her stomach. But as she approached their bedroom, even with the door ajar, she could see him lying on the floor.

Rushing over, she tried to push open the door to get inside but couldn't. Using every last bit of strength she had, the fear and adrenaline of seeing Alexander lying there almost unconscious on the floor, she pushed it just enough to squeeze her way through and step over his prostrate body.

"Alexander, my darling, wake up my love, please, I'm here," she said as she leaned over him, then noticing the dried remains of vomit on his lips.

"Alex," he started to say, his words slurred, almost as if he were drunk.

"Yes, my love, I'm here, tell me what's wrong," she implored him as she worriedly took in his bed clothes soaked through with sweat, his labored breathing.

"Serket," he managed to get out.

Alexandra was about to ask what was he possibly talking about but then it dawned on her, and she fell back so suddenly it was as if someone had pushed her. She started to hyperventilate then, her head spinning, the room going round and round. Feeling as if she would vomit herself, she started touching him, looking for any signs of a sting site. She frantically pushed up his clothes first on his left arm, his left leg, his right arm, and then there on his right calf she saw it. She screamed with a gut-wrenching cry.

He started twitching then but before succumbing for good and journeying to the afterlife he managed to get out the garbled words, "I loved you from the moment I first saw you," as he looked into her eyes, his perfectly shining and clear until they no longer were.

PART II
ELEANOR & ELENI

CHAPTER 13

Cairo, Egypt
June 1939

The heat. God, the heat- it was simply unbearable Eleanor thought as she feebly attempted to cool herself with the rattan fan she had purchased the day before from a costermonger on the street. How did they put up with it, Eleanor wondered, as she stood under an archway that offered a parcel of shade, while gazing out at the passing locals who didn't seem the least bit bothered by the fact that it wasn't even 9 in the morning yet and already the temperature was more than 100 degrees? Beads of sweat ran down her face, her white linen blouse clinging to her damp skin; she felt as if she had just taken a hot bath and immediately dressed without bothering to dry herself. Eleanor almost laughed then, remembering all of the horrid ice-cold baths she'd had to endure back in their freezing flat in Spitalfields when the coal ran out and there had been nothing to warm the water but her mum had insisted that a weekly bath before church the next day was still in order. And look at her now- complaining about being too hot while serving as a companion to a proper countess.

Lady Stratton was old, cantankerous, and entirely too opinionated. But she had given Eleanor the chance of a lifetime when she offered to take Eleanor with her to Egypt to serve officially as a lady's maid, due to Eleanor's lack of social standing, but truthfully she was really a companion. Eleanor's aunt, who had been a widow for more than 20 years and was recently bereft by the loss of her only child, was Lady Stratton's cook since Eleanor had been a child, and who had "volunteered" her favourite niece to accompany the older woman to Egypt where she was to spend the winter, as she did every year. Aunt May was well aware of Eleanor's admiration of the finer things in life and knew her niece was different from her sister's other children, namely that she had a genuine penchant for learning. When Eleanor's mum had insisted that Eleanor leave school at the age of 13 as her three older siblings had done before her (well, her brother Tom had left by age 10) to go out and work, it was Aunt May who had intervened and who had said SHE would give Eleanor's mom the money Eleanor would make so long as her niece remained in school, learning. The fact of the matter was, Aunt May gave her mum a lot more than Eleanor would have earned working in a factory but that was just how much she believed in her young niece; she wanted Eleanor to have a life beyond what had been determined for her at the time of her birth, determined by the sole fact that she was a daughter of Spitalfields as her mum had been and her mum before her. Girls in Spitalfields were born into nothing and most died having nothing and in between led a hard life filled with one pregnancy after the next in rapid succession, often burying babes who never lived to see their first birthdays, never enough food or coal, and a husband who was more trouble than he was worth. May Nichols couldn't save all of her nieces and nephews from a preordained life of poverty and hardship but she could at least save Eleanor. And Eleanor had stayed in school until she was 18 and graduated.

When Aunt May had first mentioned the idea to Eleanor, she was both excited but also petrified at such a prospect. Imagine, her, Eleanor Mews serving as a proper lady's maid, no wait, a companion she had thought. Lady Stratton had been amenable to the idea and decided to take Eleanor on for a trial basis, meaning she would come to Lady Stratton's elegant home in Mayfair three times a week and help her with her correspondence and also read to her. Neither Eleanor nor Aunt May were entirely sure why but Lady Stratton had taken an instant liking to the young girl. When Eleanor had proffered that perhaps she reminded the older woman of her daughter, Aunt May had immediately dismissed the suggestion, adding that Eleanor was no more like Violet Stratton than water was to vinegar (being a cook she was forever invoking food analogies). Aunt May thought perhaps Eleanor reminded Lady Stratton of herself at that age, although she would never dare say this in front of her niece or employer- she would have been undoubtedly dismissed without a reference if she were to say a poor girl from Spitalfields was the modern-day version of a countess.

Normally, Lady Stratton wouldn't leave for Egypt until November at the earliest, in which she would begin the long journey from England to the south of France where she would then board a vessel to Alexandria. But talk of impending war had everyone spooked, namely because of the person everyone called the 'mad man of Europe.' All Aunt May said in regards to Adolf Hitler was that she wished he'd just "piss off." You could take the cook out of Spitalfields but you couldn't take Spitalfields out of the cook, at least not entirely when it came to Eleanor's aunt. When news of the Munich Agreement broke last September, a settlement reached by Nazi Germany, Great Britain, France and Italy that permitted the German annexation of the Sudetenland, it seemed all of London and the country had breathed a collective sigh of relief, feeling that this would finally appease the 'mad man' and that his antics would come to an end. Not to mention, what did people like her and Aunt May care about a place they had never heard of before and certainly couldn't care a fig about the lot of Slavic people either, even if Hitler did claim they were German. But it was Jones, Lady Stratton's driver, who Eleanor thought had the saddest eyes she had ever seen, who seemed to be the only person she noticed that wasn't happy at the news. In the servants' quarters one day while visiting and talking with Aunt May, Eleanor had overheard him telling Whitmore, the butler, that they had just given away the free world on a silver platter to that Hitler. Forgetting her place, Eleanor asked, "whatever do you mean Mr. Jones?" And he turned to her then with those haunting, melancholic blue eyes and simply said, "the war to end all wars was never that, it was just the precursor of what's to come." And he got up and left the room without saying another word.

Later as she was leaving it was Aunt May who had told Eleanor the root of those sorrowful blue eyes- "Both of Mr. Jones' sons were killed at the front, both falling at the Battle of the Somme, both dying within three days of each other. And then his poor wife, succumbing to the Spanish Flu only a couple of years later." She whispered into Eleanor's ear then, "and he's never been the same since."

After the newspapers reported that Hitler had renounced the German-Polish declaration of non-aggression the following spring, "a whole lot of fancy words" Aunt May had called it, Lady Stratton had decided to leave by the start of summer for Egypt. "War is coming, I can feel it in my bones," she had stated in her nasally voice in a way that only the upper classes were capable of. "Hitler and his brood of Jerry miscreants won't stop until they control the continent and I simply won't stand for it. As if I in my advanced age could put up with more of those ghastly Zeppelin raids," referring to the aerial bombardments by Germany that had terrorized London and its residents during the Great War.

And so, preparations began in great haste to prepare for the journey. "Won't you come?" Eleanor had asked her aunt as they gazed down at the contents of her nearly full trunk that Jones would be collecting later that day. "If what Jones and Lady Stratton's talk of Zeppelin raids is true, it will undoubtedly be safer abroad than here," she added, a small pit forming in her stomach over the prospect of saying goodbye to the only true constant in her life, the only person who had ever really been there for her. Nobody had ever cared about her future in the way that her aunt had always done. "My dear girl, I've never had a desire to journey to the continent let alone a dark place like Africa with all their witchery and ill-begotten clothes, ladies showing their stomachs, can you imagine?" she said, tsking. "Besides, Lady Stratton is enormously fond of her cook there, an Egyptian man who loves the English more than some English do," she said, chuckling. "And someone needs to look in on your mum and brothers and sisters, wouldn't you say?" gently wiping a small tear that had escaped her eye and started to roll down her cheek. "This will be the chance of a lifetime for you that you may never get again."

"If I don't die from the heat first," Eleanor thought as she mustered up the courage to face the blaring sun again.

"Count your blessings that you didn't arrive during the *khamaseen*."

"The what?" Eleanor stuttered, her head feeling as if it were going to explode if she heard one more foreign word she didn't know the meaning of, let alone know how to pronounce it.

"The *khamaseen*," the young boy said patiently as if Eleanor were the pupil, and he the schoolmaster. Edward was a few years younger than she and according to Lady Stratton had "mixed blood." It was only after the older woman had left the room and the maid, Noor, had whispered to her in broken English that Edward's father had been a British soldier and that his mother was Egyptian had Eleanor understood the veiled words. But for whatever reason, Lady Stratton had taken a shining to the young boy with piercing blue eyes and skin the color of café au lait. He also spoke impeccable English without the least hint of an accent so naturally that afforded him an even better position in Lady Stratton's eyes. He performed a motley array of tasks for Lady Stratton including fulfilling her shopping at the British stores in Cairo including Davies Bryan, when she was precariously low on her Huntley & Palmer's biscuits. Although in the same breath she would also bemoan the fact that the store was an "utter shell" of its former self, more or less implying that how dare those Bryan brothers have the audacity to leave this earth.

"It's from the Arabic word for fifty," Edward began. "They're dry, sand-filled windstorms that blow sporadically here over a 50-day period in spring, hence the name."

"That doesn't sound so bad," Eleanor replied, thinking how utterly peculiar it was to use a number to describe a weather activity.

To that Edward just gave her a look that basically implied that she was a damned fool if she thought that. But being the aspirational young British gentleman he continued, "the storm can last for several hours and once it passes, it brings with it great quantities of sand and dust from the deserts with speeds up to 140 kilometers per hour. And even during the winter, the temperatures can still rise above 113 degrees. So imagine the heat that you complain endlessly about, mixed in with so much dust you could choke on it. It just hangs in the air with the flies and the patches of the putrid hot summer stench. You never feel entirely clean during it."

Eleanor wanted to reply that one look at all the cripples whose open wounds and festering sores made her feel instantly sullied. Or the recent time she and Lady Stratton were returning from tea at Shepheard's. They had passed a cart in which the bodies of two men whose skin was so black it reminded her of the tar they would lay down to patch the streets back home, were covered by a swarm of flies. Eleanor had wanted to retch in the back seat of the car right there and then until Lady Stratton had said in a stony voice, "look straight ahead Eleanor, what is out there on the streets is none of your concern." And that was that.

CHAPTER 14

May 1940

"WAR! It's War!" It had been eight months since those words had been exclaimed by the BBC announcer, when England had declared war on Germany following the latter's invasion of Poland and yet in those eight months, life here in Cairo was more or less exactly the same. Those familiar smells of exhaust fumes, over-worked pack animals, cheap incense, and manure that could be found in any Middle Eastern city still permeated the air; the decrepit Thorneycroft buses and trams were still as battered and lifeless looking as the donkeys they ran alongside on the streets; native children and adults alike still put out their hands at regular intervals to anyone with pale skin and white linen attire who passed them asking for "baksheesh," regardless if a service or good was proffered; and tourists and residents still came to the Khan el Khalili bazaar to shop for everything from faience beads, silver, alabaster, rugs, spices, and perfume. It was only by the invasion of khaki and additional cars, motor-bikes and military trucks on the street that the effects of war were felt.

"Whoa there!" a man's voice said as his arms went out to steady Eleanor.

Eleanor looked up, her face streaked with tears to see a man staring down at her, a look of concern in his eyes.

"Are you okay miss?"

Realizing she was entirely at fault here, nearly having knocked this soldier, no wait, he was entirely too posh sounding to be a mere soldier she thought, she rushed to apologize. "I do apologize sir, I wasn't watching where I was going. If you'll forgive me," as she started to walk off.

"Was it bad news?" he called out to her.

"I'm sorry?" she said, half turning around to face him.

"In the letter," he said, indicating his head towards the paper she still held with a deathlike grip. "Did you learn something upsetting?"

Eleanor would never know what possessed her to answer this complete stranger but she said, "My youngest brother, he just enlisted. He enlisted on the same day he turned 18. My mum is beside herself. My other two brothers, they've already gone to join the war."

The man didn't say anything for a moment, perhaps sensing by Eleanor's tear-streaked face that now wasn't the moment to deliver a "for king and country" patriotic declaration. Instead he just said, "I'm Lieutenant Antony Greaves," extending his hand.

Not expecting this, Eleanor studied the outstretched hand, momentarily forgetting what one did when in a situation like this. But then collecting herself, she said, "Eleanor Mews" placing her much smaller and equally warm hand in his.

"May I take you for a coffee, Miss Eleanor Mews?"

Was she dreaming? Was she, Eleanor Mews, a girl from the streets of Spitalfields, really being asked out for a coffee by an officer in His Majesty's Army? But then this was Egypt after all, where it seemed anything was possible. And where England and talk of war seemed as many miles away as the stories of *One Thousand and One Nights*).

They went to Groppi's, a quite fashionable café on Adly Street that Eleanor was familiar with, at least by name. Groppi's was the sort of place that a girl like Eleanor would never frequent. It wasn't that it was like the Gezira Sporting Club, a place off-limits to her solely because of her social position or more aptly, her lack of one, or the Continental's rooftop restaurant whose cabaret Lady Stratton disapproved of entirely and would be aghast if she were to learn Eleanor had been. No, Groppi's was out of her reach for the simple and timeless reason that it was too expensive. And yet here she was, enjoying a delicious coffee and cream cake.

"I grew up here, you know," Antony said, as he took out a Woodbine cigarette which he offered her first and then, at the slight demur of her head, lit for himself. Taking a long drag, "In Egypt that is, I don't mean to say here in Cairo."

"Are you being serious?" Eleanor asked, thinking he was perhaps having her on.

"Quite. I lived here until I was ten and was sent back home to the 'mother country' for boarding school. And yet, I spent my first ten years thinking this here was home," he said, waving his arms around to refer to where they were. "It took quite a bit of time to come to terms with the fact that I wasn't to consider Egypt my actual home ever, that I was British and must act the type. Needless to say, I got into quite a few or dozen scuffles those first few years at Eton, away from everything I had ever known."

Before she could help herself Eleanor said, "my God, you really are one of those lords and ladies types? Pausing then she added, "You're not a lord, are you?"

He looked at her bemused, and Eleanor thought to herself, God he was. And he was having her on.

"Look, I may not come from Mayfair but I can stand on me own two feet and I will not be made a fool by the likes of Lord whatever you are," Eleanor said, standing up, her voice rising, her tone utterly indignant. "I don't know what salacious motives you have in inviting me here but just because I grew up in the East End, I'm not your girl!" and turned to go, as she realized that everyone in the café was staring at them, no, staring at her.

He grabbed at her arm then, his fingers touching her bare skin. And all he said was, "My mother was from Shoreditch."

Her face flushed a crimson pink realizing what an utterly horrific scene she had just made. And she lowered herself back into her seat, desperately wishing the ground would open up beneath her.

"It was your accent," he began. "My mother lived her entire adult life surrounded by the finest things in life, but she never shed her East End accent. She told me how she had even tried elocution lessons, anything that would hide where she had come from, mask the fact that she didn't belong amongst as you called them, the 'lords and ladies' but it was always there. I think eventually she just grew to accept it. It helped once they moved here, away from the prying eyes and wagging tongues of London society. In Assouan, they were truly in their own little world, one where being one's own Eliza Doolittle didn't really matter too much after all."

"Assouan, that's where you grew up?" she asked, trying to imagine a childhood such as his in Egypt.

"Yes," he said, his eyes meeting hers, having returned from the recesses of his filed away happy memories. "It was simply marvelous."

"Was your father an archaeologist?"

"Oh, heavens no," Antony answered, laughing softly. "They came for his health. You see, he was badly wounded in the Great War. Well, no, wounded isn't really the right word. Horribly disfigured. Half of his face was obliterated at Passchendaele. But they also came to escape the world that was post-war England, one where an entire generation had been killed and where the remaining few were regarded as horrific monsters by those who couldn't begin to fathom what they had gone through. Their maimed faces and bodies served as a constant reminder that their sons and brothers and husbands would never come home again." Silence then. "But in answer to your question, I don't think my father cared a fig about ancient Egyptian anything," Antony added, laughing once more.

"Was he a good father?" Eleanor asked, not able to help herself. But before he could answer, she admitted, "Mine wasn't. I mean he was par for the course in a place like Spitalfields. His experiences during the war were like so many others. He was gassed, you see. His body was intact but his mind was never the same. Or so my mum would say, each time after he hit her or found the money she had been hiding to spend on drink. She would tell me, 'Nell, you can't blame him. It was the war, what he experienced in those god-awful trenches that did this to him. The drink just fuels it, he doesn't mean to.' She'd say this time and time again, all the while nursing a swollen lip or blackened eye until one day she didn't anymore, because he left one night and never returned. And then she turned to the drink herself."

Eleanor didn't know what possibly possessed her to share such intimate but also unseemly details about her and her family. His mother may have grown up on the streets of Shoreditch but she had married a lord. She was still just Eleanor Mews at the end of the day with barely 10 quid to her own name. He must think she just stepped out of a doss house.

But he surprised her once more when he took her hand in his and said, "Come with me to the pyramids?"

It was there atop the Great Pyramid of Giza that Eleanor had her first kiss, her first proper kiss, she should say. Antony had hired a horse-drawn gharry and Eliza watched in fascination as the outline of the city disappeared and in its place sprang mud-brick villages, canals, and fields recently harvested of their crops of beans, barley, and wheat.

"I remember as a young boy, my parents hiring a *dahabiya* to sail from Assouan to Abu Simbel in what had once been Nubia. My mother had said she had done the same journey as a young woman with her American friend once. A journey of the utmost urgency."

"Why was this?" Eleanor asked, bemused over hearing this childhood anecdote.

"A journey of love apparently," Antony said. "This American friend was trying to find a lost love."

"And it happened to be here in Egypt?" Eleanor asked. "How perfectly romantic. But she found him?" saying the last part with hopefulness in both her tone and heart.

"Oh yes," he answered, smiling at her. "They got married. In fact I remember going once to their house in Luxor, Auntie Alexandra and Uncle Alex, as he asked to be called, were scores of fun. Now, he was in fact an archaeologist. And he took my brothers and me on the most marvelous of visits to Luxor and Karnak."

"Are they still here? I mean do they still live here in Egypt?"

His face clouded over then. "No, he um, he died in a most bizarre way. He was stung by a scorpion and succumbed to it. Alexandra left Egypt shortly after and my mother lost touch with her. Apparently, she moved to Constantinople but that's all my mother ever learned."

Eleanor paused then, thinking which bit of information he had just told her upset her most- that this reunited couple would suffer such a cruel twist of fate in the place that had reunited them or that he had been stung by a scorpion which apparently was very much a thing here. Something she hadn't given pause to until now.

"I know I'm not your mother, well, heavens, grandmother is more apt here, but be careful, my girl. It's effortless to get caught up in one's own 'wartime romance' but no war lasts forever, only its damning, painful effects which last a lifetime."

Eleanor looked up in shock at Lady Stratton, then immediately returned her eyes to the words on the page of the novel she had been reading aloud, as was their custom each day in the late afternoon. But her cheeks now turned a deep, crimson red. Lady Stratton was quite keen on Agatha Christie books, although *Appointment with Death* would have to wait until this mortifying exchange was done with.

"You know what I'm referring to, Eleanor?" Lady Stratton asked her, for some reason persisting in this overly embarrassing topic.

Yes, Eleanor wanted to scream back. Yes, I know exactly what you're referring to and it's certainly not a topic I want to go to great lengths discussing with you of all people! But she just demurely replied, her eyes still raptly held by the words on the page that at this moment appeared to her like an incoherent jumble, "Yes, Lady Stratton, I do. But I would never do anything to bring shame or disgrace upon your good name."

"Heaven's, girl," the older woman answered, her tone now sounding moderately indignant. "This isn't the 16th century where I would cast you out simply for being a young woman taken by a handsome young man, and in your case, a handsome young officer which is even better. I know it's hard to fathom but I too was young once, and had many a suitor, including one or two even improper ones that even my dear, meddlesome mama was not privy to. Before I married Lord Stratton, I had a beau who fought in the Boer War. He was killed there. I never saw him again. Only a few stolen kisses and hidden letters to remember him by."

Eleanor didn't know what to say then. For lack of a better word, she was rendered speechless. She couldn't have ever imagined that

Lady Stratton would confide in her like this, let alone regard her like a granddaughter, a member of her family.

"With war comes loss," Lady Stratton said. "And change that can occur in the blink of an eye. So you see, my girl, sometimes it's the emotional heartbreak and devastation that hurts more than any animate *thing*," saying the last word with such precise pronunciation it reminded Eleanor of a snake. And she realized then that Lady Stratton hadn't been only referring to becoming with child but also the pain and hurt if the person you loved with all your heart never came back to you.

CHAPTER 15

"Have you thought about life after the war?"

Antony was headed back to the front in a few days' time and he had told her this time would be for more of a long haul. Gone would be the days where he'd materialize every few weeks for a couple days of R & R and where Eleanor would feel like the vivacious young woman she had always dreamt of being.

Was he going to propose, here, now Eleanor wondered? There certainly wasn't any spot more beautiful. Ever since Antony had first taken her here, the Orman Garden had fast become one of her favorite spots in all of Cairo. And why shouldn't it be, having been established by the Khedive no less. But when she glanced over her shoulder, she could see his long frame still gingerly reclining on the picnic blanket, his head propped up by his arm. No down on one knee, holding a tiny black box she could see.

Stifling a small pang of disappointment Eleanor collected herself to say, "No, I can't really say that I have."

"But would you want to stay here? In Egypt I mean?"

Eleanor turned again to look at him, this time equal parts quizzical and surprised. "I hadn't really given it much thought," she answered. "I mean, there's nothing back in London, back home, I mean to go back to," inwardly shuddering at the thoughts of returning to her mum's dark, dank, miserable flat in Spitalfields. And unlike Aunt May, she had no sought-after or prized skill. She was what, a lady's companion? But what would that get you in 1940, when the great families like the Strattons, with their once great houses, were a skeleton of what they had once been, long, long ago. They were very much a dying breed. Eleanor knew this. But staying on in Egypt, even after Lady Stratton returned to England or heaven forbid, passed, she could possibly be someone here, not just defined as being a once 'wretched thing' from the East End.

Returning to the present and dispelling the whimsical notions she had entertained just moments earlier, her mind having taken an imaginary knitting needle to each of them, she said, "But don't you have to go where the army says?"

He burst into laughter then, making Eleanor feel as if she were a small child who had just asked the most ridiculous question. "Of course I do, my dear girl, all soldiers do. But if the last few months have shown me anything, it's that war is folly. And I don't want a whole career or lifetime spent amongst it. Not being the heir, it was my preordained path since birth, as all males in my class and rank have done. But that was before I met you," he added as he pulled her towards him. She almost lost her balance but he caught her, she knew he would always catch her, and kissed her.

"I too, would like to stay here. It would be as if I had come full circle, the prodigal son returning home to the land of his birth," he said smiling, as if their minds and inner thoughts were one.

Antony had been gone for almost three weeks now and never had Eleanor felt so lonely. Lady Stratton, as if sensing Eleanor's loneliness, was keener now to do more activities outside her home, although she regularly bemoaned the increase of both noise and those insufferable 'wild colonials' as she referred to the ANZAC soldiers. But they routinely went for ice cream at Groppi's, dinner at Shepheard's, they had even taken in a movie at the Metro Cinema where they saw the American epic, *Gone With the Wind*. Even Lady Stratton had adored it and requested that Eleanor purchase the book, which they promptly started reading the next afternoon as was their daily custom following afternoon tea. "Oh that no good Rhett Butler," Lady Stratton had said countless times, which made Eleanor smile. Although Eleanor had been smiling more and more when it came to her employer. She was simply amazed by the utter transformation that Egypt brought out in Lady Stratton. Gone was the cold, older woman who rarely smiled and seemed peeved by the slightest thing. She had been replaced by a happier one who didn't appear as weighted down by the many personal losses she had endured. Here she was simply free. And while Eleanor bemoaned endlessly about the oppressive heat and scorching sun, those were the ingredients that appeared to make Lady Stratton thrive. And she supposed that's why she had come here all these years, why Egypt had always been her second home.

29 May 1940

My dear girl,
    In my last letter to you, I promised that I would give you a taste of 'military life' as you called it, so here it is. Many will say that in the desert, sand is one's greatest enemy but clearly they have never met the dreaded desert fly. And lest you think it's the same variety as the

ones we have back home, think again. Not only is it smaller but it's also more aggressive, perhaps compensating for its smaller size. If I'm being honest, we spend just as much time (if not more), brushing them from our eyes, lips, foods, and as my dear mama would say, our 'cuppa' as we do engaged with the enemy.

Food, while not what I would call 'good', is if nothing else, plentiful (although yes, I fully acknowledge that as an officer my rations are of a higher caliber than what the average 'Tommie' is receiving. Food is heated on what's called a Benghazi burner- these my dear are large petrol tins filled with sand and soaked with petrol. Other petrol tins filled with sand act as filters, they are for those fleetingly rare moments when there's enough water to wash or shave in. But believe me, those are far and few. It is the desert after all...

It's strange, I suppose it's nothing more than a byproduct of having grown up here, but what the other men find so strange and exotic, just seems normal to me. Although I suppose the young pimps offering up their 'sisters' and saying they're 'pink inside like Queen Victoria herself' is a tad peculiar. Although I've heard from other officers that VD is proving to be one of the number one ailments of our men, so clearly these sisters are not that pink. Forgive me for being cheeky, but I didn't think you would entirely mind my sauciness here.

I anxiously await until I can see you again, my dear girl.

Yours, Antony

August 1940

Eleanor had never been there but when she heard that Paris had fallen to the Nazis on June 14, she immediately burst into tears. Of course, this was mere days after Italy had aligned itself with Nazi Germany and declared war upon France and the United Kingdom, making the raids that Antony and his men had been conducting on Italian positions in Cyrenaica all that spring seem like child's play, and life now hauntingly real.

When Eleanor had asked Lady Stratton if she would be amenable to the idea of Eleanor volunteering at the 9th General Hospital as a VAD, the older woman had surprised her by immediately agreeing, even going so far as to say she thought it was a 'fine idea.'

The following week on her first day there, Eleanor wasn't so sure it really was a fine idea after all when a horrible stench invaded her nostrils. She must have been making the most awful of faces because a young sister around her age stopped and coldly said, "burnt flesh" and walked away without another word. Eleanor quickly came to the realization that there was no smell more horrible in the world than that of burnt flesh mixed in with the oppressive Cairo heat. But she chided herself for being squeamish and reminded herself any number of the boys here could be any of her brothers or even Antony and she wouldn't want some namby-pamby looking after them. Well, the non-nursing side that was, since a sister she was not.

Some days later, a different and much kinder sister explained that for the burn victims (of which there were endless numbers; so many patients suffered their horrific injuries after stepping on a mine or being caught in a tank when it was blown away) there was no way of adequately washing them so the nauseating smell was always there. One of the burn victims, a young soldier who appeared younger than she, noticed that she had been studying his arm and told her he had been 'brewed up.' In a thick cockney accent, he explained that's when a tank was blown up, a fire was lit in order to brew tea. Eleanor felt like she was going to be sick but stifled the bile she felt forming in the back of her throat and feebly smiled instead, the young soldier all smiles as if he hadn't a care in the world.

But most of the men inside the 9th's wards were those who had contracted a disease- malaria, dysentery, mumps, and VD. The last one elicited the most tsk-tsks from the sisters on duty, grumbling that Clot Bey needed to be razed to the ground. Not wanting to appear ignorant on the matter, Eleanor later asked Edward about it, who reddened and responded that no well-bred lady should ever go there let alone speak of it. Eleanor assumed that it was an area of prostitutes. Eleanor also thought that must be the British part of him.

The days that Eleanor spent volunteering were filled patrolling the wards, laden with tea, sandwiches, cigarettes and books. *The Grapes of Wrath, The Big Sleep,* and *Rebecca* proved to be especially popular, although most men wanted *Blighty Parade;* Eleanor blushed when she discovered it was primarily a pin-up magazine although with some cartoons and stories. Some sisters were less strict than others and would allow torn pages of famous American actresses to be affixed next to their beds or lovingly placed on bedside tables. Of these, Rita Hayworth was undoubtedly the most popular.

Each night Eleanor and Lady Stratton listened in rapt attention to that day's BBC report on the wireless of the events of what they were calling the 'Desert Campaign.' Eleanor always remembered what Antony had told her once, that reports from the front were generally one of two things- highly exaggerated or grossly downplayed. She always hoped for his sake that it was neither.

November 1940

"I wonder if I shall ever see England again."

Eleanor looked over in shock at Lady Stratton who, out of character for her, was leaning back in her peach-colored velour armchair, almost slouched really.

"Are you not well, Lady Stratton?" Eleanor asked, rising to come and stand closer to the older woman in case she needed assistance getting up and going to her room.

"Oh, I'm fine. Don't fuss," she chided, but playfully. "In the last war, they said it would be over by Christmas. And it went on for more than four years. Who knows how long this one will last. With the progression of time comes the advancement of innovation, new ways for grown boys to kill each other."

Eleanor's mouth was agape. Never before had she heard Lady Stratton speak so openly, even with the thawing of her temperament and personality over the last nine months. It was almost as if she had become a defeatist, a stark contrast to the stiff upper lip stoicism she typically exhibited. Fearing what the older woman would say, Eleanor hesitantly asked, "Do you think the Allies will lose?"

"The war? Oh heavens no. But I'm an old woman now. I just don't know how many years I have left. And I won't lie, I yearn for the day when I am reunited once more with my children. A mother no matter the circumstances should never outlive her child or in my case, all her children."

And then as if she were reciting at a school pageant, she spoke, tears brimming in her eyes-

> *With proud thanksgiving, a mother for her children,*
> *England mourns for her dead across the sea.*
> *Flesh of her flesh they were, spirit of her spirit,*
> *Fallen in the case of the free.*

They went with songs to the battle, they were young,
Straight of limb, true of eye, steady and aglow.
They were staunch to the end against odds uncounted:
They fell with their faces to the foe.

They shall grow not old, as we that are left grow old:
Age shall not weary them, nor the years condemn.
At the going down of the sun and in the morning
We will remember them.
They shall not grow old.

"For the Fallen" by Laurence Binyon" Lady Stratton said. "Never have truer or more eloquent words ever been spoken."

CHAPTER 16

November 1940

While war raged throughout Europe, one country after the next falling to Hitler and the Nazis, as if a nation and its people were nothing more than a cheap pack of dominoes, life in Cairo was still the same. For the Egyptians, their only source of consternation was the arrival of the Australian soldiers. Many remembered the sheer havoc they caused through their rampaging of the capital streets at the end of the last war. The Egyptians wanted neither their businesses nor their daughters' reputations destroyed by the arrival of the men whose English accents were so peculiar.

Outwardly, the Egyptian government and monarchy were grateful for Britain's help in keeping the Italians out of their country (or as Lady Stratton referred to Il Duce, 'that thug Musso or something'). Many were fearful that their country would suffer the same fate as that of Ethiopia, their neighbor to the south, which Italy had invaded in '35 and had occupied ever since. But from Antony, Eleanor had learned that Egypt had no wish to be involved in the war between England and Germany. In fact, he had also told her rather 'hush hush' that many Egyptians, even those that were high up in the government, secretly admired Hitler. That they saw the German leader's rise to the top from humble beginnings to where he now stood, going up against the most powerful country in the world, as a parallel to the Egyptian people's own struggles in wanting to finally have complete independence from that very same leader.

But for Eleanor, news from home had become increasingly sparse over the past months. Although her mum had never been much for letter writing to begin with, her once weekly missives to her daughter had trickled down to one, possibly two a month. And they were always the same- the same trite words in each letter, almost as if she were copying them from a play and couldn't be bothered to write anything new to her very own daughter. But Aunt May dutifully still wrote to her each week, sometimes twice. She didn't go into great detail but spoke on how difficult life had become in London, what with the food shortages and rationing for those articles one could still find in the shops. And then of course there were the bombs that rained down in the capital and other English cities morning and night, which had been going on for months now. It had all started back in September. 'Black Saturday' Aunt May had written, was what the papers had called it when the German bombers attacked London for the first time, leaving hundreds dead and scores more injured, not to mention all the homes that had been destroyed, lives and memories completely snuffed out, just like that. Eleanor wondered if she'd even recognize the place where she'd grown up with all the destruction around it now.

In her last letter, Aunt May had written that the bombing attacks only seemed to occur at night now and she half-feared that she would never again enjoy an uninterrupted night of sleep in her lifetime. She wrote about her work at a local soup kitchen where she volunteered as the cook, feeding the many East Enders whose homes had been reduced to rubble by the falling Luftwaffe bombs. "The guests are a bit different than those who attended Lady Stratton's fetes that I used to cook for, but it's me doing my part for the war is what I tell myself," she had written. She always ended her letters reminding

Eleanor to be kind to her mum and that it was triply hard having not one but three sons fighting in the beastly war.

"I wonder if I'd even recognize her anymore."

"Who, Lady Stratton?"

"Why, London," she replied a bit exasperatedly, as if another of Eleanor's duties was to be a clairvoyant. "Friends write to say the city is being terribly bombed each night. Not that we'd know it from the wireless. It's a bit too much of the whole 'stiff upper lip' attitude if you ask me."

Just like her aunt's letters, the BBC rarely went into great detail about the Blitz bombings back home, but they did say that the damage and loss of life was greatest in the East End. Eleanor felt immense irritation then, resentment even starting to build within her. Lady Stratton's friends, undoubtedly posh aristocratic ladies from the West End who had never once set foot in the East End, who if they did have their home destroyed in the middle of the night, would have their country estate to escape to and ride out the rest of the war. What would any of them know about tragedy and loss, Eleanor angrily thought. But guilt set in then, guilt over herself when she remembered the champagne and Battenberg cake she had enjoyed a few weeks ago at Shepheard's where Antony had taken her following a night of dancing at the Continental. She really was immune to all of it, living in Cairo, Eleanor thought, picturing the full kitchen pantry and icebox, all of which, should it become empty, could be restocked at a moment's notice with a quick visit to any of the Greek grocers. She even still had the luxury of adding not one but two lumps of sugar to her tea each afternoon, along with a dash of cream. Bitter, both literally and figuratively, was not a term she'd had to become accustomed to here in Egypt. And then she remembered Aunt May's final words from her last letter-

It's always those who have nothing to begin with, that lose the little they do.

Cairo
December 1940

"Marry me."

Eleanor whipped around to see Antony kneeling before her on one knee, his hands holding a small black box that contained the most exquisite ring she had ever seen. She felt lightheaded, thinking this couldn't possibly be real, that all of this was just a dream, a perfectly splendid dream. But she pinched herself then, quite hard, only to see Antony still kneeling there before her, along with a cacophony of voices emanating from just inside the ballroom to their right, party revelers who were just getting started in the night's festivities. And his smile, his perfectly wonderful and infectious smile, and she knew yes, it was indeed real.

"Yes, yes," Eleanor answered, half-sobbing as Antony shot back up, engulfing her in his arms as he passionately kissed her, her shaking body gradually subsiding to feeling so wonderfully alive. And as he placed the ring on her finger, it fitting like a glove as if she were always meant to wear it, she thought, how can any of this be real? A child of Spitalfields- when one grows up in a place like that, you never imagine that you'll go anywhere else, be anything or anyone else. That your place of birth predetermines your life's path. And yet here she was, a modern-day Cinderella complete with her very own Prince Charming, although Lady Stratton was hardly the Evil Stepmother.

"I don't want to wait until the war is over."

"I don't understand," she said, unsure of what he meant.

"It could go on for years and life can change at the…" his words trailed off, but Eleanor knew his meaning. This was war, when a life could begin and end just like that. Nobody was guaranteed there would be a tomorrow, the only instance when money and social rank couldn't change a thing. Antony served with the 11th Hussars, a rather prestigious cavalry regiment that had already been stationed in Egypt when the war started and as such was one of the most battle-seasoned units in the 7th Armoured Division, as well as the most adept at handling armour in the desert. The 'Desert Rats' they were called. Although it was easy to pretend that he was just 'away on business' when she wouldn't see him for weeks, sometimes more than a month at a time, that business was, in fact, war. But each time he had gone away, gone back to the all too real game of war, he always came back to her, came back to lowly Eleanor Mews from Spitalfields.

"And your family?" she tentatively asked.

He looked at her, confusion apparent on his face, until moments later it cleared and his smile turned upward. "I only telegrammed Mother to give her the news, but she's delighted. Truly. She can't wait to meet you one day. As for the rest of the lot," (Eleanor knew he had two older brothers and three younger sisters), I know they'll be thrilled too." And as if sensing the fear that still inwardly plagued her he added, "And no one cares a fig about your 'origins' as you call it. I was never the heir, and now with William having two sons of his own, I'm so far down the line, you'll never have to worry about stepping up to the pitch," he finished, smiling broadly at her. "We'll be able to just live our lives as we want," and then he kissed her once more, this serving as both a form of reassurance and also a sublime pleasure. "Wherever the desert winds may take us."

For all of December Cairo had been awash in both triumphal

jubilation and a carefree existence, a dazzling *joie de vivre* that made Christmas of 1940 seem even more special, more simply wonderful. All of it stemmed from the fact that the Italians had been pushed out of Egypt that autumn and that they had also failed to take Greece. And so every Brit and Greek in Egypt, regardless of their class, title, or rank, celebrated like the war was over.

Eleanor had never felt so much happiness as she had that night at the Red Crescent's Christmas Ball, when Antony asked her to marry him and when the war itself seemed like it would never come to Cairo. But all that changed in a cruel twist of fate when on the last two days of the year, Eleanor received not one but two telegrams bearing heartbreaking news- her mum was killed by a bomb that struck her flat, and her younger brother Charlie died at sea when his destroyer, the HMS Acheron, struck a mine and sank off the Isle of Wight, taking nearly 200 of its crewmen with her. War may not have come to the doorsteps of Cairo but it had certainly come to her.

CHAPTER 17

"Eleanor, may I come in?"

For the past three days, Eleanor had remained voluntarily sequestered in her room. She had neither an appetite nor the desire to see anyone, Lady Stratton included. Eleanor was inwardly glad this was 1941 and not a century earlier when, had she experienced the loss she had now, she undoubtedly would not have been able to completely ignore her employer as she had been doing; in fact, she probably would have been dismissed. She wasn't sure who laid out a tray at her door each morning and evening, only heard it being placed on the floor followed by a quiet perfunctory knock and then silence. Eleanor knew she couldn't stay like this forever nor could she ignore Lady Stratton, who now stood on the other side of the door.

"Yes, Lady Stratton," she replied.

The door opened and Lady Stratton entered the room which was awash in the late afternoon's setting sun. And then she sat on the edge of Eleanor's bed, taking her hand in hers.

"Each life is precious, each death is different, no two are ever the same. Don't let anyone ever tell you differently. We must all grieve in our own ways at our own time. Life will still be here when you are ready."

Unable to say anything, she merely mumbled "thank you" as she took her damp cuff and wiped it once more over her wet eyes.

Lady Stratton studied her then, her long thin face scrunched up, appearing as if she wanted to say more but wasn't sure if she should. As if she, the Countess of Hertfordshire should be concerned with being improper to her young employee, a girl from the East End.

"Have you written to your beau?"

"No," she whispered.

"I think you should tell him."

"I don't want him to worry."

"You're his fiancée, and war or not, if you are to be his wife, you must confide and tell him of important matters, especially ones of such a heartbreaking nature. And besides," she said, rising from the bed, "not writing to him at all will only cause more worry."

But Eleanor ignored Lady Stratton's words and remained silent. She dutifully wrote to Antony but kept her letters short and for her, jarringly sweet. It wasn't just that she didn't want to worry him when he was at the front, she didn't want to hear any more lifeless, conciliatory words that although they were uttered with heartfelt meaning, only left her feeling more hurt and alone and at times, angry.

"To die will be an awfully big adventure."

As children, Eleanor and Charlie had adored the book, *Peter and Wendy*. It had been a birthday present from Aunt May to Eleanor the year she turned nine and she had read it out loud to Charlie each night, who struggled with reading and preferred being read to.

She thought of that line a lot in the weeks after learning of his death.

Adventure was what he had always wanted out of life, why he had joined the Royal Navy. He had envisioned himself a Peter Pan, off to have his own adventures just like the leader of the Lost Boys had had on the mythical island of Neverland. Would he see them now, Eleanor wondered? Was there still life after death? Or will his biggest adventure in life having been that he died, and so young? And not even in a far-off distant land but on an island in the English Channel.

Winter, 1941

Eleanor's immense grief aside, it seemed that perhaps 1941 was going to be a good year; perhaps the war would even be over by Christmas. The fighting in neighboring Libya was going in favor of the British. They overran Tobruk after a brief battle and mere weeks later in February, they took Benghazi. And for all his fiery speeches, that "Musso or something" was more air than smoke and no match for the might of the British Empire. But all of that changed after February when a German general arrived in North Africa. Erwin Rommel soon became known as "The Desert Fox," a nickname bestowed upon him by his enemy. And soon his prowess amongst the vast swatches of empty desert made it easy to see why he was called that.

August 1941

"Am I dreaming now, sister? Does this mean I'm dead?"

Eleanor turned, startled at the voice coming from the hospital bed, that for the last three days was still breathing, but had been otherwise dead to the world ever since he had been brought in from Tobruk, bandages still covering his eyes.

"No, private, this is real," Eleanor said, squeezing his lifeless hand that rested almost carelessly at the edge of the bed as if to reassure him this wasn't a desert dream. And then realizing she didn't want him calling her sister again, lest one of the actual sisters overhear and think Eleanor was behaving improperly she added, "I'm not a sister, just a VAD."

As if he hadn't heard her, he asked, "where am I?" looking around in a mixture of both amazement and confusion. "There's no sand."

Tobruk was a port city on Libya's coast that had been under siege since the beginning of April. Eleanor knew from Antony's letters that the desert conditions could be just as harsh and brutal an enemy as the actual one. Add a siege on top of that with constant artillery and air bombardment, ever dwindling supplies of food and water, and the ever-present flies, fleas, and illness, it was hell on earth. And it was still going on.

"You're in Cairo, at the 9th British General."

"And my mates?"

"I'm not sure," Eleanor replied, completely at a loss what to say. "The siege is still continuing. Reports say that the Australian forces have been replaced by the British 70th Division."

"Why are my eyes covered?" he asked, sitting up in his bed, becoming visibly agitated, making Eleanor worry he was going to start thrashing about and rip his eye bandages off.

More feelings of being at a complete loss. "I'm sure the sister on duty and doctors will be around shortly to talk to you about your condition," Eleanor answered, hoping this would mollify him, having no idea if the bandage coverings meant his lack of vision was a temporary thing…or a permanent one.

"You know what we called ourselves?" he asked, more relaxed now as he reclined once more against the crisp, stark white sheets of his bed. "The Rats of Tobruk. You see some British whacka broadcaster who works for those Nazis, he described us as being caught 'like rats in a trap' in one of his broadcasts. Called us the 'poor rats of Tobruk.' Well, we took it as a badge of courage and honour and started calling ourselves the 'Rats of Tobruk. Because I'd rather be a rat than a dirty fascist any day."

"You are indeed a most courageous lot," Eleanor said, squeezing his hand once more, and trying not to think of those who remained. The Desert Fox was many things but a defeatist was not one of them, as evidenced by his determination to take Tobruk.

3 March 1942

My dear girl,

They call the desert area below Bir Hacheim the 'Cauldron' as if it's a proper place. Never was there a more appropriate name to describe what I think of as hell on earth. I'm almost inclined to think that Dante's inferno would be preferable to this cesspool of pure misery - searing dusty winds that scorch the lungs the moment one draws even the slightest of breaths and scour one's eyes and skin until they both are raw.

I always prided myself on being made of tougher stock than my men and fellow officers who had never left England before, never had a foreign posting. I always referred to it as my 'desert stock,' the childhood I had spent in Egypt that looking back on it now seems like an absurd fantasy. But I feel that romping around ancient ruins, having picnics prepared by cook and nanny at the monolithic feet of Ramses II is ridiculous when one considers that in these same vast desert sands, men are dying in droves, their lives ended by bullets and bombs and all the other horrors that the modern armies can inflict upon their fellow-man.

I feel there's a reckoning coming. My only hope is that I live to see it. To see you again. To go to the pictures with you and have a coconut ice cream at Groppi's after. I hear Suspicion is quite good.

With all my love, Antony

A reckoning. But what on earth did he mean by that, as Eleanor stared at the letter she held in her hands, the other words a jumbled mess on the page except for that one. What did he know that he wasn't saying, or Eleanor stopped to remind herself, couldn't say due to the censors. Even months after the siege at Tobruk had ended, the BBC still carried on as if that was the greatest victory, never mind the fact that Singapore, one of the crown jewels of the British Empire, had fallen to the Japanese. Antony had once told her that the BBC was notorious for overhyping the British military's modest victories and understating its catastrophic losses, all to not dampen the morale of the British people back home, never mind they were the very same people who were living right in the thick of it.

But for Singapore to have fallen to the Japanese, the British Army surrendering to what it deemed a vastly inferior one comprised of inferior people in the mindsets of many, how could it not be anything less than a horribly stinging defeat? Was one in Egypt or neighboring Cyrenaica not far behind? Before, Antony had never talked like a defeatist, so why now? They say a cat has nine lives. Did Antony feel he was out of his?

"Every time I'm at the hospital, I fear I'm going to be walking down the wards one day and see him there lying in bed, only it's not going to be the Antony I remembered, for his face will be horribly burned, or his leg maimed from a bomb."

"Would that make you love him any less?"

Lady Stratton had invited Eleanor for tea at Shepheard's, which the younger woman had eagerly accepted, anything to take her mind off Antony's worrisome words in his latest missive. And yet the moments their cups were filled with hot steaming tea, Eleanor couldn't help but relay the contents of what he had written.

"I'm not sure, I never really thought about it, never thought about Antony being anything but the man I know."

"You know, my dear," Lady Stratton said as she rather unceremoniously plopped another lump of sugar into her cup. "After my boys were killed, I often asked God why he didn't let them live, that wouldn't living be preferable to death, wouldn't it be better to still have them there with you in some capacity than never seeing them again at all? But I had too many friends whose sons did come back from the Front- missing an arm, a leg, an ear, or even worse, paralyzed. And I think would that have really been preferable? Would it have been better for my greed to surpass them no longer having the chance to have a normal life- to marry, have children, to lead a rich and complete life. Is it better to be able to remember my boys are they were and not a permanent reminder of what war does?" She looked at Eleanor squarely then before adding, "I'm not saying you are a vain little creature who would abandon the man she loves if he bore horrific scars on his person. I'm just saying you are too young to live the life of a nursemaid and nothing else. But in times of war, all we can do is pray, pray that all our loved ones return to us safely and pray that this horrible war comes to an end."

When the Battle for Tobruk began, it was only then that Eleanor realized that war was nothing more than the grown-up version of a children's fight over a beloved toy. First, the toy is that child's but then another child takes it back and so the tussle goes. And this was Tobruk , the port city in neighboring Cyrenaica which had been Axis, then Allied, and now was at risk of falling into Axis hands once more.

And Antony was right there in the thick of it all. The reckoning he had foreseen.

"Oh, Eleanor, do turn the wireless on. Let's see what London has to say about this Tobruk."

"Tobruk, the port city in eastern Cyrenaica might be lost but it's not terribly important anyway."

"Did the bloody announcer really just say that? Say it's not really that important?"

Eleanor thought she had screamed this statement of outrage in her head but upon seeing Lady Stratton's bemused look and raised eyebrows, Eleanor realized she hadn't. "I'm so sorry Lady Stratton, I didn't mean to be so vulgar."

"Oh, do hush, you silly girl. I dare say I was thinking the same thing since I think it's quite important to the thousands of families whose fathers, sons, and husbands are fighting there right now at this bloody moment," she said, smiling warmly at Emily as almost a form of encouragement.

But by June 21, it was all over, the Desert Fox getting what he had come for, the taking of Tobruk. And for the first time ever, the British in Egypt were genuinely scared of what was to come.

CHAPTER 18

1 July 1942

"Good heavens, would you look at all that smoke!"

Eleanor looked up from the book she was reading, *A Farewell to Arms* by that American fellow, Ernest Hemingway, to see Lady Stratton standing in the open doorway to the courtyard with its inner gardens. Rising from the settee to join her, she too was amazed to see the already typically hazy sky ablaze with a thick layer of smoke that seemed to alternate between billowing and lightly swirling, making Eleanor think that these great plumes of smoke resembled dancers as 'black snow' rained down.

"Do you think it's the Germans? That they're already here?" Eleanor asked, her voice quavering as she spoke aloud her biggest fear, forced occupation and life under the Nazis. She knew that this was a way of life now for virtually the whole of Europe and that weren't it for the bravery of the RAF, London and all of England would be bedecked with that ghastly Nazi flag. But she couldn't fathom it. Although Antony and his fellow soldiers had been fighting the 'Desert War,' as it was called, for years now, it still had seemed far enough away to not really register that in truth, it had always been an absolute reality. How did that phrase go, "ignorance is bliss?" Had she been completely ignorant of the fact that just because she wasn't on the continent, she was safe, immune even from the dangers of this new world war? Look at Singapore, how quickly it had fallen to the Japanese, how even the farthest corners of England's colonial empires were now under Japanese rule. And then there was Antony, whom she hadn't heard from since Tobruk had fallen.

"I'm not sure, I'm really not sure," Lady Stratton replied, her eyes still fixated on the sky.

"The wireless said Alexandria suffered horrible air raids a couple of nights ago. Do you think we're next?"

"I feel that Alexandria is to the Germans what Manchester or Liverpool is to us- nice enough cities but not the crown jewels. Not what Cairo is."

"They say tens of thousands of soldiers and the like were taken at Tobruk. Do you think that's why I haven't heard from him?" Nearly two weeks had passed since the catastrophic defeat at the port city and nary a word from Antony.

"My girl, I am not Apollo to be asking these sorts of questions." But Lady Stratton hadn't said this unkindly or without feeling, more an air of defeat that seemed to be pervading all those who swore allegiance to God and King. A feeling of utter helplessness. "Capture is still a better fate than death, which is permanent," she added, gently placing her hand atop Eleanor's. "And as egregious as those Nazis are, they are still bound to honour the Geneva Conventions where prisoners of war are concerned." It wouldn't be until well after the war ended, did Eleanor learn how the Japanese had not honoured the treaties of the Geneva Convention and that her brother Ralph and thousands of other captured POWs had suffered more horrifically than one could ever imagine. But of course, Eleanor hadn't known that then. Nobody did.

"I'm getting myself on the train to Palestine."

"Don't be absurd, Diana, go to South Africa, away from all this madness! If the Jerrys can make it to our doorsteps here, Palestine will be next. Only going to the very ends of the earth will be safe anymore!"

It was a few days after what had been dubbed Ash Wednesday, when it was rumoured that the embassy and GHQ had burned vast quantities of files in preparation for the German invasion. But the capital had been in a dreadful state of unrest ever since. Lady Stratton hadn't forbidden Eleanor from leaving the house, but she also knew that she wouldn't be happy to learn she did so. Braving the heat, Eleanor had snuck out when she knew Lady Stratton would be taking her customary nap during the hottest part of the day. And found herself at Groppi's a short time later, although her heart felt like it was constricting every time she looked in the one corner where she and Antony always sat. And whom she still hadn't heard from and was indeed fearing the worst, that he had been captured by the enemy. Eleanor knew there was no escaping from either war talk or the war itself, even in Cairo now, but was dismayed to hear that was all that people were talking about. One saw it everywhere too- on the dirty and beleaguered faces of the soldiers who had managed to escape the snares of the Desert Fox and were now streaming into Cairo by the thousands. And for every soldier that Eleanor had passed, for that fleeting moment she wondered if it could be Antony. But it never was.

"Do you think we should leave Cairo? Head to Palestine or South Africa?" Eleanor asked later that night over dinner, echoing the words of the two women she had overheard earlier.

"Oh, heavens no! What a silly notion. No one forces me from my home, not the heat of Cairo or the likes of that Hitler."

Eleanor couldn't help but smile at the older woman's bravado which knowing Lady Stratton, she knew to be entirely genuine.

"But that's not to say that you mustn't feel like you need to stay here with me if you wish to go. I will of course provide for your passage wherever that may be."

"No, Lady Stratton," Eleanor quickly replied. "My place is here with you. I mean, I want to remain here with you." Eleanor wondered if she could read her mind, what she was also thinking- this is the only place where Antony knows to find me.

"Good, I'm happy to hear that. Which leads me to my next point," she said rather business-like, like she had when Eleanor had first started working for her. "I've had my will changed and I'm leaving you the house. The house here in Cairo, I mean," she quickly added when she noticed Eleanor's mouth that had fallen agape.

"But Lady Stratton," Eleanor said protesting, trying to wrap her head around what the older woman had just said. "You can't, you mustn't, I, I," she said stammering, "I don't know what to say."

"I think in your time here, you have fallen just as much in love with Egypt as I did back as a young girl all those years ago. Now it wouldn't be proper for me to leave you the house in London, but one day this dreadful war will indeed come to an end and perhaps you and Antony can make a proper life here as his parents did."

And then in a rare moment of emotion for someone of Lady Stratton's station, she said to Eleanor, looking her squarely in the eye, "I've come to think of you as a daughter. There is no greater heartache than a mother outliving her children and I've outlived all of mine. But at this late stage of my life, I feel as if I was given a second chance by having you come into my life and for that I shall be eternally grateful."

"And I you, Lady Stratton," completely breaking tradition and societal norms and hugging the older woman.

When Eleanor started seeing the closure of Jewish businesses that she had frequented numerous times, others doused with red paint and the vile Nazi swastika painted on their fronts, she immediately thought of the Rogarshevsky family. They had been a Jewish family, Orthodox she remembered how they referred to themselves, who'd immigrated to England after a pogrom in what was it, Poland? Ukraine? The parents kept to themselves, the mother rarely venturing outside except to go to the synagogue. The father had always scared Eleanor, what with his dreadfully long beard and the strands of hair on either side of his haunted face, sidelocks they were called. Eleanor thought then of something her mum had once told her, one of the kindest, most authentic things that had ever come out of her mouth- "Just because they don't look like you and me doesn't mean they're bad people or people to be scared of. They're just different. But different don't mean that it's bad neither." They lived in a neighboring flat and even paid Eleanor's brothers, first Tommy then Willie once Tommy had left, a bob to come to their flat each Friday at sunset to light the gas lamps for their Day of Rest since they were forbidden from doing any work. But one day, the family was gone, their flat completely cleared out. Willie said that the old man had killed 'em all (he was a butcher after all) and thrown all the bits into the Thames but their mum had whopped him on the side of his head and said 'stuff and nonsense,' that they had merely gone to America.

For months, Eleanor had seen the newspapers that spoke about the 'Jewish Problem' in Europe. The articles said that the Jews of Germany and other occupied countries under Nazi rule faced greater restrictions with each passing week and how many were being relocated to work camps in the East for 'their benefit.' Could the same thing happen here to Cairo's Jewish population? She thought it positively dreadful that her countrymen were so peevishly concerned about the Germans taking over Egypt when they weren't at risk like the Jews clearly were.

But all thoughts of the Rogarshevskys and the Jews of Europe were quickly forgotten when there came the sound of something hitting her bedroom window. Pushing aside the heavy damask, she looked out only to see what looked like a vagrant standing on the ground beneath her window. She was about to call out "scram" but then it dawned on her, why was it her window in particular they had chosen to throw the rock at? And then they looked up and even against the moonless night, the weeks' worth of a beard, the khaki fatigues so dirtied they almost looked black, she knew it was him. And Eleanor flew out of her room and down her steps, wondering if she was perhaps dreaming until she opened the door, and reaching out touched his grimy, sunburnt face, grains of sand caked in his beard and shaggy hair. And then she kissed him but not before he leaned back from her, even going so far as to hold her at arm's length.

"I'm positively filthy," he said, still keeping her at bay. "You mustn't."

"I must," Eleanor replied, reaching out to wrap her arms around his body. He remained almost stiff as he kept his arms at his side, no doubt not wanting to dirty her pristine white nightgown until his resistance broke and he engulfed her tightly in his. And it was as if she had been fed a magic tonic for the moment she felt his might around her, Eleanor felt as if she could take on the world, perhaps even Hitler himself. Or at least the dawn of a new day.

As they were exchanging a passionate kiss, Lady Stratton startled them from behind by asking how long this public display was going to last? Until dawn? prompting both Antony and Eleanor to jump back. Lady Stratton, even at 3 in the morning, looked to be the essence of elegance standing there in her lavender silk dressing gown and then, without even bothering to turn back, said over her shoulder, "come along, Lawrence of Arabia looks like he could use some actual food, more than the standard rations of bully beef and beans."

And then she surprised them both even further when she took out a skillet and made scrambled eggs, toast, and rashers.

"Will you permit me to speak frankly, Antony?" Lady Stratton asked, blowing on the cup of tea she held within her hands that had undoubtedly cooled off ages ago.

"Of course, Lady Stratton," Antony replied, sitting up straighter in his seat, as if he were seated at a dinner party for 20 and not in a kitchen in Cairo.

"I'm not sure what your orders are. I would hope they'll give you officers R & R after your hellish retreat back from the desert." Antony blanched when she said the word retreat, the fall of Tobruk still a source of bitter and dazed shock for the British people as a whole, but especially its army. "But before you return to the front, I want you to marry this girl here."

Silence. Such quiet one could have heard a pin drop.

"You did say I could speak frankly, my boy," Lady Stratton went on, a mixture of both sarcasm and directness in her tone.

"No, that's not it," Antony answered, his eyes cast down, fixated on his hands which rested atop the wooden table. And then in a whisper, his eyes never once looking at Eleanor's, said, "I don't want her to be a widow when she's barely been a bride. It's war, Lady Stratton. I can't do that to her." And then more emphatically stated, "I won't do that to her."

"But think, my lad. You die next week, next month, Eleanor gets nothing. She's chalked up to being nothing more than a wartime romance."

"I've never once behaved improperly towards her," Antony called out, emotions and anger rising within him. "And besides, my mother would do the right thing by her."

"But wouldn't it be better to do the right thing by her, by you in the first place? Not counting on anyone else but you to take care of the woman you love more than anything?"

At those words, Eleanor finally dared to look at Antony and saw that he was staring at her. Still looking at her he said, "You are the most important thing to me, my love," as he rose from where he was sitting to come and stand in front of her. "I'd marry you tomorrow if that's what I thought you truly wanted," he added, taking her hands in his.

"Oh heavens," Lady Stratton cut in. "Now I didn't say a wedding the very next day, but even in the midst of war, I need a little time to plan a fete."

They all laughed then, the tension in the room now broken, the anxiousness they had all felt in the past couple of weeks- the fall of Tobruk, the worry that Cairo would be next, not hearing from Antony- it had all given way, gone into the air as quickly as a sand storm did once it passed through.

"Yes, I want to marry you," Eleanor said. And then for the first time in her life she was greedy and added, "It's entirely what I want," as she placed her lips upon his, throwing her arms around him once more, her already sullied white nightgown now a permanently brown one.

They were married less than a week later at All Saints Cathedral with only Lady Stratton and the priest serving as their witnesses. Eleanor wore a simple shirtwaist dress the color of cornflowers along with a fascinator in a similar shade of blue while Antony was dressed in his uniform. It wasn't at all the wedding Eleanor had thought she'd have, or dreamt as a little girl she might have, but it was war and even though luxury goods like yards of silk and nylon stockings could still be found in the Cairo shops, it didn't matter to her anymore. Eleanor wished that Aunt May could have been there and of course Antony's mum, her fellow East Ender, but it couldn't be helped. As Lady Stratton had reminded them, in times of war, nothing was guaranteed, not even the chance of tomorrow. Eleanor knew it must have cost her a small fortune but Aunt May sent them a telegram congratulating them on the wonderful news and saying how much she couldn't wait to meet her dear niece's new husband.

As both the British Army and government continued to nurse their wounds from the staggering defeat at Tobruk and plot its next moves against the Desert Fox, Antony had been given two weeks holiday leave for his wedding.

And it was he who had surprised her with the greatest gift of all- a honeymoon sailing on a *dahabiya* up the Nile. A *dahabiya*, Eleanor learned, was a type of Egyptian passenger boat and was told by both her husband and Lady Stratton that it was the best way to see the sights of ancient Egypt. Antony had also said that it was a *dahabiya* that his mum and her American friend had sailed on all those years ago when in search of the American friend's lost love. Eleanor found it all terribly romantic and now found herself alone with only her husband, a cook, cabin boy, and captain for company.

The further they sailed, the more they retreated from the capital city and its surrounding environs, the omnipresent noise and chaos of Cairo replaced with the quiet and serenity of a floating village life, the more Eleanor was able to imagine that it was the war that was imaginary, and that this life on the *dahabiya* with Antony was what was actually real.

"I don't think I've ever seen so many stars before," Eleanor said one night where after dinner, they had come up on deck, placed two chairs next to each other and sat in, holding hands, as they gazed up at the night sky. "When you grow up in a place like Spitalfields, stars are almost as make believe as fairies."

Antony softly laughed then, still gazing up intently at the sky. "My father, he, um, he wasn't the most demonstrative with us children. I don't think it was necessarily his upbringing that he was like this." At her confused look he said, "You know, men of his station, their only interaction with their children was the hour or so each day that nanny brought them into the parlour to see him. I think he was honestly horrified what his own children thought of him, because of his war injuries, his facial deformities, at least when we were young, that is. Like it was almost as if he envisioned himself to be a scary monster to his own children and so he stayed away from us. But stargazing was one thing he always did with us, did without mama's prompting. 'Come along children, a quid to the first of you lot who can find Ursa Major and Orion.' It was only when I was older did I realize that stargazing meant darkness, and he could hide his scariness from us under the cover of darkness."

Eleanor didn't quite know what to say. They both had had absent fathers, one literally, the other figuratively. But it didn't mean either absence hurt any less.

"As a grown man, there are so many things I wish I could go back and tell him now, but especially now as a soldier and all that I've seen."

"From wherever he is," Eleanor began, "he knows," she said, squeezing his hand. "He knows how much you loved him."

As they made their way up the Nile, Eleanor very much wished she could go back in time to when she had learned about the ancient civilisations. Antony was a fountain of knowledge, spouting historical fact after fact when they visited the ruins of Karnak and Luxor.

"How in heavens did they build these, I mean there's so many of them!" Eleanor said in disbelief, as she posed next to a colossal statue of Ramses II as Antony had identified for her while he took her picture with his Leica Model A camera.

"The wonders of ancient Egypt," he replied, holding out his hand to her to take to continue their exploration of ancient Thebes.

"Are they all like this? I mean, are they all so grand and enormous?"

"Wait till you see Abu Simbel, it's location right on the Nile, it's simply breathtaking. Possibly my favorite spot in all of Egypt. Although I must say I'm pretty partial to obelisks too," as they approached one.

"Who's this?" Eleanor asked, staring in amazement at the intricate and fascinating hieroglyphics that were carved into it.

"Hmm," Antony said, narrowing his eyes to more closely examine it. "Either Hatshepsut or Thutmosis I. I'm a bit rusty. My classics instructor would be most disappointed in me right now."

"Do you want to hear something funny? Although you may think less of me once you do," Eleanor added.

"I highly doubt that."

"I must have passed by Cleopatra's Needle dozens of times. You know, back in London along the Victoria Embankment in Westminster? It was only right before I left for Egypt did I learn what it's called, I mean what it is. An obelisk. And it was my Aunt May of all people who told me. I felt like such a blockhead."

"My dear girl," he said, pulling her into his side and playfully squeezing her waist. "You could never be a blockhead and I dare say there are plenty of oblivious lords and ladies who don't know what they're called either, beyond that 'pointy thing' by the Thames. And yet here you are, a lady of Egypt, now standing next to another one. I think you've done quite well for yourself," he said, gently kissing her on her cheek.

"Excuse me," Antony said, suddenly calling out to a man in a pith helmet and what were they, jodhpurs Eleanor wondered. "Would you please take my wife and my photo?"

"Most certainly!" the man said in an astutely marked upper-class British accent as he came towards them to take the Leica.

Click.

CHAPTER 19

Growing up in the East End, Eleanor was all too familiar with superstitions. Cockneys didn't believe much in the way of schooling; they reasoned the best school was what their mum and nan taught them and what their mums and nans had taught them before. Books had no place on the streets of the East End, except maybe to kindle the fire or when you needed to go to the loo. But superstitions, that's where you'd want to pay attention so as not to have bad luck or have the devil and witches pay you a visit.

Eleanor was eight when she first realized that superstitions were pure poppycock. She had been hit in the face with salt which, according to her nan, had been meant for the devil's face but instead had gotten Eleanor since the practice was to throw it over your left shoulder. And then there was the hagstone her mum kept on an iron key ring by the front door of their flat. The hole in these stones supposedly symbolized a passage through which only good luck and prosperity could pass. Witches, fairies, and evil thoughts were too big and would therefore be kept at bay. But one time her older brother Tommy had taken the hagstone after a particularly nasty row between him and their mum. He wouldn't tell her where he had hidden it and after getting his ears boxed a second time, he had off and stayed away for days. All Eleanor knew was that in the almost week that the hagstone hadn't been hanging by the door, no witches had passed through.

But if there was one superstition Eleanor should have paid attention to, it was that bad things always come in threes. And it was already too late by the time she did.

It was just a cold, allergies even. That's what the doctor said. "Fit as a fiddle" he told Eleanor when she privately voiced her concern over the general state of malaise Lady Stratton had been exhibiting for the last couple of weeks.

"War fatigue," he had said as Eleanor handed him his hat. "We all have it and I dare say it's a bit much for anyone's nerves, let alone a woman of nearly 70. Have her continue to rest in bed as she's been doing and she'll be as right as rain."

Eleanor sat with Lady Stratton for most of the day. When she wasn't sleeping, she would read to her and when she was, Eleanor wrote endless letters to Antony, putting them into two piles. One pile contained the letters she would send, the other were ones she would never post, never have him or anyone else read her inner-most thoughts and fears. She didn't have much of an appetite, which Eleanor knew only contributed to her heightened state of weakness, nibbling on dry toast without any butter or marmalade and almost tentatively sipping her tea. Each night cook would prepare a full plate for Lady Stratton but it was never touched; the older woman delivered almost the same habit each night by taking one look at the plate of food and simply shaking her head and saying, "oh I can't." And so, she grew frailer and weaker with each passing day, making her resemble more a woman deep into her 80s and not like the robust woman who had so intimidated Eleanor all those years ago.

And then one day she was gone. Eleanor had brought in the customary tray of toast and tea and saw that Lady Stratton was still sleeping. Setting it down on the edge of the bed, she saw upon closer examination that her employer had an almost a blueish hue to her complexion. Eleanor, swaying then, grabbed onto the bed's column so as to steady herself. Her hand trembling, she took the older woman's hand, its grip as cold as ice and without feeling a pulse, Eleanor knew.

When she heard that her mum had been killed, Eleanor had grieved for the figure, but not the person. The circumstances of her upbringing exasperated by the abject poverty she had been born into gave her a childhood both difficult and tumultuous. That was something she couldn't change, just as she couldn't change the fact that her father had abandoned them. But her mum, she **chose** the bottle over her children, she chose everything else in life **except them.** And for that Eleanor had never been able to forgive her. But with Lady Stratton, she felt that she had lost her 'mum.'

"You can be with them now," Eleanor whispered as she leaned down, gently kissing the woman's forehead. As she went to leave, she took in the contents of the room, her eyes then briefly settling on the row of three black and white photographs in ornate brass frames. Three individuals, taken from this earth when they were barely more than children, three sets of eyes that appeared to be staring right at her. A quarter century had passed since she had lost all her children but for Lady Stratton, it might have as well been yesterday.

"Take good of your mum. She never stopped loving you. And I'll never stop loving her," Eleanor said to those same three sets of eyes, slowly closing the door behind her.

Eleanor had never been close with her youngest brother, George. He had been diagnosed as having a heart murmur when was just a boy and spent all of his childhood wanting or seeming to compensate for it, forever starting fights, constantly getting clocked by the schoolmaster until he had stopped going, not wanting anyone around him to think he was less. It only got worse the older he got.

Because of this Eleanor was glad he wouldn't be able to fight in the war. She could see him being killed his first day on enlistment by a fellow soldier who couldn't stand his pugnacious manner anymore. Before she left for Egypt, Eleanor had heard he was working for Cunard on one of its ships as a crew member. In the beginning, long before she met Antony, Eleanor would think of George at times, hoping he was safe and out of harms way, especially since the Atlantic was littered with U-boats and mines. But then her life had changed so much and she hadn't given the brother who had caused so much trouble and difficulty for all those who knew him little more thought. He was safe. Or so she thought.

When the newspapers and the BBC first reported on the sinking of the RMS Laconia by a German U-boat in the Atlantic off the African coast, for a fleeting moment she worriedly thought 'what if George was on it?' It was after all a passenger ship of the Cunard Line. But then she chided herself for being silly. She would know if he had been. Aunt May would have told her. At the hospital that week, the Laconia incident, as it was being called, was all anyone could talk about.

"Imagine surviving the sinking of a ship, on the precipice of being rescued, only to be killed by aerial bombs and strafing from your own side."

"Those Yanks don't have the sense that God gave a canary. I'm hardly saying a German POW camp is the optimal place to be but it sure beats a watery grave."

They were referring to the American aircraft that, upon sighting the German U-boat that was rescuing the Laconia survivors, had opened fire on it, forcing the submarine to crash dive, thus casting the remaining survivors she had rescued into the sea where they were sitting targets for the unparalleled might of the U.S. Army Air Corps.

But the rest of September had passed and Eleanor heard nothing from Aunt May. And she thought nothing more of George. She had been too preoccupied with thoughts of Antony. He had been to see her at the end of September, telling her that this would be it for a long while. Eleanor never liked when he said this, for left unsaid was the painfully hard truth that she could very well see him again soon, but not in the way she would ever want.

"Shall we live here when the war is over?" she asked him. They were in the garden, the air still horridly hot but the now darkened sky providing a welcome respite from the day's soaring temperatures. Twenty-four hours he had been here with her, twenty-four more to go before he returned to the front where a new battle would ensue now that both sides had had plenty of time to lick their wounds and re-group.

"Would you like that?"

"I dare say I think I would," she replied. "And after a couple of years living here, I've even become accustomed to the heat. Not sure if I could ever take another English winter."

He laughed then, the sound of his laughter as wonderful a feeling as a cup of hot tea with honey on a sore throat. "I remember my first English winter, when I was sent away for school the first time. The stiff, scratchy wool coats and sweaters, having to wear shoes that pinched my toes. Mama always hated it when I went barefoot; she was deathly afraid of scorpions, you see. She'd always say, 'That's how Mister Alexander died and you wouldn't want that now, would you?' But I didn't care. Going barefoot was my way of rebelling against the tyrannical Headmaster Owens, although looking back on it now, I dare say he wasn't that bad of a bloke really."

"Would we need to return to England?" she asked him. "I mean to live, that is. Of course, we would visit," thinking how much she longed to see Aunt May again.

"As I've said my dear, that's the beauty of being neither the first born or the heir. I and now we have the supreme pleasure of doing exactly what we want to."

"And we'll travel?" she hopefully asked.

"Plotting out the next 50 years?" he replied in a playful banter.

"I am the Major General here. You, after all, are merely a lieutenant," she said, kissing him smartly on the lips.

He laughed uproariously then, pulling her backwards onto his lap. "And children?" he asked, whispering this into her ear.

Eleanor paused then, glad that the night's darkness provided a cover for the look of apprehension that had passed across her face just then. She thought of her miserable and bleak childhood, over the many days and nights she was hungry, of having shoes she was forced to wear that were more often than not beyond repair or pinched her toes so they caused blisters, of the countless things she was forced to go without, most notably a caring and loving home. But she knew that life with Antony was none of those things, would never be. Nevertheless the thought of becoming a mother scared her deeply, a fear she had never really shared before with him.

"Just come back to me," she whispered back as she kissed him, this time with all the feeling and passion that tonight might be their last and hoping that her response would mollify him for now.

24 October 1942

Word came of George when she was least expecting it. The BBC had reported that the Second Battle of El-Alamein had commenced the day before, so all her thoughts and prayers were on Antony. The first battle had ended in a stalemate and Eleanor knew, even though a military strategist she wasn't, that there would be no third. This would be the battle where for better or worse, one side would emerge the victor. The desert was not the Western Front, only it would be the true victor in the long run with its harsh and unforgiving conditions, where one careless, stupid move could prove fatal, just like that. Eleanor just hoped it would occur on the right side.

"Ma'am?" Eleanor turned at the sound of the voice. She saw the cook standing there, holding a folded white piece of paper. "This came earlier when you were out."

"Thank you, Ahmed," she said, almost lifelessly taking it as she went to stare out the window. "Please close the door behind you."

"Certainly, ma'am," he said, slightly bowing as he went to leave.

Upon hearing the gentle click of the door, Eleanor let out a huge breath and fumbled her way over to the desk chair where she sat as if her legs were on the verge of giving out beneath her. Steeling herself she unfolded the paper and felt dizzy when she saw the name Aunt May and not Antony. Aunt May and George. The words appeared a jumbled mess on the paper except for the line-

RECEIVED CONFIRMATION THAT GEORGE DIED ON LACONIA. I'M SO SORRY.

She started shaking then, heaving uncontrollable sobs, her body wracked with not only immense pain but also guilt. Guilt for that initial feeling of relief knowing that it wasn't Antony's name in the telegram but just a brother. Just. She had already lost one, another's fate unknown in a Japanese POW camp. And now she had lost another one. The brother she barely knew, the brother she had cowered from when fits of rage overtook him, the brother she would never see again.

Once her tears had subsided, a sickening horror dawned on her. Was there to be a third? A third bad thing, a third death? And if so, who or what would it be?

2 November 1942

Eleanor had barely slept in over a week. She nibbled at food and this only due to the cook's urging. He no doubt remembered Lady Stratton's demise and the belief that his culinary prowess would cure everything. She remained glued to the wireless at all hours, hoping that a report would come in announcing victory at El-Alamein, that the Desert Fox had been defeated. There were rumors that the Yanks would be in North Africa soon, doing their part to rid French North Africa of its occupiers. Was there any substance or truth to them, she wondered? But was there ever really any truth in war at all?

10 November 1942

The broadcasters were saying the battle was nearly at an end, that the sly and cunning Desert Fox had been defeated at El-Alamein, that the threat to Egypt and control of the Suez Canal and the Persian oil fields was over. The Yanks had landed in French North Africa only days earlier, which many felt was the final knockout blow. Lieutenant-General Montgomery or 'Monty' and his Eighth Army needed to emerge the victors. The might and support of the American forces joined the already three-year old war. And yet, Eleanor had still not heard from Antony.

She wondered if she'd awaken in the middle of the night to see him standing there, saying to her, "my dear girl, I'm home" before taking her in his arms in a crushing embrace. She had no one to confide in that her worst fear was what had happened with George, that she would be lulled into a false sense of peace and happiness that he had survived the battle, only to receive weeks later news that a body has been misidentified, that it was indeed her husband, Lieutenant Antony Greaves. That superstitions ultimately always proved right.

11 November 1942

Eleanor wasn't one much for religion but as she had every year since she had been in Egypt, she attended the service of remembrance at All Saints' Cathedral on Armistice Day. It was the only time that Lady Stratton would ever display emotion whilst in public, for normally she wore the steely hardened face that aristocratic women of her generation so often exhibited. But when she heard her boys' names being recited from the list of the fallen, she would softly start to cry. Her very first year there, Eleanor had quickly taken her employer's hand in hers and squeezed it in a show of both comfort and solidarity, knowing she was never alone in her grief. She hadn't at the time thought how entirely improper this was of her to do, but the older woman had surprised her by squeezing back. Eleanor always thought it was that moment which had cemented their friendship, helped it transcend beyond the confines of an employer, servant relationship.

"Have you received word from your husband yet?"

Eleanor turned to see one of the sisters speaking to her, Sister Grace was it, she wondered? All of the sisters always looked the same to her in their crisp, immaculate woolen uniforms, only their perspiring skin showing the least bit of discomfort from the ghastly temperatures and lack of circulating air inside the 9th.

She gulped, not really wanting to answer and have her thoughts and inner fears fixate on the fact that she still hadn't.

"No, I'm still… still waiting on word. I'm sure I will any day now."

If there was one thing Eleanor couldn't stand it was pity and that was exactly the look that had passed across the sister's face when Eleanor spoke. "Yes, my dear. I'm sure you will. Any day now, just like you said," and just like that she was off, ruling her wards with equal parts empathy and efficiency but also with an iron fist.

Later that night

And then it came, in the form of a telegram. A horrible, staccato missive that said he was missing in action, and presumed taken prisoner by the Germans.

Eleanor had gasped for air at reading those words, the walls around her looking like they were closing in. And then on the cold tile floor of the entryway, she had sunk to her knees and doubled over, howling in pain, indifferent to whoever might see her prostrated body stricken by the worst grief she had ever felt.

CHAPTER 20

Cairo, Egypt
Fall, 1943

Eleanor frequently let the cover of darkness consume her- not only her body and also her thoughts. And so, for weeks now, ever since Aunt May's telegram about George and the start of the battle, she would consume multiple G & T's in the garden only when it was completely dark out. She would make her way to the garden through the darkened rooms of the house when the sun had just set and there was still that sliver of light where one could see, armed with her bottle of Gordon's gin and tonic water.

Eleanor couldn't bear to see herself in the light of day, feeling too much like both her mum and father with her drink, feeling too much that she was careening more than ever down a precariously dangerous slope. She would drink until she was nearly numb but still coherent enough to fumble her way to her bedroom without injuring herself in the process.

But today, she had thought about it. Ending it, ending her life, lowering the curtain on the whole bloody production as she had come to think of life. For months, ever since she had received word that Antony was missing in action, the cognitive, still functioning part of her had implored and reminded the other half that she mustn't give up, that she must still have hope he was alive. That he had been wounded and had suffered memory loss and didn't know who he was, what his name was. That sort of thing. But that had all ended today. The tragic, irrational, saddened state had won out in the end when the doorbell rang earlier that day, bearing the confirmation she had both so wanted but equally dreaded.

Eleanor didn't know how long she had been out there in the garden, having eaten nothing all day. She wasn't sure if she was on her what, second? third? but Eleanor could have sworn she heard a rustle in the towering hibiscus trees that adorned the back wall. And yet there wasn't a breath of air blowing. She sat up in her chair, attempting to focus her already unsteady eyes on the corner, thinking there was something there. Not hearing anything more, she chided herself, knowing she must be in her cups.

But then there it was again, this time quite distinctly.

"Hello?" Eleanor called out, unsteadily rising to her feet. "Is anyone there?" She wanted to go right to those trees and pull back whatever it was but felt a wave of fear over the prospect of it being a rabid animal or worse, an intruder. Cook, she knew, had long since retired to bed and once asleep, not even an Avro Lancaster could wake him.

If she had not been so deep into her cups, Eleanor would have thought to break the bottle of Gordon's and use that as a weapon but at this very moment, she didn't have an ounce of intelligence coursing through her veins, just sheer dread.

"This is ridiculous," Eleanor muttered to herself as she marched over to the corner of the garden expecting the worst, only to come face to face with a child.

The two of them looked at each other in complete fright. Neither of them spoke nor moved. Eleanor's numbness from the gin had evaporated and with clearer focus she could see the child was a girl, perhaps around eight or nine. She was dark with a swarthy complexion but she didn't look Egyptian, she had more European features. Perhaps she was mixed, Eleanor thought? She was dreadfully skinny, her dark brown eyes looking enormous against the rest of her. And she was filthy, dirt and grime covering every inch of her. Eleanor's eyes focused on something that was glistening on the girl's chest. Bending closer to examine it, she went to touch it, only for the girl's bony hand to snap up and slap at Eleanor's arm.

"I'm sorry, I just wanted to see your necklace," Eleanor said kindly to the girl. But the girl didn't answer, didn't even look like what Eleanor had just said to her had registered. Her soft wide eyes which looked so beautiful just a moment earlier, now had a hard glint to them, her little hand still fiercely clutching her necklace.

Was she a mute, Eleanor wondered? Leaning down so that she was eye-level with the girl she drew out her own necklace which she wore and said, "My husband gave this to me," letting the girl touch the beautiful sapphire pendant, which she then lovingly caressed. "May I see yours?" she asked, pointing to the little girl's own necklace. Slowly the child uncurled her fingers and even in the darkness Eleanor could see that it was a Star of David.

"Beautiful," Eleanor told her.

"Be-you-ti-ful," the little girl slowly echoed in heavily accented English.

"Eleanor," she said. "I'm Eleanor," she said, pointing to herself. "Eleni."

And that was how the little Jewish refugee girl called Eleni came into Eleanor's life, although Eleanor didn't then know anything about her except her name. She came into Eleanor's life on the very same day she received confirmation that Antony was indeed dead, killed in action, not taken prisoner as previously thought for all those agonizing months. He had been killed on the last day of the battle…that he had suffered the worst kind of death when the tank he had been riding in hit a mine and he hadn't been rescued in time before burning to death. Burned bodies- that's why it had taken so long to identify him. But he hadn't been meant to be riding in the tank either.

Eleanor hadn't known any of it. She just knew this. Bad things really do come in threes. And it was a superstition she would pay close attention to for the rest of her life.

9 November 1942

My dear girl,

I dare say I've never been so exhausted in my life as I have been these last few weeks. Victory is nearly ours, it's so close everyone from private to Monty himself can taste it. But I know it comes at a great cost, a great cost to both sides. I count myself incredibly lucky that I come away from this latest battle unscathed. But it just goes to show that you, my real-life guardian angel, continue to watch over me.

For the last year I've been worried that this 'desert war' has ruined the life I wanted us to have together after this horrible war is over. That all the death and suffering man and modern wargames can inflict upon his fellow man would make it so that I could only see those things here against the infinite desert sands. But then just last night the most breathtaking of sunsets appeared (I had wandered off a ways you see, but not too far as the Jerry minefields are omnipresent and it wouldn't do much good to come home to you a one-legged man). You know me, I'm not one for talks of spirituality but if there was ever a moment for me to embrace the divine, it would have been seeing this perfect creation from both God and nature - the most dazzling array of colours - splashes of mint green, baby blue, light grey, and peach all so wonderfully infused together. It gave me the fortitude I so desperately needed at that very moment.

Ever thine, ever mine, ever ours.

Antony

CHAPTER 21

Island of Corfu, Greece
March 1943

"I'm taking Eleni!"

The hushed but angry sounding voices had awoken Eleni from a deep sleep. Crawling over to the stair from her bed, careful so as not to disturb her younger sisters Eirini and Areti, she could see the shadowy outlines of Mama and Papa against the fire.

"And go where? We're safe here. The Italians are a nuisance but they leave us alone for the most part."

"*Bavajadas*!" Papa fired back, his nostrils flaring, his eyes bulging. Eleni could see that it was taking every ounce of strength for him not to completely erupt. Papa only spoke in Ladino, the language of their Jewish ancestors who had fled from Spain in the 15th century, when he was incredibly angry. But Eleni also knew that Mama wouldn't like being told she was speaking nonsense either. "Tell that to Stavros, whose son they killed!"

Mama hushed then, the truth of Papa's words resonating against the darkness of the room. They didn't want her knowing but Eleni had often heard Mama and Papa discussing things on the island. She knew that Stavros wasn't the only Corfiot who had died since the Italians occupied the island in 1941. Many had been arrested, while others had their livestock and harvests taken from them. Eleni had even heard Mama saying to *Yiayia* that a farmer's daughter had been violated by two drunken Italian soldiers last month. She wasn't entirely sure what it meant but knew it wasn't good by the way they clicked their tongues together in a disapproving way. *"As if any man would marry her now, knowing what everyone knows," Yiayia had said.*

"Egypt."

"Egypt!" Now it was Mama's turn to look like she wanted to explode. "What, you just plan to float on a fishing boat all the way there? Like it's as easy to do as sailing to Albania?"

"Nowhere in Europe is safe for us Jews. Not even here." Papa's tone no longer angry, now just containing a trace of both sadness and resignation. "There's an Italian soldier I've gotten to know-"

"Oh, so now you're friends with the people you were just telling me are so evil barely a moment ago?" Mama interjected.

Ignoring Mama's barb, he continued. "He's a good lad, not even 20. He has no reason to lie to me. He said the Nazis are sending the Jews to camps in the east. That they're arresting them and putting them on trains to work camps in Poland. Not just men, women and children too. What's happening to the Jews in Salonika is going to happen here too."

Salonika? What did Papa mean by that, Eleni wondered.

"To what purpose?" Mama asked, her tone immediately dismissive of Papa's words. "What would the Nazis want with women and children? This so-called friend of yours is leading you on," she added.

A hard look passed across Papa's face, one of knowing but also pity as he said the words, "Look from heaven and perceive that we have become an object of scorn and derision among the nations; we are regarded as the sheep led to slaughter, to be killed, destroyed, beaten, and humiliated."

In the following days, Mama and Papa barely spoke to each other, often using Eleni and her younger sisters as their voices when they needed to ask the other a question. Eirini and Areti, who were only four and six respectively, found the whole thing quite funny, likening it to a game they would play with their friends, but Eleni, being nearly 10, knew better. This was no game. Papa and Mama were both as stubborn as Achilles, the ornery mule who would kick up his hind leg at you if you simply looked at him the wrong way. But Papa was smart, much smarter than Mama. But he wasn't just book smart even though as a young man he had spent a year studying in Venice at university there. However, he returned home after his own papa died and he had his mama to take care of. No, Eleni's Papa was the one person she knew could keep her safe.

"Dimitra says you want to take the girl to Egypt. I've never heard anything so stupid."

Everyone at the table stopped eating. Eleni and her parents and sisters had come to *Pappouli* and *Yiayia's* house for *Shabbat* as they did every Friday evening after shul. *Pappouli* and Papa had never gotten along. Eleni's grandfather was of the belief that Papa considered himself better than him since he had studied in Italy and spoke Italian, and was more than just a tailor, but most of all, because he always considered himself Greek first, and Jewish second. Never mind the fact that Papa saw an impending danger for the Jews here while *Pappouli* thought they were perfectly safe. Who was right, Eleni wondered, often at night when she couldn't sleep.

The room was so silent Eleni was certain she could hear a pin drop.

Both Mama and *Yiayia* kept their gazes lowered out of respect for the men since they were talking, but Eleni knew they must be dying to look at both Papa and *Pappouli*.

"And when they come for us?" Papa asked this quietly, but pointedly.

"Pshaw," *Pappouli* scoffed, huffily ripping off a piece of challah and using it to scoop up the *bourtheto*, the spicy fish stew *yiayia* served every Shabbat. "For all your book learning, you're no smarter than Michalis!"

Papa's nostrils flared so big then Eleni thought they might explode. Papa wouldn't abide being likened to the island's most famous drunk.

It was at that moment, with the room so heavy and thick with tension, that Eleni wondered why her parents had ever gotten married? Had they ever really loved each other? It wasn't as if their marriage had been arranged by a matchmaker. Eleni knew that on Rhodes where *Yiayia* had been born and grew up in *La Juderia,* the Jewish quarter there, *Yiayia's* marriage to her first husband had been arranged by the *shadchan*, the local matchmaker. And when *Yiayia* and *Pappouli* had married after the death of *Yiayia's* first husband, they had been distantly related, having met when *Pappouli* spent the summer visiting relatives on Rhodes. But no, for mama and papa, they of course shared the bond that they were both Jewish (and even for as modern and liberal as papa was, would never have dared marrying outside the faith) and were both Corfiots, but that's where any connection ended. They were as different and mismatched as oil and water.

Eleni then dared raise her eyes to look at Papa when he spoke.

"She's old and capable enough to make the journey. The littles-" looking at Eirini and Areti who just then were pulling each other's fingers and then plaited braids, completely oblivious to the heavy tension in the room, "are not. And besides, I wouldn't take them from their mother."

"Oh, but you can take my eldest when she's still just a mere child herself! And who's not even had her first bleeding yet?" Mama shouted, standing up so violently from the table that the chair she had been sitting on crashed backwards onto the floor.

"Dimitra!" *Pappaouli* and *Yiayia* both shouted in horrified union.

"I'm going to bleed? Why am I going to bleed?" Eleni cried out then, her voice quavering, not understanding anything that was going on now.

At that, Mama burst into tears and because she was crying, Eleni's younger sisters took one look at their mama and quickly followed suit. *Yiayia* just dabbed at her eyes with her white handkerchief while *Pappouli* silently rose from the table and left the room, only to return a short while later with a clear glass and two small tumblers. He quickly filled each and passed one to Papa.

"To hell with the Sabbath," *Pappouli* said softly enough so that neither Mama nor *Yiayia* would hear, clinking his glass with Papa's. "At least for tonight."

And then both men quickly downed the clear contents of the tumblers.

May 1943

"Papa, are we not safe here? Are the Germans going to come here, come to Corfu?"

Eleni had been wanting to ask this of her papa, ever since the *Shabbat* dinner from a few days earlier. Papa and Mama continued to not speak to each other but their tensions and discord seemed different now. Mama appeared more agitated, her eyes constantly brimming with tears, at times hysterical with Eleni and her sisters, whereas Papa seemed more withdrawn, his eyes conveying a melancholic look. When he had asked her if she wanted to have a special day with just him, she had readily agreed.

He had surprised her by having her get in the car and told her they would be going for a drive, to his favorite spot on the island. When they arrived in Afionas, the first question out of Eleni's mouth was, "have I been here before?" to which he replied that she hadn't, that this was his favorite spot in all of Corfu and that she was the first person he had ever taken here. "Even Mama?" she asked, her eyes wide with surprise at hearing this. "Even Mama," he confirmed, leaving a wonderfully warm feeling within her.

Afionas truly was beautiful. It was a small white-washed village built on a hill with a breathtaking view of the sea. Papa had taken her through its winding streets and alleyways, each one bedecked in the most dazzling array of vibrant pink bougainvillea trees and blue shutters and doors as cerulean as the Ionian below.

Now they were enjoying the picnic lunch Mama had packed for them. When she had handed Papa the basket, he had lightly grazed her cheek with his finger. She stared at him for a moment, then leaned up on her toes and placed a light kiss on his cheek.

Papa didn't answer; he didn't even look at her. He just kept staring off into the never-ending sea. "This here is the best spot to see the sunset. Right below us is Arillas Bay, Greece's most western point. You wouldn't believe the colors you see here," he said, his voice catching ever so slightly.

Eleni waited, wondering if Papa had heard her and if she should ask her question again.

"There are many people who feel that what's going on in the rest of Europe doesn't matter to us. They say, 'France, Germany, Belgium, it's so far away from us here in Greece.' But look at Salonika."

Salonika, there he was mentioning the Greek city on the mainland again, Eleni mused.

Papa stopped, noticing Eleni's confused expression. "I know you're still a child, but contrary to what your Mama and *Pappouli* and *Yiayia* think, I believe you should know. In 1941, Salonika wasn't invaded by the Italians, but rather the Germans. The Nazis," he added for extra chilling emphasis. "So yes, while we've been I won't say protected, rather cushioned by the Italians, the situation for the Jews in Salonika has always been bad. At first, maybe you could say it wasn't so bad- Jews had to turn in their radios, cafes started posting signs saying Jews weren't welcome. But a couple of months back, all Jewish men between the ages of 18 and 45 were rounded up in Eleftherias Square and were forced to do humiliating physical exercises at gunpoint. And then thousands of these same men were ordered to construct a road for the Germans, linking Salonika to Katerini and Larissa. Hundreds have died from exhaustion and disease. Hundreds. And all because they were Jewish."

"But how do you know this, Papa? Salonika is so far from Corfu."

"There is a man here, a Jew who escaped from Salonika. He was there that day in Eleftherias Square and spent almost two months where he was forced to build the road. Once he was freed, friends gave him the money to escape to the Italian zone. He confirmed what an Italian soldier had already told me, that the Germans want to get rid of the Greek Jews too."

"So they just took the men, Papa? They're done with scaring the Jews there?"

Eleni had always considered her papa to be a fighter, maybe not so much with his fists but rather his words and spirits. But in that moment, he appeared to be entirely broken. And that in turn broke Eleni's heart. But he continued talking.

"Back in March, they forced all the Jews from their homes, robbed them of their property, stole their most valuable belongings. They forced them into ghettos." Already aware that Eleni wouldn't know what a ghetto was, he added, "An area where only Jews live, often in horrible conditions. But now, just like that Italian soldier told me all those months ago, they've started emptying them. Emptying the ghettos."

Eleni felt very old at that moment, much older than her years, for she didn't need to ask what he meant by that. Emptying them as if the inhabitants were nothing more than pieces of rubbish to be thrown out.

"They were put on trains to somewhere in the east. And none have returned." He paused then before adding, "I don't know this for certain, but I don't think the Germans will let the Italians be in charge forever here on Corfu. I think Hitler is a madman, but I think he also has enough competent generals and leaders in charge to guide him. I think Mussolini is just a buffoon and I don't think he'll be around forever."

"But Hitler will be?"

Seeing his daughter's ashen face, he said, "I really don't want to scare you. I wish I could say this is all folly, all speculation, but we need to be realistic and have a plan, two things your Mama won't listen to me on. I pray more than anything that the war ends, and we are rid of the short little man with the funny mustache forever. But a seer I am not and never have been." He returned his gaze to stare out at the sea again, his eyes as deep and endless as the open water.

"All I want to do is keep my family safe. I'm not looking to be a hero, to join the partisans in their fight against ridding Greece of the occupying forces." He regarded her before adding, "when this is all said and done, I want to look back and know that I did everything I could."

Eleni started having nightmares after that day, after what Papa had told her. The first night, she woke up screaming like Medusa, Areti later told her, calling out for Mama, something she hadn't done in years. But in the nightmares, it was Papa who had been on the train tracks and had roughly lifted her into the train car, locking her inside all alone before it started to move.

It was like this for nights on end, Mama cradling Eleni on her ample bosom, rocking her back and forth as she softly crooned the words to lullabies, while Papa stood in the doorway, his arms crossed over his chest, a worried look on his face.

But one night after Mama had left the room Eleni shared with her younger sisters and quietly shut the door behind her, Eleni could hear their raised voices, having not yet returned to a state of peaceful slumber.

"What did you tell her for her to be so terrorized?" Mama angrily hissed.

"The truth," Papa vehemently spat back. "She's old enough to know!"

"Salonika isn't Corfu! Why do you insist on terrorizing her with your stories!"

"Stories, stories!" Papa said, sputtering out the words in a state of disbelief over what Mama had just said. "The Jews of Salonika are gone, gone Dimitra; how do you not see how grave a situation this is?" His words seemed to reverberate through the whole house, neither of them caring in the heat of the moment how loud they were being. Eleni looked over in the bed she shared with her sisters but saw they were both still fast asleep.

"This is no longer a war where we can bury our heads in the sand! We can no longer say it's about the Jews of Europe, the Jews of Germany, of Poland. The Jews of Greece are now unwilling participants in this madness!"

"You're going to break up this family," Mama said, her voice now subdued and tired.

"I'm going to ensure there's still some of my family left when this war is over."

CHAPTER 22

Cairo
Fall 1943

The little girl was filthy. Her skin, although naturally dark, was caked in a mixture of dirt and grime making it appear almost ashen, her bony knees and legs were covered in sores. Her dark hair ran wild down her back, everything from burrs and foxtails seemingly nestled in a tangled heap, although at a cursory glance Eleanor didn't see any lice. As a child, Eleanor's brothers constantly brought lice into their crowded flat and she dreaded the almost toxic smell of the Petrol that came in a small bottle that Eleanor's mum would pour on their heads to kill the lice and their nits.

The little girl was shy at first, refusing to undress, even though Eleanor tried to tempt her by giving her the biggest smile as she moved her hand over the bath she had drawn for her. Eleanor wished there was something she could say or do to reassure the girl, not have her look so scared, but she was stumped.

"Oh, I've got it!" Eleanor said, almost triumphantly as she hurried from the room. She came back this time with a glass bottle in her hands and proceeded to dump its flakey contents in the glistening water. And then Eleanor watched with supreme satisfaction as the little girl's eyes grew wide in amazement over the bubbles that started to form. And then without being asked again, she started to undress and stepped into the bathtub, plopping in with a big whoosh, lightly splashing Eleanor in the process. And then for the first time since Eleanor had seen the girl, she smiled.

When Eleanor left the girl, she was fast asleep in the guest room, her child size making her appear almost doll-like in the canopy bed. Eleanor decided she would tell cook and the houseboy tomorrow of their guest. She had neither the desire nor the focus to get into a discussion with cook as to why someone who was possibly a street urchin was staying in Lady Stratton's home (how cook still referred to the home even though it was legally Eleanor's). Although that thought did give Eleanor pause, wondering if she'd wake up tomorrow and all the silver and other priceless treasures would be missing. But no, Eleanor chided herself. The girl had appeared malnourished and exhausted. She had fallen asleep within moments of Eleanor pulling the luxuriously appointed sheets and blankets over her.

But where was she from, Eleanor wondered, hours later as she lay awake in her bed. She had looked blank when Eleanor asked her questions in her feeble Arabic. When she had spoken in English, the child looked like she understood but hadn't wanted to answer.

But wait, Eleanor thought, sitting upright in bed. What about French?

"*Avez-vous faim?*"

When Eleanor had gone into the room, she was startled to see the girl was wide awake, her eyes trained on Eleanor. She had come into the room carrying a pot of tea and some toast and orange marmalade for the girl.

"*Oui, j'ai faim*," she replied ever so softly, her eyes revealing nothing.

Yes, I'm hungry. Eleanor couldn't believe it, the girl spoke French, she thought triumphantly. She offered a big smile as she walked over to the bed, placing the tray on its edge.

"So, you're French," Eleanor deliberately said in English, knowing the girl would protest.

"No," the little voice called out. "Greek!"

Greek! Heavens, Eleanor thought. How on earth did she end up in Cairo? "So, you do speak English."

The little girl smiled shyly then. "I no very good."

"You understand quite well," Eleanor responded encouragingly. "And you speak French too? That's quite impressive to know so many languages and be so young."

"My papa, he speak many languages. He taught me little English. Taught me little Italian too. He studied in Venezia."

"But where did you learn French?" Eleanor asked, curious more than ever as to the backstory of this mysterious little girl.

"The Alliance Israélite Universelle."

"In Athens?"

The girl looked confused before answering, "Corfu."

Eleanor paused then, desperately trying to think back to her geography lessons and place Corfu. And then, as if she had read Eleanor's mind, the little girl said, "Ionian Sea."

"Where is your family, dearie?" Eleanor asked, no longer able to avoid the topic. "You mentioned your papa, is he with you here in Cairo?"

And then whatever lightheartedness and relaxed mood that had manifested in the room only moments earlier was gone just like that. The little girl not only burst into tears but her tiny shoulders started convulsing too, her entire body wracked by sobs.

Eleanor, not ever having grown up with maternal affection and unsure about any motherly instincts she might inwardly possess as a grown woman, took the little girl in her arms and simply said, "there there, shhh," as she gently rubbed her hand over the small of the girl's back over and over until her sobs subsided.

The little girl's face was streaked with tears, her big doe-like brown eyes blotchy and red, a sight Eleanor was all too familiar with from the last few months.

"I'm Eleanor," she said, gently stroking the girl's cheek.

"Eleni."

"I haven't the faintest idea where she's come from. Anytime I ask questions about her family, or her papa, she breaks into tears. I fear she's suffered some horrible trauma but I'm basing that on pure speculation. She says she's Greek but then why is she here in Egypt?"

Eleni had been with Eleanor for nearly a week now and in that time, she had taken the little girl to the Ninth to be checked out by one of the doctors. This in itself had caused a major ruckus with Eleni screaming like a banshee, refusing to come inside the building until a hospital attendant who had been mopping the floor noticed what was happening and rushed over, lifting Eleni upside down and tickling her, which made her laugh uncontrollably. Eleanor had frozen then, the sound of the little girl's laughter both disconcerting and joyful. What better medicine is there than to hear a child's laughter in a hospital of all places.

The head sister who had observed the whole incident gave permission for the orderly to remain with them as Eleni was examined by the doctor, preferring to be in his lap and still holding onto his hand when she had to stand on the examining table. He remained with Eleni, continuing to make the little girl laugh and smile when the doctor said he and Eleanor should step outside to speak privately.

"She has bone spurs. I feel she's walked quite a distance. Frankly, I'm amazed she's able to walk at all." Seeing Eleanor's confused look, he added, "They're hard bumps that form around one's joints. They're caused by a great deal of things but one of them can be wearing badly worn shoes and walking gait abnormalities."

"But where would she have walked from? It's not as if she would have walked from Greece," feeling this doctor, that although kind, was also of no help at all.

"A refugee camp."

"You think she's a refugee? From Europe?"

"Without a doubt."

"There's not many photos of me growing up, but this is one of my absolute favourites."

Eleanor had found Eleni in the library after they returned from the 9th, her eyes agape at the dozens of cloth-bound books that lined the floor to ceiling shelves. But now Eleanor could see the little girl's eyes were focused on the framed black and white photographs that rested atop the piano.

"Go ahead," Eleanor urged Eleni. "Here," she said picking up the frame and handing it to Eleni. "Now you can have a better look. Can you spot me?"

Eleni regarded her quizzically for a moment before asking, "That you here?" she asked, pointing to an image of a girl her own age with two braided plaits that ran down her back.

"Yes, that's me. I believe I was 10 here."

"I 10 too." A pause then before she said, "Who these?" pointing to the other people in the picture.

"Let's go sit, shall we?" Eleanor said, taking Eleni's hand in hers and leading her to the amber-coloured divan. Pulling her onto her lap, "This here," Eleanor began, pointing to the tall boy on the left, "is my eldest brother, Tom. And that's George he's holding," she added, indicating the small boy he held in his arms. "And these two," Eleanor continued, pointing to two boys of around eight or nine, "are Ralph and Charlie. They weren't twins but you would have thought they were with how inseparable they were as lads. They were barely a year apart in age. And this here," pointing to the right side of the photograph of a slightly older boy who was scowling ever so much, "is Willie. I can't even remember why he's not smiling there," Eleanor said to herself, almost musing. "You would think he would have been, that was the only lovely day I remember having as a girl. You see, mum had taken us all to Brighton for the day. It was the first time ever that I had seen the ocean. She even gave us all money to have an ice cream from Pip's Ice. We never had that back in Spitalfields."

"And this your mama?" Eleni said, pointing to a slender, worn-looking woman. A woman beaten down by both time and the life she had been given. Eleanor so rarely remembered her mum actually smiling but that day she was. Perhaps in all of us there always remains a childish spirit that can never be fully put out.

"And papa?"

And papa indeed, Eleanor thought. She hadn't thought of her father in years, so long gone and removed he had been from her life. Her relationship with her mum had been acrimonious enough growing up, what could she dare proffer on the man who had drunk away what little money he made and who ultimately decided to completely abandon his wife and eight children, all of whom would have ended up in the workhouse had it not been for Aunt May helping them to survive.

"And these?" Eleni asked, pointing to two little girls younger than herself.

"My younger sisters," Eleanor answered, her voice slightly catching. "Violet and Rose."

"I have younger sisters," Eleni said proudly. "Eirini and Areti."

"What beautiful names," Eleanor said. Then almost tentatively, fearful of how the girl would react she asked, "Where are they now, Eirini and Areti? Are they with your papa?"

A sad look passed across Eleni's face. But she didn't burst into tears or run from the room as she did before when Eleanor asked about her papa.

"With Mama. Back home."

"On Corfu?" Eleanor prodded further.

Eleni nods her head yes, her brown eyes looking so particularly large and sorrowful just then, but Eleanor pressed on. "Where's your papa, Eleni? Was it just you two that came to Egypt? Where is he now?"

"He sick in camp. Sand all around us. They took him away from me. Nurse say I can't visit till he better. But he never get better, I never see him again. So I ran away."

She had run away. Eleanor was rendered speechless at this. Eleni told Eleanor that she had snuck onto a supply truck that was leaving the camp that she knew was empty of passengers. She wasn't sure how long or far they had traveled but abandoned her hiding place in the truck when she heard the driver and another man saying they would need to make space for the new load. Lest she be discovered and sent back to the camp, Eleni had jumped down from it and run, never once daring to look back.

Eleni must have walked dozens of miles through the desert, alone, without any proper tools for survival. Eventually she came across two little boys around her age, who had been herding sheep. They couldn't communicate for they shared no common language but they must have taken one look at her beleaguered appearance and beckoned her to come with them. Eleanor supposed that the innocence and trust a child places in its fellow man was a universal trait, not tied to any one culture or country. So she had gone with them. They walked a short while before coming across a squat, almost open-air building. Older women, one who Eleni had guessed to be the boys' mama, completely covered except for her eyes in a loose-flowing black Arabian dress, had started yelling at the older of the two boys in a peculiar sounding tongue. But then the woman stopped, regarded Eleni more kindly, clucked her tongue in such a way that Eleni wasn't sure if it was one of pity or disapproval or both, but Eleni was given cup after cup of water because for now, Eleni could barely speak for how thirsty she was. And then a plate of beans with onion, garlic, and tomato. The smallest boy passed her a type of flat bread that Eleni looked at quizzically, puzzled by its unusual appearance. But then he took it back from her and pushed it into the food on the plate, indicating that she was to use it to scoop up its contents.

Eleni wasn't sure how many days and nights had passed since she had been with the desert family, but after a time, the father, a man Eleni was scared of, had roughly woken her one night. The sky was still black outside, the stars visibly pronounced against the dark sky. He beckoned her to come with him. For a moment, Eleni thought a terrible harm was going to come to her, that after all she had done to survive, she would truly never see her mama and her sisters again. She solemnly walked out of the mud hut, lifting its flap up to see the father and the two sons sitting in a wagon. The older of the boys lifted her up. And off they went, Eleni thinking then that as much as she missed her beloved Ionian Sea and Corfu, there was nothing more beautiful than seeing the desert and its golden sands silhouetted against a crescent moon.

It was the sounds that first woke her. At some point in the journey, Eleni had fallen asleep, her head resting against the younger of the two boys, who in turn had fallen asleep onto his older brother's shoulder. Eleni woke with a start to the sound of blaring horns, animals voicing their displeasure, whips being brandished on the backs of those same animals when they weren't moving fast enough, people yelling in a multitude of voices and tongues- sheer chaos. And then the smells. Eleni had become accustomed to the smells of livestock and manure and of course, all the weeks spent in the camp, the odiferous smells of unwashed bodies and putrid misery. But this was different. She saw now that she was in a city, a very big city and she looked around in both sheer panic but also excitement for she had never been to a city before, not even Athens.

The father continued to drive the cart through the streets of what Eleni guessed must be Cairo until he pulled up in front of a train station, turned around and spoke to Eleni in Arabic. She didn't know or understand the words' meaning. She looked at him for a moment, not understanding. But then he turned back around, stared straight ahead, saying nothing. The boys climbed into the seat beside him. And only the little boy peeked back at Eleni, his eyes sorrowful and brimming with tears. It was then that she understood. She was to get out, and they were to return to the life they had before this strange, foreign girl invaded their home. She hopped down and within a moment, the cart pulled away, Eleni staring after it like her life depended on it. She stayed in that spot, transfixed as she watched its retreating form appear farther and farther away until she could no longer see it, oblivious but also immune to the goings on around her.

Eleni spent several days wandering, although here in the city it was much easier to find food, or in Eleni's case, steal food from both shopkeepers and waiters who had their backs turned. Eleni passed by what she knew were churches and thought about going inside but was too scared that perhaps there were Nazis there. Back on Corfu, Papa had told Eleni that Egypt was safe for Jews, that Germany hadn't occupied it. But that was months ago now, and Eleni had no idea if that still held true. And she was not about to take any chances, lest she be sent back to the camp. She saw people eye her curiously as she passed them on the streets, some with looks of scorn and revulsion, but others with pity and compassion. One day as she was sitting on the steps of a building, she saw a nun start to come towards her. She had seen nuns before on Corfu, but this one's black dress and white headpiece frightened Eleni. She took off running, convinced that the nun was going to come and send her back to the camp. She ran and ran until her little legs couldn't take her any further. And that's how she came across the house with the beautifully painted turquoise door. Eleni was transfixed by it for it so reminded her of the beautiful homes on Corfu. And then she saw her chance. A dark man suddenly appeared at its front door and stood there as a shopkeeper unloaded cart after cart of goods. When both of their backs were turned, as they conferred over something in the cart, Eleni darted into the house with the bright blue door and kept running straight back as she noticed a garden was there. She laid down then, hidden amongst the vast tropical flora and fell immediately asleep, enjoying once more the precious, carefree sleep of a child.

CHAPTER 23

Cairo, Egypt
1945

When the BBC announced the death of Hitler on 1 May, by suicide the broadcaster said, Eleanor should have felt joy. And in the following days when evening programs were routinely interrupted with news that the Germans had surrendered in Italy, then Denmark, she should have felt excitement, knowing that this conflict that had ravaged Europe for almost six years was all but over. But then on the evening of 7 May at 1800, the BBC told its listeners that the Prime Minister would not be broadcasting that night, which Eleanor had found rather peculiar. She was dumbfounded when a mere couple of hours later, the program she and Eleni had been listening to was interrupted. The following day would be the first VE Day. Victory in Europe. The war was really over.

Eleanor stared blankly at the wireless at hearing those words. Over. That one word kept repeating in her head, as if it were a ricocheting ball. Eleanor could hear the screams of joy carrying over the wireless' waves from the BBC newsroom all those hundreds of kilometers away back in London. But the only thing she felt was numbness. Numbness that Antony wasn't with her right now to celebrate, to mark the time and date that would be forever recorded in history.

And Eleni, dear sweet Eleni, had even put down the doll she was playing with to focus on the words coming out of the wireless.

"It's over?" she asked almost incredulously. "No more fighting?"

"Yes, my dear Eleni," Eleanor responded, trying her best to keep back her tears, tears that were not ones of joy but rather anger and jealously from consuming her. At least not now in front of this child who had lost more than anyone she knew. "It's all over. Well, at least in Europe. I fear the fighting in Asia may still go on." For some time, she wanted to add but didn't, knowing that the topic of war was complicated enough for most children without adding to the many intricate differences between the European front and the Asian one.

And then Eleni proceeded to do the most childish thing she had done since Eleanor first met her, more than two years ago. She jumped up and down, shrieking in pure joy at the top of her lungs. When the little girl held out her hand to Eleanor to join in with her, Eleanor wanted nothing more than to say, "I can't. I'm too old for this, we're being much too loud, and besides, what would the servants think." But she didn't. She just took her hand and joined in. For Eleanor knew that's what Antony would have wanted her to do. Not just for Eleni but for him. He would always want her to jump for the things in life worth jumping for.

But the euphoria felt in Cairo that night and in the coming days in the rest of the Empire and the rest of the free world, was of course short-lived, for the horrors of the Nazi concentration camps was yet to be known and the war in the Pacific would last another brutal three months, finally ending with the dropping of two atomic bombs over Japan.

Cairo
March 1946

"Excuse me, but does an Englishwoman by the name of Eleanor Greaves live here?"

Eleanor stared at the stranger, wondering how this tanned man with the jet-black hair and oval-shaped onyx eyes knew her name. She stood there, neither moving nor acknowledging that she had heard him, instead thinking how much he reminded her of someone. And then it dawned on her, making her blurt out, "You're him, you're Eleni's father, aren't you?" Eleanor couldn't remember if she said this in the form of a question or an accusation.

Now it was the man's turn to appear startled, clearly not thinking he would be recognized so quickly and only confirming Eleanor's sinking suspicion. He's come to take her from me, she thought bitterly, everything and everyone I love.

"Yes, I'm Spiro Algazi," he said, clearly wishing her to reciprocate with an introduction of her own. He said this kindly enough but a look of impatience started to flash across his darkened features.

But Eleanor still didn't speak, rendered immobile by the appearance of a man she had long thought dead. Maybe she was dreaming, maybe this was all just a terrible dream and she was to wake up any moment now. So Eleanor closed her eyes and waited. But then she heard his voice and knew it was no dream.

"Miss? Are you her, are you Eleanor? Is Eleni here? Do you have my daughter?"

Have your daughter? I saved your daughter, Eleanor thought, fully appraising the man, Eleanor's supposed father. Had I not taken her in, heaven knows what would have happened to her, where she would have ended up. But rather Eleanor said the first thing that came to mind.

"The war's been over for nearly a year," Eleanor said, softly, but with an accusation of guilt attached to it.

His face, jubilant only moments earlier when Eleanor realized he must be Eleni's father, was now shattered. She immediately regretting her choice of words. Clearly the man had been through a lot. Regaining herself, she said, "Yes, I'm Eleanor. Won't you come in?"

So she led him through the darkened, cool hallway back to the inner garden where she indicated he should sit on the wrought-iron chair. "I'll ask cook to bring us some lemonade." She took the chair opposite him and began. "It was here, in this very garden where I first met your daughter, nearly three years ago now."

The man looked overwhelmed now, his eyes brimming with tears. "So she's here?" he asked Eleanor, his voice trembling.

"Yes. I mean, well no, not at this very moment. But yes, she lives here." Lived, Eleanor thought. "She's at school right now."

"Mr. Algazi, won't you tell me…" Eleanor began, but her words trailed off, unable to say the words, "where have you been all this time?" So instead she said, "Eleni thought you were dead."

"And I her," he proffered, quietly.

Cook then appeared with a pitcher of lemonade and lemon shortbread biscuits, the latter of which he had long since perfected making. Judging by the way he slowly lowered the tray onto the small table and the snail-like manner in which he poured each glass, Eleanor knew he no doubt wished to eavesdrop on the conversation between her and this man whose skin was only slightly less dark than his own. But Eleanor would have none of the old man's gossipy machinations today, not before she learned the truth. "That will be all, thank you, Simbel," Eleanor said, rather dismissively but her tone brokering no further discussion. The cook looked at her slightly surprised at her tone, so unlike her, but he slightly nodded his head as a sign of deference and left the garden.

"Please, Mr. Algazi. Won't you begin?"

His sickness had been the measles, caught no doubt from the overcrowding and horrible conditions found at El Shatt. He had been isolated from the others upon an official diagnosis, his being one of the first confirmed cases at the camp, officials there no doubt concerned over an outbreak but also unrest amongst the refugees if word were to get out. And in the beginning he had been much too sick and delirious to inquire after Eleni. When he finally came around and asked about his daughter, Eleni was long gone and camp officials, understaffed and overworked, didn't have the faintest idea where a little Greek refugee girl was and couldn't be bothered to investigate. But the furtive glances that passed between the officials, the things they didn't say to him, told him what he couldn't dare think- that she was dead, that there was no way a child could compete against the desert and live.

When he had mustered enough strength, he escaped from the camp one night since the British government didn't let you leave the complex without a pass and he had no valid reason to obtain one. However, he returned on his own volition two days later, his sickness ravaged body no match for the desert. Life inside the camp in the desert of the Sinai Peninsula was bleak and miserable, but the refugees were given water and meager food rations. In the desert, he was entirely on his own and knew he would die a quick death if were to stay out there. What good would he be for his daughter if he were dead, his body forever lost to the desert sands if he pursued such a deadly folly. So, he returned to the camp, biding his time, waiting for the war to end. Deep in his heart, he never gave up hope that she was still alive.

When news of the Allied landings at Normandy reached the camp, he reacted with glee and jubilation along with everyone else. And then little by little, Europe was liberated, cities and countries that had been under Nazi occupation for so long, were finally free, including Corfu in October of '44. And from a British soldier who had liberated the island but was now working at the camp after VE-Day, he learned the horrifying truth. On June 9 in 1944- only four months before the Nazis withdrew from Greece- all of Corfu's Jewish residents were ordered to meet in the Kato Platia, the main square of the old town, before being taken to the old Venetian fortress nearby. Days later, roughly 1800 Jewish men, women, and children were transported on three boats to Athens. And from Athens, they were taken by train to Auschwitz.

"My wife, her parents, and my Eirini and Areti. All of them, gone," Mr. Algazi said, his voice hoarse, his put-together reserve finally starting to break. "Gassed upon arrival. A journey of nearly 2,000 kilometers all just to be murdered." He said this second part with a chilling, stony voice.

Eleanor was stunned, not sure what to say. She had heard about the camps where the Jews were taken, killing centers they were called. But Eleni's own mother and sisters, murdered.

"But how do you know?" Eleanor asked, wanting what he had just told her to not be true. "How do you know for certain that they were killed? This British soldier you say was on Corfu, not in Poland. How would he have known any of this?" she asked imploringly.

He regarded her then as if she were a child, one utterly ignorant to the cruelty of the world and what man is fully capable of.

"After I left El Shatt, after we were 'permitted' to finally leave that fiery hell-hole," he began, his tone now hardened, "I returned to Greece. To Athens that is. The British Red Cross told me that's where Greek Jews in the camps were being sent after they were liberated.

Well, those that had survived, that is."

He was silent then, but Eleanor knew she must allow him to continue telling the story at his own pace, when he was ready.

"I had never seen anything like it. The survivors I mean. They were living skeletons, they had –" but he broke off, tears starting to finally fall until he began to sob uncontrollably. Regaining himself he said, "There were lists of survivors, boards with notices asking for news of a loved one or more often the case, ones. I went every day, telling myself at the start of each morning, that today I would get the one thing I had prayed most for, that I would be reunited with them once more. But each day, my prayers were never answered, my hopes so bitterly dashed. Until one day, I recognized a neighbor from Corfu. She had been on the transport from Athens with Dimitra and my girls. She told me when they finally arrived at Auschwitz, they were ordered to go left, Dimitra's parents too, along with other women and children and old men. The woman, she was young, in her twenties, not married, no children. She, along with other women, was told to go right. She never saw Dimitra or my children again. Days later when she asked an SS officer about the Corfiot Jews she had arrived with, for she spoke German, she said he had laughed menacingly at her and simply pointed to the chimneys before walking away. And she knew. She knew that those who were told to go left were killed immediately."

Mr. Algazi got up from his chair and walked away, his back to Eleanor now. "Four months. Four more months and the Germans would have been gone forever," he said in almost a hushed whisper.

"How did you find me?" Eleanor asked. It's not that she wanted to change the subject, but rather she was at such a loss as to what to say to someone who had lost so much. She had endured loss after loss in the war and it was tragic and incomprehensible to bear, but Antony, her brothers, her mum, none of them had been murdered, systematically murdered at that. Her losses were something every individual throughout history had experienced during war.

He turned around, smiling wanly at her now. "I had remained in touch with that Tommy soldier after I left for Greece. He had friends in Cairo you see, he made some inquiries."

"Clearly they were fruitful," Eleanor responded, partially laughing. "I had no idea I was so well-known."

"This went on for months. But then he inquired with a doctor at the 9th, a doctor who had examined a foreign child with black hair who was brought in by a beautiful fair-skinned British woman."

"Ahh," Eleanor replied, knowing that for as vast and expansive as Cairo was, for the white, English-speaking population, it really still was an incredibly small place after all.

"So you've come to take her home?" Eleanor regretted her choice of words the moment she uttered them. Of course, he's come to take her home, he has every right to. He's her father, after all.

The look he gave her then was one of pity. "I no longer consider Corfu home," he began. "My family lived there for centuries, ever since they were expelled from Spain in the 15th century. But my home there is gone, my possessions taken by people who I thought were my neighbors." He said this bitterly.

"Then where will you go?" She wanted to add, Eleni is a child; she's been through so much, she needs a stable home like the one I've given her for three years now. But she didn't. She couldn't say this, ever. Eleanor had no claim, legal or moral, to the little girl. This was to be the end of the road for her and Eleni, a road where their paths would never cross again.

"Somewhere that the scars of the past can be erased, their cruel memories never allowed to manifest again."

CHAPTER 24

27 November 1947
Cairo, Egypt

Antony's mum was coming here. To Egypt. To finally meet her after all this time, all these years. Although Aunt May had been asking Eleanor to return to England, to finally come **home** after all this time away, she never had. But now Eliza had written to Eleanor out of the blue saying she would be arriving in Egypt on the 27 November. She hadn't written Eleanor asking if she could visit, rather she'd just announced it, leaving no room for discussion or refusal.

More than the sudden announcement from Eliza, Eleanor was even more surprised to hear from her at all. Although she wrote a couple of times a year, one always around the anniversary of Antony's death, she'd just assumed communications would become sparser with each passing year, each one more removed from the sole connection they'd once shared. Antony. Eleanor was Antony's sole heir, and had been informed a trust had been set up for her back in England in the event of Antony's passing. But Lady Stratton had left her more than comfortable in her own will. So why on earth would Eliza be coming here now?

As Eleanor waited nervously in the terminus of Cairo Station, she wondered if she'd recognize her, Antony's mum. Antony had said that once the war was over, they'd travel back to England for a proper how do you do, meet the 'clan' as he often referred to his brothers and sisters and long widowed mother. But of course, that had never come to fruition. Although she'd seen a few pictures of the older woman over the years, those photos themselves were outdated, as they depicted a much younger woman in the essence of her youth, not a middle-aged one in her mid-50s.

"I'd recognize you instantly," a female voice said from behind Eleanor, with the faintest lilt of the East End, giving her a start. Eleanor whirled around, almost losing her footing in the process, to see an older woman with auburn hair lovingly gazing at her.

"Lady Greaves," Eleanor said, nervously.

"Oh heavens, don't start that with me," Eliza said, in a mock tone of horror. "I'm plain old Eliza. Come here and let me give you a proper hug," and the older woman took Eleanor in her arms in an almost crushing embrace. Letting her go, she said, "Do you know I haven't set foot in Egypt in more than 25 years."

"I didn't know it was that long," Eleanor said, her head still whirling, her mind trying to place Antony with this woman.

"Yes, when my late husband passed, I just couldn't bear to be here without him anymore. Everything reminded me of him."

Is that how all those who still lived felt about their loved ones who'd passed before them, Eleanor pondered. Permanent members of a club we never asked to join?

"Although, I never lived in Cairo, always Assouan which I much preferred," Eliza continued on, oblivious to Eleanor's inner musings about life and loss. And heartache. "I already have a porter attending to my luggage so onward we go," Eliza said enthusiastically, taking Eleanor by the arm and leading her towards the exit as if she were the local resident and not the other way around.

"I'm sure you're wondering why I've come here after all this time," Eliza said, stirring her coffee and then gently placing the demitasse spoon on the saucer.

They'd just finished dinner in the formal dining room and Eleanor had suggested they retire to the gardens where they could take their coffee.

Taking a sip of the beverage, Eliza sighed contentedly. "Oh, how I've missed this. Nothing quite compares to Egyptian coffee."

Eleanor smiled, wondering why she just didn't buy some imported beans back in England. Surely she had the money.

"I did wonder, yes," Eleanor answered politely.

"Well, you see my dear, I am dying." Eliza said matter of fact.

Eleanor stared at her, rendered speechless by this admission. This she had not been expecting.

"Cancer, the doctors say. I've been seen by all the best on Harley Street and they all say the same, that nothing can be done. And in so many words, I am to make my peace with the world and be ready for the end."

"But surely you shouldn't have undertaken such a taxing journey then," Eleanor said, upset that this woman who was sick would endure so much travel for her. "I mean, the crossing alone from Europe to Alexandria," remembering then how seasick she had felt on the rough seas all those years ago.

"Stuff and nonsense," Eliza said, smiling. "Believe me, the more taxing part was convincing my children to let me do this."

Antony's siblings must hate her now, Eleanor thought, even though she'd never asked for Eliza to come. "Then why on earth now?" she asked again.

"For Antony," she said simply. "I owed it to him to meet the woman he fell so madly in love with in the land of his birth. To meet his beautiful young wife who was widowed much too soon. To the beautiful soul who made my son so blissfully happy for the time he got to share with her," Eliza replied, smiling warmly now at Eleanor. Coming over to stand next to Eleanor, she took her hand in hers and said, "I've come to terms with the fate that awaits me. I've led a life that I never expected to, one filled with more riches and wealth and opportunities than a girl from the East End would have ever dreamt of. Just like you, Egypt allowed me to reinvent myself, become someone entirely new. I think that's the magic of this place; anything is possible. The last piece of the puzzle was coming here and finally seeing you face-to-face so that when I meet up with my dear boy once again in the afterlife, I can tell him what a wonderful wife he'd had."

At this, Eleanor started to cry, covering her eyes with her hands so Eliza wouldn't see.

But very gently, Eliza pulled Eleanor's hands from her eyes and said, "There's nothing shameful or wrong about crying. And I dare say, living here all alone, no family around you, you've never had the chance to properly cry. Do so now, my girl. You've earned it."

They stayed like this a while, Eliza comforting Eleanor with a warm mother's care, something that she'd never had growing up, and only started to enjoy as an adult with Lady Stratton. But she cried now to say a more proper goodbye to Antony, one not laden with heartbreak and devastating shock when she'd learned of his death back in '42. She would never really get over losing him, but now she'd at least accepted it.

Cairo, Egypt
January 1952

"I know I'm not a sophisticate like yourself, but when are you coming home? It's clear as day they don't want us here anymore."

Aunt May had been in Egypt for all of five days and already had become quite the expert on British-Egyptian relations. Never mind the fact that this was her first time here even though Eleanor had been imploring her to visit since the war's end and even that was going on nearly seven years ago. But she was here. Finally. And with a litany of both constant complaints and uninformed biases.

"It's a bit more complicated than that, Aunt May."

"What," Aunt May scoffed. "You returning to your home country?"

Eleanor wanted to respond that it hadn't been home in a long time. The land of her birth, her difficult and bleak childhood. But home? No, Egypt was home to her. Egypt had been home for more than 20 years now, more time than she had spent in England. But Eleanor knew she couldn't fully ignore what was going on around her. The rising anti-British sentiment. Although British troops had been withdrawn to the Suez Canal area in 1947, that still hadn't appeased the nationalists who wanted all things British gone from their lands, namely, who wielded power and controlled the Suez, but also the country as a whole. And that included the nationalists' disdain of the Egyptian monarchy and its loathsome King Farouk, whom they saw as just another puppet of the British.

"Aunt May, let's not quarrel, please," Eleanor said imploringly. "You've-"

"Eleanor." Aunt May said her name sternly, as if she were still the little wisp of a girl she had once been. "You were always the smartest and most sensible of all my sister's offspring, God rest their souls. But you're being daft if you think you can remain here, head in the clouds, thinking that what's happenin," pointing to the parlour window from where she sat, her thick Cockney accent manifesting itself more during heated discussions, "is not going to affect you in here. Just look at what happened in India!"

Eleanor knew she was losing this battle. India, the crown jewel of the British Empire for nearly a century, was no more. The Indians had been clamouring for independence since well before the Second World War and had not been mollified with measures like greater autonomy and promises of independence as soon as the war ended if the Indian nationalists cooperated in the war effort. And then it seemed independence happened just like that. After the long years of war, the exhaustion of both Britain's coffers and its citizens, and the restlessness that persisted in the Raj, along with native forces no longer being a source of dependability to quell any unrest in the provinces, India was no longer something worth fighting for to the British. It had to go and in early 1947 Britain announced its intention of transferring power no later than June 1948. But as independence approached and hostilities increased between the Hindus and Muslims, the British army, entirely unprepared for the possibility for increased violence, moved up the date for the transfer of power, allowing less than six months for a mutually agreed plan for independence. Nearly 100 years of British rule, and less than six months to plan a future, post-independence. To the old guard in Cairo, those that still nursed their gin and tonics at Shepheard's and Mena House, who rehashed the newspapers and BBC's coverage of the partition, Britain's withdrawal from the Indian subcontinent was a success. Although so much of British rule in India had been marked by revolts and brutal crackdowns, their leaving of the place was basically bloodless. But the accounts of what happened to the Indian people, neighbour killing neighbour because they were a different religion, never mind the fact they had lived peacefully next to each other for hundreds of years, families displaced and separated due to the ill thought out and rushed and harried independence plan, had horrified Eleanor. Could that really happen here, she thought, Aunt May's words echoing in her head.

"Egypt is not India," Eleanor flatly stated.

"My girl, the last war was just the beginning. A new world is upon us, one in which the order of the past will not be the order of the future," Aunt May answered, saying this as if she were a soothsayer. But maybe she was, Eleanor thought. Maybe you reach a certain age like she had and you are able to see into the future. But Eleanor didn't want to think of a future if it was devoid of the only memories she had of Antony. And that was here. That was where home was.

"I'm not saying this isn't lovely, my dear," Aunt May began, her head tilted back on her rattan chair, her eyes closed, basking in the golden warmth of the January sun. In her will Lady Stratton had left Aunt May, a valued and even beloved employee of hers for more than 30 years, a tidy pension for her to live comfortably for the rest of her life and Eleanor was glad of that. She had worked so tirelessly throughout the war, never refusing to cook for those who were rendered homeless from the bombing. For the first time in her life, it seemed that May Drummond was finally relaxing.

They had come to the Mena House for afternoon tea following their excursion to the Great Pyramid. Although initially opposed to the idea of climbing it, "what, an old lady like me climb something like that?" she had said, completely serious, when Eleanor said they could hire a native to help her up, she had acquiesced. And her face had come alive when after much sweating and panting, they had finally reached the top and she looked out at the vast arid landscape in front of her and seemed genuinely speechless. "I can't believe someone like me is really here," she had said in almost a whisper. And it was then that Eleanor had noticed tears in her aunt's eyes, the first time Eleanor could ever remember her aunt displaying real emotion. And it was this that rendered Eleanor quiet. Her beloved Aunt May, who had always treated her like a daughter, been a mother figure when her own mother was nowhere to be found.

"But it just ain't real."

"But it is to me," Eleanor replied. "It's always been real to me."

"But you have nothing keepin' you here," Aunt May said, her tone slightly annoyed. "You have no family!"

Eleanor was about to ask what family she had back in England besides her, but she stopped herself, knowing that would be cruel. Aunt May, Eleanor knew, was lonely. And what right did she have to deny an old lady some final years of joy and happiness.

"I'll plan a proper long visit, very soon," Eleanor said, taking her aunt's hand in hers. "And I'll tell you what. I'll come and visit every year."

But Aunt May, as if she were a small child who hadn't gotten her way, shook free of Eleanor's hand and turned in her chair to face away from her.

I can't leave him, she wanted to say but didn't. Even after all this time she couldn't bare her soul to anyone, not even Aunt May.

26 January 1952
Cairo

The day started like any other. The morning air was cool and crisp as Eleanor went out to water her plants. But the sky was its usual striking, picturesque bright blue, the air alive with the endless possibility of the day.

But as the afternoon progressed, Eleanor started to smell smoke. So did Aunt May. And as the sky above them turned black Eleanor thought back to the war, to that day they called 'Ash Wednesday'

when half-burnt pieces of paper British officials had hurriedly tried
to burn in advance of the rumoured German invasion, rained down
on the capital. And then came the endless barrage of firetrucks.

"Heavens, is all of Cairo on fire?" Aunt May asked jokingly as they
took their afternoon tea in the parlor, the air too thick with smoke to
be outside but the sounds of chaos and havoc still coming through.

But then Ahmed, Eleanor's faithful cook for all these years,
appeared in the doorway, his face ashen and serious.

"Yes, Ahmed, what is it?" Eleanor asked, wondering whatever was
the matter for him to appear now. Wafaa, Ahmed's young nephew,
was the one who usually brought and cleared the tea.

"Ma'am, I implore you and your auntie to not go outside. At all.
It is not safe right now."

"Whatever do you mean, Ahmed?" thinking he was possibly
joking, even though Eleanor had never known Ahmed to make a joke
or laugh in her presence. He was the beacon of the seen but never
heard servant. And he also loved all things British, having spent most
of his adult life perfecting his second language.

"Riots, ma'am. All over the city. Against the...." He paused then
before continuing. "Against the British."

At that, Aunt May drew in a sharp breath. And Eleanor sat back
down, groping for the front of the chair to fall down into.

Ahmed looked frightened then, unsure if he should continue. But
he did. "Shepheard's is destroyed, ma'am."

Shepheard's, the unofficial crown jewel of the British Empire for
nearly a century although it had only existed in its current state, the
one Eleanor had become acquainted with it so intimately, since the
1890s. The place where she'd had so many wonderful moments with
Antony. Gone.

"The Casino Opera club, the Automobile Club. The Rivoli, the
Miami" (two cinema houses Eleanor had always adored and

frequented), Ahmed said in almost a monotone voice. "Groppi's."

And at that, Eleanor felt like her feet had been knocked out from under her. Groppi's, the ice cream parlour where she had first met Antony. Gone.

"So when are you booking passage home? For you can't really think a place that has destroyed all things British as home anymore, can you?" Aunt May asked coolly, not the least bit ruffled by what Ahmed said, but more determined than ever to prove her case.

PART III
JIMMY, ELEANOR & LUX

CHAPTER 25

Egypt 1997

"You weren't scared about coming here? What with all the terrorist activity and such."

"I could ask the same of you," Lux said in response to Eleanor's question, rather haughtily, Jimmy thought.

Eleanor appeared startled then, clearly not expecting this. But then she said quietly, looking directly into Lux's eyes, "I used to live here."

Jimmy was amazed by this. Although she had proved to be more agreeable than Lux, he still hadn't found either woman at last night's dinner to be overly warm. He had taken the older British woman to be just that- your stereotypical elderly woman who had a clipped English accent. But lived here? Lived here when, he wondered? Here in Cairo? Elsewhere in the country? Not to mention, there had been something odd about the way she had reacted when he told the story of how his *yiayia* had fled to Egypt during the war and survived. It was almost as if she had been stunned by this. But why, he asked himself? What would his *yiayia,* who had been a little girl then, have to do with the elderly British woman? Never mind the fact that Eleanor hadn't even greeted him this morning when their tour group convened in the lobby before they were to board the coach that would take them to Giza, to see the last remaining Seven Wonders of the Ancient World.

Yet now here she was, breaking his reverie (and Lux's too, by the way she seemed lost in her own trancelike stupor) of the most incredible sight he had ever witnessed in his life by starting the day talking about terrorists?

"Well, I dare say you know how to liven things up in a totally macabre way," Lux said, walking away to where their Egyptologist stood.

"I apologize, I didn't mean anything by it," Eleanor said to Jimmy, although her eyes were still trained on Lux's retreating figure. "I just meant we can't go a month without reading about the latest terrorist attack in Egypt."

"You don't need to apologize," Jimmy said, smiling what he hoped came across as charmingly at her. "I understand. A bit apprehensive, well, my mom more so than me. But I like to think my *yiayia* is watching over me, keeping me safe."

Eleanor didn't answer, she didn't say anything. So Jimmy went back to his reverie then, marveling at how even though one of the most populated cities in the entire world was little more than 10 miles from where he now was, you would never know it standing here. It was just as easy to believe that it was 1897 and not 1997 considering how much the vast desert landscape must appear the same as it always had, ever since the time of the Pharaohs. He could have stayed like that forever, or at least until his supply of water ran out. But the 30 minutes allotted for that picture perfect view of the Great Pyramid and the smaller (but still equally massive) pyramids that surrounded it went by entirely too fast and soon they were being herded back onto the coach that would take them to their next ancient wonder.

Jimmy knew his *yiayia* had never seen the Great Pyramid or any of Egypt's famed ancient sites. He knew Egypt had saved her in the sense that she had been kept safe and survived the war. But her views of Egypt had been limited to those found inside the refugee camp where they had been penned like animals for the duration of the war. A refugee camp in the middle of the desert, a childhood completely devoid of any fun or joy. But as she had always told him, ever since he was little, "I survived, I lived to see the end when so many of our people didn't."

"This is for you, *Yiayia*," Jimmy whispered before snapping one final picture with his camera.

But not before he heard Eleanor quietly whisper the words, "Are you here too, Antony?"

"I simply must ask, where are you from? Your accent is one I can't place."

Lux looked at Jimmy only to see him indicate his head towards Eleanor, that it was she asking the question of her and not of him. The three of them were seated together again at dinner, the three lone single travelers forced again to socialize. Although the other travelers in their group were friendly enough, their even numbers paired with his, Lux's, and Eleanor's odd ones meant they were always going to be the outliers.

Lux sighed, for some reason perturbed by this question. Jimmy wondered to himself if she was asked this a lot. Not that he would have dared ask it. She intimidated him.

"My nationality is American. But I was raised in Istanbul and have spent my entire life there."

"Heavens," Eleanor replied. "How on earth did you end up there?"

"I always thought British people were supposed to be beacons of good manners. You seem anything but with your prying questions."

"I'm sorry?" Eleanor replied, her tone slightly offended now.

"I don't remember seeing anything in the tour itinerary that said becoming chums with our fellow tour members was a daily activity."

"If you'll excuse me," Eleanor said, stiffly rising from her seat. "It's been a very long day and I know we have a dreadfully early rise again tomorrow," as she left the dining room.

"Go ahead, scold me," Lux said to Jimmy after Eleanor had gone, although he wasn't entirely sure if she was being serious or not. "As I said, I'm American in nationality. Both my parents were American so I supposed I inherited the mannerless Yank bearing. Mind if I smoke?" she asked, removing a packet of cigarettes from her purse.

Although he detested the smell of cigarettes, Jimmy didn't want to incur the mild wrath he'd just witnessed, so he nodded affirmatively. She offered him one, but he shook his head no, politely he hoped it came across.

Lighting one, she took a long drag then released the smoke as she lifted her head back.

"I suppose it's just a bit much for me. This place. Being here. Being to a place that runs in me, and yet one I had never been to either."

What? This woman truly was an enigma with her constant cryptic phrases when she wasn't being snippy or abrasive. He would love to ask what the hell she meant by that, but didn't want to be accused of prying. So he just politely nodded his head, smiling in feigned agreement.

"So what was your favorite thing we saw today?" she asked, taking another deep drag. The cigarette, Jimmy observed, was clearly having a calming effect on her. She was almost, he dare say, pleasant?

"Giza. I mean the views, were just –"

"Like nothing like it," she filled in.

"I kinda wish I hadn't given up art as a kid," he said, half-jokingly. "I would have liked to sketch like Bouc does when Poirot meets up with him at Giza."

She laughed then, the first genuine laugh he'd heard from her since they met. "You know your Christie," she added, approvingly. "I loved Giza too, don't get me wrong, but for me I'd have to say Saqqara. I have a thing for places that hold world records."

Saqqara, only a short drive from Giza, contained the oldest complete stone building complex known in history. Jimmy had thought it neat but to him it hadn't the same visual allure that the Great Pyramid did. Maybe that's why he had never heard of it before.

"Well, that and the fact that it was my father's favorite place in Lower Egypt," Lux added. "Or so my mother told me."

The following day Eleanor kept to herself, walking around with an almost melancholic look to her. Jimmy felt bad at this since at Giza the previous day she had seemed almost giddy, excited to be there. Today, they had been in the capital city the whole time and Jimmy wondered if this was somehow contributing to her mood. Surely, she couldn't be bothered with what the abrasive Lux had rudely said to her the night before?

"It was never this bad. The smog I mean."

She was right about that. The sweeping views offered from the Citadel of Saladin, a medieval fort, were undoubtedly the best in Cairo due to its incredible location at the top of Mokattam Hill.

When Jimmy had noticed Eleanor sitting down on a stone slab that overlooked the city, he went to sit down next to her. She hadn't looked at him when he sat down, just stared straight ahead, transfixed almost at the sprawl that was Cairo. A city of over 10 million people, all living on top of each other, it seemed. All with nowhere else they wanted to be but in Cairo.

"You said yesterday you used to live there," Jimmy began, taking a moment alone to learn more about her. "Since Lux isn't here," he said jokingly. "If you don't mind me asking, when was this?"

Eleanor answered by way of a deep sigh, her eyes Jimmy noticed, filled with pain. "A lifetime ago it seems. Right before the Suez Crisis. I left in '56."

"Wait, were you a refugee too during the war?" Jimmy asked this a moment before realizing what a stupid question it was.

As if she could read his thoughts she said, "Not stupid at all. I know the timing certainly seems more than coincidental. No," she sighed again, her eyes looking forward once more on that overwhelming view. "I came as a young girl, working as a companion to a countess who had a winter home here. We ended up staying for good when war broke out."

"Did you come across many refugees during the war?"

Eleanor jerked back her head then to look sharply at him. She looked like she wanted to say something, but shook her head, adding, "No, not really."

And then it seemed like she shut down, or perhaps her mind was in another time, Jimmy thought, studying the elderly woman who became completely oblivious to his presence.

"Eleanor, I want to apologize if I came across as rude the last two days. I'd like to blame my behavior on jet lag, but coming from Turkey, I can't really play that card," Lux said, smiling. Jimmy had arrived at the restaurant for dinner the same time as Eleanor and had planned to sit with her but before they could even confer with the maître d Lux had waved them over to where she was sitting.

Eleanor appeared completely taken aback by this public apology and seemed at a loss for words.

Jimmy always fulfilled the role of mediator it seemed, at home or abroad, with his parents and with still-almost strangers. He broke the ice by raising his glass and saying, "To my *yiayia*, the reason why I'm here today, both literally and figuratively."

Clink.

"To my parents."

Clink.

"To Antony."

Clink.

Just when Jimmy thought there was nothing that could remotely touch the wonderment that was Giza, the next day they flew south, although he had to keep reminding himself, it was technically Upper Egypt.

"I guess you could say I'm living my best Agatha Christie life," Jimmy joked as the three of them walked along the Avenue of Sphinxes at Karnak. "Although being here, I really wish I had studied archaeology. My profession seems incredibly lame."

The two women both laughed. "What is your profession?" Lux asked.

"Stockbroker."

"Ahh," Eleanor politely responded. "Well, I'm sure you make a good salary."

"My father was an archaeologist. My mom, well, an amateur one on paper, but a genuine one in her heart and brain," Lux added, stopping to admire the statues of Ramses II as Osiris, leaning her head back to fully take in their monolithic height.

"How extraordinary," Eleanor said whimsically. "Did they do excavation work here?"

"Oh yes, scores of it. They lived here too. My father was one of the few archaeologists to live here year-round, not 'summer' elsewhere, not go on a dig in other parts of the world."

"Was this before you were born?" Eleanor inquired, walking to an area of the temple that offered the least bit of shade from the intense, late morning sun.

"Yes. As I said, I've never been here before now," Lux answered stiffly, walking away.

"Your grandmother," Eleanor tentatively began. "How old was she when she came to Egypt? As a refugee, I mean."

They were at Luxor that night, having arrived just as the sun was setting, so that natural occurrence paired with the flood lights that were scattered throughout the site that in ancient times was the city of Thebes, provided a most spectacular backdrop. Once it was dark, Jimmy had noticed Eleanor stepping more cautiously so he had offered her his arm, which she immediately accepted.

"I think she was about 10."

Jimmy thought he felt her pause but must have imagined it.

"You know, I lived here for years but never left Cairo. It's a country replete with so many astounding sites and I never saw any of them, until now. Antony and I had so many things we wanted to do after the war."

Antony. There was that name again. "Who's Antony?" Jimmy asked.

And then her sad, melancholic face took shape. With a deep sigh and slight tremble of her lips, she said, "My husband. He died during the war, killed in action."

"I'm so sorry," feeling there was no phrase more trite in the

English language but what else could he say.

"As I routinely say, a lifetime ago. For a long time, I felt as though I had lost him, that with each passing year, he, my memories of him, were slipping further and further away, deep into the recesses of my memory that I won't be able to access anymore. But somehow being back here, back in Egypt I mean, I feel as if I'm a young woman of 20 again, about to get dressed for a night of dancing and G & T's at Shepheard's." A pause then, "They were always his favourite."

Jimmy had no idea what any of this meant but just nodded, letting her speak.

"Ever since I arrived here, I feel both haunted but also reinvigorated by the memory of him."

"I wonder if your path ever crossed with my *yiayia*."

"I wonder that too. You have no idea."

CHAPTER 26

Lux's story

"Breathe."

Lux commanded herself as she studied her reflection in the stateroom's bathroom mirror. As a child growing up, Lux's mom had always said Lux had one of the most indomitable personalities, her very own shield if you will. But she had also been scrappy, industrious when she needed to be. Lux had never lacked for anything growing up, with the exception of maternal affection.

Lux knew that her mother loved her, would have done anything for her, but she had never been warm or demonstrative. Lux's mother had expected her daughter to be self-sufficient, even from a young age. She had also severely regimented Lux's reading habits, having her read the classics as a child instead of popular titles of the day like the *Little House* books and Betty Smith's *A Tree Grows in Brooklyn* as any young girl would have preferred. In fact, for Lux's 12th birthday, her mother gave her a copy of a new, hardbound edition of Homer's *The Odyssey* and told Lux she expected to be able to discuss and have a discourse on the previous day's reading each night at dinner.

Her childhood spent in Istanbul had been very 'avant-garde.' Her mother wasn't exactly what you would call bohemian in the traditional sense, but maybe she was. Instead of returning to the States where she had grown up after a personal tragedy had struck, she made a new home in another exotic corner of the world, one where she spoke neither the language nor was fully accepted because of her gender. But she did it anyway. She thrived and Lux did too in her own way.

Lux had never met her father. When she was old enough to ask her mother why she didn't have one, her mother simply told her that he had died before she was born. She said this quite bluntly and entirely without feeling to a seven-year old. The next time her mother went out and Lux was left in the house with only the housekeeper for company, Lux tried snooping through her mother's things, thinking she must have a photograph or memento of him. But she found absolutely nothing which left her more confused than ever. Her mother wasn't one for displaying photographs. In the whole of their house, there was only one sitting portrait of the two of them.

But the following morning at breakfast, Lux's mother had completely surprised her when she said, "I see you've acquired a propensity for detective work."

While she was quite a precocious child but still only seven years of age, Lux simply stared at her mother uncomprehendingly.

"You have nothing to say to the matter?" her mother quietly demanded, noisily stirring the sugar cube she had just dropped into her tulip-shaped tea glass. Taking Lux's silence to mean she did not, her mother continued. "When you are sixteen, and not a day before, then and only then I will tell you the full story of your father."

Lux was confused. Sixteen, why sixteen she wondered to herself. It seemed like such an arbitrary number.

"That was how old I was when I first met him." Then, looking directly at Lux and further surprising her when she took her small hand in hers, she said, "I need to know you are emotionally mature enough to learn about the past."

"But it's MY past," Lux said in a defiant tone. "I deserve to know it."

But her mother was unswayed by Lux's plea. She merely rose from her chair and walked over to the sideboard where the breakfast dishes had been laid out by the housekeeper. Only then did Lux notice a small, leatherbound case at one end. Lux's mother reached into it and retrieved what Lux could see was a photograph.

She returned to Lux's side and surprised her again she lowered herself so that she was almost eye-level with Lux and handed the photograph to her.

Lux held it in her hands as if it were a fragile treasure but then looked down in amazement at the figure in the image.

"My father," Lux whispered, not saying it as a question for she already knew who the man in the old-fashioned attire staring back at her was.

So Lux had waited, biding her time, anxiously awaiting the day when she would turn 16. She had obeyed her mother all those years, never once bringing up the subject of her father or asking questions about him except that one time they'd had an usually bad row. Lux, still only a child and not aware of the emotional effects one's words could have on someone, told her mother that she wished it had been her who had died, and not her father.

And all Lux's mother had said in response was, "So do I." She had walked away then, but not before Lux saw for the first time in her life, tears streaming down her mother's cheeks.

Egypt
1997

"Is Lux short for anything?" Jimmy asked.

"Awful, isn't it?" Lux wryly remarked.

"Oh no," Jimmy said, quick to answer. "I didn't mean anything in the least by it. Just that it's quite-"

"Unusual? Since I went to an international school in Istanbul I wasn't teased like I'm sure I would have been in the States."

"Unique," he said, hoping that his answer was diplomatic.

"It means 'light' in Latin. Although that's not why my mother chose it."

Jimmy waited, wondering if she would offer the reason her mother named her that or if he was to inquire further.

And then looking at him with a smirk on her face she said, "Where we are is the inspiration."

"I don't get it," Jimmy said, thinking she was the ultimate prankster, not with actual pranks but word teases. But then comprehension dawned on him. "Wait, Lux is short for Luxor? Your real name is Luxor?"

"God no. It thankfully and legally is just Lux. But the inspiration coming from yes, the Egyptian city of Luxor," she said, waving her arms to gesticulate towards their current surroundings, the former ancient city of Thebes. "Thank God I wasn't a boy, she might have named me Thebes," she said, in mock horror.

"Your dad wasn't around?" Jimmy asked, hoping he wasn't being too forward.

Lux sighed then and Jimmy could have sworn he saw a tear start to fall down her cheek. But quickly brushing both the corner of her eye and then cheek she said, "No, he died here. I never knew him. And the really messed up and tragic part?" Lux said, turning to fully face Jimmy.

"He didn't even know my mother was pregnant when he died. And for that matter, neither did she."

Lux's mother kept her word. On her 16th birthday, she gave Lux a beautiful Florentine leather journal. Upon opening it, Lux saw it contained the keys to her past.

The journal was a combination of both passages her mother had written as a young girl on her first trip to Egypt, complete with a random assortment of pasted in paper mementos- a napkin from Shepheard's, a sheet of papyrus depicting a series of hieroglyphs and then, Lux discovered, a collection of black and white photographs. Lux carefully studied each one, wondering as her eyes took in the people's faces if any of them were her father. They were sitting next to each other, out on the terrace that overlooked the Bosphorus. Her mother hadn't said anything at all since handing Lux the journal, but then she started to tentatively speak.

"Those are my parents, your grandparents," she said, indicating a striking older couple posing in front of the pyramids, Giza she presumed. The man, sporting a mustache that was the fashion at the turn of the century, Lux knew from history books, had a kind face, one where he looked what, at peace? In his glory, Lux wondered? The woman was beautiful, that much was clear. Even in her outfit, which looked comically out of place against the backdrop of the desert sands, made her appear as if she had just come from a dress fitting at a famous Parisian *atelier*. "My father was a wonderful man, always happy to indulge my every whim and curiosity. I was a girl, not the son that I'm sure deep down he had always wanted, but he never treated me differently, never made me feel as if I shouldn't demand more from life in terms of knowledge."

She regarded Lux then, looking as if she wasn't sure if she should continue her ramblings.

"And my grandmother?" Lux asked, wanting to hear more.

Lux's mother sighed heavily then before looking away. Her eyes focused on a yacht that had just come into view on the water. "My mother was a horrible woman. She was constantly derisive of me, constantly battling with my father on what **she** believed a young lady's education should and should not consist of, and I think deep down she was also horribly jealous of the close relationship my father and I shared."

"What brought you to Egypt?" Lux asked, feeling this deep family revelation was veering off course and further away from learning about her father.

"My father," she replied, giving Lux a genuinely happy and carefree smile, something she hadn't remembered seeing on her mother's face for a long time. "He simply adored ancient Egypt, always said that if he hadn't been a doctor, he would have liked to become an archaeologist. They, my parents I mean, had come to Egypt on their honeymoon. My mother apparently detested every minute of it. But my father, he fell in love with the country and its past."

"And they came back? With you I mean?" Lux asked, thinking her grandmother sounded like any number of the evil witches from Grimm's fairy tales.

"Yes." A long pause then. "You see, when I turned 17, my father found out he had cancer, that it was incurable. My mother, for all her loathsome qualities, did grant him his last wish, to see Egypt again and for me to see it with him." Another pause. "He just didn't expect me to fall in love when I was there."

"Wait," Lux said sitting up rather excitedly. "You mean to tell me you met my father when you came to Egypt?"

"Yes. It's true when I say that Egypt runs in your blood," she said, smiling wanly at Lux. "Read through this," she said, touching the top of the journal that Lux still had open on her lap. "And then once you're finished, I will give you part two of your origin story, as I like to call it." She stood up then and Lux could see her eyes welling with tears. "I never meant to keep this secret," she began, waving her hand to indicate the journal, "but it seemed easier to bury it than to talk about it, let alone talk about it with a child."

"Can we go one day, to Egypt I mean?" Lux asked. "Show me where you and my father lived?"

"No!" Lux's mother said this with so much force and vehemence, Lux was stunned. "I will always answer any questions you may have but I will never go back, never," she said, saying the last word emphatically. "I had such happy memories there with your father for so many years until he was suddenly taken from me. Going back would make me have to relive it all again."

"What happened to him?" Lux asked, many horrible images and scenarios running through her head just then.

"An insect bite," she replied, her words sounding just as poisonous as the thing itself.

There were so many times Lux had thought about going to Egypt as an adult. It was right there, she would tell herself, studying a globe, seeing how incredibly close Istanbul was, just a short plane ride away. And while she knew her mother wouldn't have forbidden her from going, especially once she was an adult, Lux couldn't do it. She couldn't bring the pain upon her mother that she knew her going would cause, even if her mother would never say any of this out loud. And so after she finished at uni, she went east, embarking on what would become infamously known as the 'Hippie Trail,' starting in Istanbul and visiting such exotic locales as Beirut, Amman, Teheran, Kabul, Katmandu and ultimately ending in Goa, a beautiful beach town in southern India. But no matter how far she traveled, how many breathtaking and wondrous sights she saw, she couldn't put ancient Egypt out of her mind. Especially since it was completely connected to her father.

And so she waited, biding her time for the day when she would feel emotionally free to be able to go there. She had long since returned to Istanbul after retiring her faded maroon rucksack from her backpacking hippie days, feeling nowhere else was really home in the sense that the once great capital of the Ottoman Empire was. Her mother never said out loud how pleased she was to have Lux back, but her face conveyed her happiness. As her mother aged, she became if nothing else, more 'motherly,' more the warm woman Lux had so desperately craved as a young child.

Lux taught at an English language school in Nisantasi, teaching her high-school pupils classical studies. And while the curriculum she was required to teach predominantly focused on ancient Greece and Rome, it was ancient Egypt that captured her heart. She had eagerly devoured both Lady Duff-Gordon's *Letters from Egypt* and *Last Letters from Egypt,* utterly captivated by such vivid descriptions of the land in her beautiful prose-

"Cairo is the Arabian Nights; there is a little Frankish varnish here and there, but the government, the people- all is unchanged since that most veracious book was written."
"The view all round my house is magnificent on every side, over the Nile in front facing north-west and over a splendid range of green and distant orange buff hills to the south-east, where I have a spacious covered terrace."

Lux nearly envisioned herself becoming a modern-day Lady Duff-Gordon of the 20th century- moving to Egypt as the English author had in 1862, settling in Luxor, learning Arabic, and sharing with the world the wonder and beauty that was Egypt. But this was the 1970s, not the 1860s, Egypt was no longer 'new' and undiscovered by the Western masses as it once had been in history. And besides, Lady Duff-Gordon had died so tragically young, she was only 48. Not exactly something she wanted to aspire to.

She told herself that when her mother died, she would finally go there. But unlike her father, who had died so prematurely young, Lux's mother seemed to have drunk from the fountain of youth. Sure, she physically aged with each passing year but her mind, wit, and physical health were just as robust as they had been when she was younger.

But then on the eve of her 99th birthday, she had simply passed in her sleep. She had gone onto the next journey in her life from her own bed and for that Lux would be forever grateful. Lux had many friends whose parents had seemed to age overnight and they routinely bemoaned all that came with having an unhealthy, aging parent, where hospital stays occurred with as much regularity as a full moon.

And then some weeks after the funeral, a courier had delivered to the house a small, locked box. The accompanying letter had been from her mother's longtime lawyer. It hadn't revealed much, simply that Lux's mother had wanted her to have the contents of the box upon her death. As Lux opened it, not sure what she would find inside, she was surprised to see nothing more than a leather-bound book etched with the words-

The Ancient Egyptian Adventures of Alexander & Alexandra

"I'm going to admit what's probably an unpopular opinion but I'm not at all a fan of *Death on the Nile*."

"The film or book?" Lux asked Eleanor.

"Wait, there was a movie of it?" Jimmy asked, his youth now showing to the two older women, who looked at each other then and laughed. No one was exactly sure why or how but there had been a sort of *détente* between the two women. But one didn't seem to take umbrage over every little barb or question, and the other was more at ease with talking about herself and her past. Unlike most of the people in the tour group who had come to Egypt for no other reason than to see the treasures of one of ancient history's greatest civilizations, the three of them had all traveled there for personal reasons, because of a connection that bound them to this place. They were all inextricably linked to it.

"Ohh, look the sun is starting to set. Shall we go outside?" Eleanor asked excitedly in the voice of a school girl, as she looked out the window of the dining room where they were seated.

"Let's," Lux answered, rising from the table.

"You know," Jimmy began. "I've never been really a religious guy, I guess I've always preferred to keep religion out of-" his voice trailed off as he struggled to find the right word.

"Life?" Lux and Eleanor both chimed in perfect unison.

"But standing here now," he continued, "on a boat on the world's longest river, watching what almost looks like a painting come to life, I can see why some people invoke God with images like this."

"You can be religious in your heart with what you see around you," Lux said, taking his hand and gently squeezing it. "If nothing else."

Eleanor sat down on one of the wicker chairs that graced the deck of the Karnak.

"Antony was so good with words, the beautiful things he'd say without a thought to them," she said, her eyes transfixed on the glassy and calm water before her, so deeply lost in her thoughts and entrenched memories. "Even from the battlefields, he'd write me the loveliest of letters, as if he were on holiday somewhere, and not about to mount a major offensive. I feel I did nothing but whine in mine, or simply complain about such mundane and trivial matters. But if he were here right now he'd describe this as a 'blaze of color- the sunset painting the sky with a bushel of peaches."

"You know, my parents came here by *dahabiya*, back in the '20s. Well, multiple times I think, but long before they moved the temples, when you could still come right up to the shore."

They were at Abu Simbel today, an ancient temple complex in Upper Egypt that had once been the *pièce de resistance* of the ancient kingdom of Nubia. Unlike the characters in *Death on the Nile* and of course Alexandra's own parents and Eleanor's mother-in-law, visitors to the site of these two massive rock-cut ancient temples flew south from Aswan to almost the Sudanese border and from the airport, boarded a motor coach to a parking lot brimming with tourists comprising nearly every language and nationality.

"Oh right, when did they move it?" Eleanor asked, graciously accepting Jimmy's outstretched hand as she navigated the slightly uneven, downward path. "I remember reading about it some time ago. Didn't even Jackie Kennedy become involved?"

"Hmm, that I don't recall," Lux answered. "I just remember at the time reading that the venture cost millions back in the '60s."

"Bit more romantic doing it that way," Eleanor mused as she turned towards the hordes of visitors descending upon the ancient temples. "It had been on our list," she continued, almost a bit wistfully. "To visit I mean. After the war. So much we never got to do."

Neither Jimmy nor Lux spoke, but each took one of Eleanor's hands and lightly squeezed it.

"You're here now," Lux said. "You're here for the both of you, you in the flesh, he in spirit with you."

"Wait, I still don't get why was it moved?" Jimmy asked. "And how the heck do you even go about doing it?"

"Back in the '60s, Egypt built a dam along the Nile," Lux answered, ever the schoolteacher. "To help with the annual flooding. But doing so meant the temples here and countless other Nubian treasures would eventually become submerged in the newly minted Lake Nasser," she said, waving her hand in front of her to indicate the beautiful glistening cerulean waters that so reminded her of the Turquois Coast back home in Turkey.

"So, if they hadn't moved them, they'd all be gone?" Jimmy asked, stupefied now.

"Reduced to the annals of history," Eleanor said dryly, making Jimmy smirk and Lux smile wanly in response.

"To survive thousands of years, withstanding the test of time, the elements, war and more, only for modernization to get you in the end," Eleanor said, that wistful look back in her eyes again.

"Well, almost get you," Lux clarified.

"Do you think these places will always exist?" Jimmy asked, gazing out onto Lake Nasser as he spoke but not before turning to admire the more than 3000-year old structure once more.

"They will so long as there's always someone who cares."

CHAPTER 27

"I've wanted to ask for days now but you hadn't seemed ready, or what I mean to say, in the right frame of mind-" Jimmy cut off his words now, realizing he was uttering nonsensical ramblings.

"Right frame of mind?" Eleanor looked up at him from the chaise lounge she was sitting in up on deck with a bemused look in her eyes. "I know I'm getting up there in years but I hardly think I'm in the mentally doddering stage yet," she replied, her tone light and jocular.

"Refugees during the war. That is the Jewish refugees," Jimmy added, clarifying. "Did you know some? I just feel every time I've brought up my *yiayia,* well, when she was here in Egypt I mean, you always looked like you wanted to say something, ask me something."

Without looking at Jimmy, her gaze still focused on the signs of life that lay just beyond the banks of the river, lush green vegetation at its edge, shepherds out with their grazing animals, women and children carrying jugs of water back to their homes for cooking, the dark golden sands of the desert the least bit further in, she asked, "What was your grandmother's name?"

Jimmy looked at her a moment before he answered, "Calliope. Calliope Doukas."

Eleanor sighed then, or did it sound more like a sigh of emotional defeat, Jimmy wondered. "Did you know my grandmother?" he asked.

"No. I never met your grandmother. But I did know another Greek refugee girl during the war. I took her in, in fact," she said, turning to him now, her face tired and haunted looking. "Into my home. I treated her…" her voice trailing off. "I treated her like a daughter. I even hoped to adopt her after the war. We had both lost so much but somehow in the midst of it all we found each other. But then in 1946, her father came. And he took her away. And I never saw or heard from her again. And in all this time, there's never been a day that's gone by where I haven't stopped and thought of her. And I always wondered did she ever think of me? At least in the early years I mean. I'm not vain enough to think she would still remember the English woman she lived with in Cairo during the war 20 years later."

"And you thought my grandmother could have been her?" Jimmy asked.

"It happened once before," Eleanor answered. "Two strangers whose paths would have never crossed had it not been for extenuating circumstances."

"Yeah," Jimmy began, "but you can hardly consider a tour to Egypt in the 1990s the same thing as people being thrown together because of the events of war." Jimmy instantly regretted his choice of words, feeling they were nothing more than belittling to an elderly woman who had clearly done a wonderful thing during the war by taking in and caring for a Jewish child. "I just mean the odds would have been one in a million."

"Haven't you ever read Dickens? The literary master of improbable odds," she replied, offering him a sad smile. "I just thought that coming back here as I'm nearing the end of my life, that I would finally be able to give a proper goodbye not just to the memory of Antony but Egypt, the country itself. Something I had never really been mentally ready to do until now. But then on our first night here at dinner when you told me the story about your grandmother, I thought that my coming here had been for a reason, to be reunited with a descendant of Eleni's, a testament that she had lived a long life and prospered by establishing new roots in her new homeland."

"That was her name?" Jimmy quietly cut in. "Eleni?"

"Yes," she answered. "Eleni and Eleanor. If you want to talk about odds, what are the odds that two people with basically the same name will be brought together?"

"I'll give you that," Jimmy said. "It's a beautiful name. My grandmother always hated hers, Calliope. She said Americans never said it right so most people just called her Cathy."

Eleanor laughed at this, wondering if Eleni as a grown woman had the same spirit and pluck that Jimmy's grandmother clearly had.

"Did you ever try looking for her?" Jimmy asked.

"For who? Eleni?" Eleanor answered.

"Yes."

"No, I never dared. When he came for her, her father wanted to give Eleni a fresh start. I would have always been a reminder of-"

"A reminder of the English woman who saved her? Who made it possible for her father to find her again after the war?" Jimmy interrupted by saying.

Eleanor thought no, a reminder of the period in her life when she was all alone, having left behind her mum and sisters, her grandparents, the only life she had ever known, to come to a foreign country where they were penned in like animals, only to flee where she could have perished in the unforgiving desert had it not been for her smart wits and good fortune. No, it was good if her father made her completely move on, erased that part of her memory. And then as if he was reading her thoughts Jimmy said, "And yet if she were to erase that part with you, then she'd have to erase her memories of her life before the war too, now wouldn't she?"

"I'll tell you what," Jimmy said. "When I get back home, I'm going to start looking for her. So you can finally learn what happened to her after you said goodbye. And you can have that closure for yourself."

Eleanor stayed silent, making Jimmy wonder if she'd heard him. "Eleanor?" he asked.

"Never say goodbye because goodbye means going away and going away means forgetting." Then turning to look directly into his eyes she added, "Always remember that."

CHAPTER 28

Valley of the Kings
16 November 1997

Jimmy had never been one to stop and take a moment to pause in his life. He wasn't one to stop and admire a rainbow that had just appeared after a rain shower; dogs that most people would remark "how cute" when passing by, Jimmy would be indifferent to. And sunsets- well, a girlfriend had actually dumped him after a trip to Mexico because he had said he didn't want to leave the resort just to take a cab all so that they could watch the sunset at a famous overlook. Of all the reasons to break up with. His refusal to watch a friggin' sunset? Well, that had rendered him speechless and clearly confirmed a long-held suspicion that all women were certifiably nuts.

He hadn't been brought up to be religious. After the war, after his *yiayia* had immigrated to America with her father, she eventually married an American man. He was "the only Gentile who actually liked gefilte fish," his *yiayia* liked to joke, referring to the dish made from a poached mixture of ground deboned fish that was a fixture in Ashkenazi Jewish households, not the Sephardic ones where she had grown up. When Jimmy was a little boy, she had actually served it to him and laughed in pure glee when she saw the look of disgust on her small grandson's face. Both she and he loathed the dish.

Yiayia, wanting nothing more than to fit in her new American life, had converted to Christianity. Jimmy's grandfather had been raised Presbyterian and so that's what she became, dutifully attending services each and every Sunday and becoming a fixture in the church community- always the first to volunteer or organize whatever needed to be done. Jimmy's mom, of course, had been brought up as a Presbyterian but it was only in high school, when she learned what had happened to *yiayia's* family during the war, their extermination in the Holocaust, did she begin to question the whole institution of religion, any religion that is. Like so many of the post-war generation, children of the survivors, children of the soldiers who had liberated the camps, she couldn't understand how if God really existed, how could He have allowed such a thing to happen? She was done with organized religion.

It greatly upset *yiayia* and *pappou* when Jimmy's mom and dad hadn't had him or his sister baptized. But *yiayia* wasn't the stereotypical Greek woman, overly pushy, overbearing, needing to make their opinions known on just about every topic imaginable even if it wasn't any of THEIR business- the decisions her grown, American children made, she may not have agreed with them, but she respected them. Perhaps this was due to her having left her land of birth when she was still just a child and more importantly, having lost her mother so young too.

Yiayia always said she believed that religion was what you felt deep in your heart- that you didn't need to go to a brick-and-mortar structure and hear someone talk to be religious. Before she died she told Jimmy that she could no longer remember the faces of her mama and little brothers and sisters, that they were nothing but blurred memories so deeply receded from her memory. But she said she knew she would see them again, see them once more on the other side when she passed. Jimmy had only been 14 then and wanted to ask, "But when you see them again, will they have grown to be old like you?

Or will you be once more a child as you were when you left them?"

He had so deeply felt his *yiayia's* presence the whole trip, from the moment he had landed in Cairo. But today, standing here in the Valley of the Kings, he felt for the first time in his entire life, the presence of a higher being. For the first time ever, he just wanted to stop and take it all in.

When they had first arrived at the Valley of the Kings, Jimmy was surprised to see such a vast and desolate space before them. Although Luxor was situated just across the Nile, a modern city teeming with business, people, and of course, ancient ruins you couldn't help but come across, here there was nothing, at least to the naked eye.

Noor, their Egyptologist, had told them that the barren space had been chosen on purpose, that the kings of the New Kingdom, fearing for the safety of their rich burials, had adopted a new plan of concealing their tombs in a lonely valley in the western hills behind Deir el-Bahari. And so there, in tombs sunk deep into the heart of the mountain, pharaohs were interred along with several queens, and the numerous sons of Ramses II, the beloved ruler who had constructed Abu Simbel. Although each burial chamber greatly varied from one to the next, all featured a descending corridor that was interrupted by deep shafts to baffle robbers, and by pillared chambers or vestibules. "Not that it worked," she had said adding, "virtually all of the tombs in the valley were cleared out in antiquity, a combination of some having been partially robbed during the New Kingdom but all the rest having been systematically denuded of their contents in the 21st dynasty, an effort to protect the royal mummies but also to recycle the rich funerary goods back into the royal treasury."

Growing up, one of Jimmy's favorite movies had been *Lawrence of Arabia*. For Halloween one year, he even dressed up as the infamous Brit turned de facto Arab leader, wearing a flowing white sheet with a cut-up pillow case adorning his head to serve as his *keffiyeh,* the traditional Middle Eastern headdress worn by men. Jimmy knew T.E. Lawrence had certainly been to Egypt. He wondered, though, if he had ever visited the Valley of the Kings, stood where he was standing right now. Jimmy had spent his entire life surrounded by people- he had grown up in Philadelphia, attended college in New York City where he stayed after graduating. But here was the most "alone" he had ever been, no signs of the coming 21st century anywhere. What a marvelous feeling it was.

"Now if you think these tombs were impressive, wait till tomorrow when we visit the Temple of Hatshepsut and you see it in the early morning light," Noor said after they all had boarded the bus. "There's nothing else like it."

17 November 1997
Temple of Hatshepsut- Deir el-Bahari

8 a.m.

Unlike in the Valley of the Kings where the tombs were built so elaborately and deep into the desert valley, you would never know they were there unless someone told you, here everything was prominently visible in a spectacular "look at me" fashion. The entire structure was designed to blend organically with the surrounding landscape and the towering cliffs. Its three massive terraces seemed almost to rise above the desert floor and into the sheer, stark cliffs of Deir el-Bahari.

"It almost looks Greek to me," Jimmy said aloud as they came upon the temple, its pillared porticos making him think of his *yiayia's* birthplace, not that to his knowledge, Corfu had any ancient Greek temples still standing.

"Yes, it's undoubtedly a unique blend of Ancient Egyptian and Classical Greek architecture," Noor said from behind as she hurried to get to the head of their group.

"I'm so glad I'm still able to do this," Eleanor murmured as she, Jimmy, and Lux began their ascent up the first of the three terraces.

When they got to the middle terrace, pausing to allow Eleanor time to rest, Lux asked, "Shall we take a picture of us here?"

"Let's," Eleanor replied.

8:45 a.m.

"Do you hear that?" Eleanor asked, a slightly worried look on her face.

"Hear what?" Lux and Jimmy both asked at the same time.

"I think someone's shooting at that dog that was bothering people when we came in," Eleanor said, looking over the terrace wall towards the entrance below. But then she saw the dog, still angrily barking, but not at all in harm's way.

She tried to place where she had heard the pop-popping of automatic rifle fire coming from and then she looked down in confusion when she noticed two tourists who had been standing on a ramp taking pictures, all of a sudden drop over like rag dolls, like dominoes. She tried to make sense of what she had just seen when a rush of horror came over her at the sight of two men sprinting up the ramp, each carrying an assault rifle.

And then it was Lux who cried out in horror when an Asian tourist was shot in the face at close range by one of the assailants, her face seeming to explode in a million bloody pieces.

"We need to run and hide, now!" Jimmy screamed, grabbing

Eleanor's arm, not caring how rough he was being. Lux was rendered frozen in place, horrified at what she had just seen.

"Lux, now!" Jimmy yelled at her.

And it was the sound of Jimmy screaming her name that finally broke her from the nightmarish trance she had been in.

She ran after Jimmy and Eleanor, who was being almost dragged by Jimmy, so determined was he to find a safe place for them, all while the sickening sound of gunfire mixed with screams and commands and what sounded like rallying cries in Arabic was being heard.

"Here," Jimmy called out, quickly clambering over a wall and then reaching out his hands to help pull Eleanor over and then Lux, where they crouched down. Lux could see they were in a small ruined enclosure and it dawned on her the irony in that moment, that she'd escape death at the hands of Islamic terrorists only to die from a scorpion bite. Just like her father had all those years ago, just across the river from where she was now.

"Jimmy, will you do something for me? One day?"

Jimmy was at his yiayia's bedside, the hospice care staff saying that it would be any day now. His yiayia had always seemed tiny to him, even as a kid, but now lying against the big, fluffy, white pillows, her frame reduced even further by the spreading cancer in her body, she looked even more so.

"Anything, Yiayia." Jimmy said, siting down on the edge of the bed, careful as not to disturb her, taking her frail, withered hand in his. It was cold even though outside it was a hot 90-degree day.

"One day, I want you to go to Egypt. For me. It will all be paid for, you won't have to worry about that."

"Egypt?" Jimmy was confused, not sure if it was the morphine talking since never once had she mentioned Egypt before. The last couple of weeks she'd seemed out of it, more often than not, once even calling him James, his grandfather's name and who he was named after. But looking into her eyes, Jimmy saw they were alert and focused directly on him.

"Why there?"

She ignored the question and went on. "Do you remember when you were a child, you saw that man who had the numbers tattooed on his arm and you asked me why he had those numbers and what did they mean?"

"What??" Jimmy wondered if he should go and get his mom because none of what she was saying was making any sense, alert eyes or not. Is this the end he wondered? Is she going to die any moment now? Slip into unconsciousness, never to wake up? But he looked at her again, and she was still staring intently at him. So he played along.

"Um yes. I remember you telling me that your family didn't have numbers because they had all been killed. That only those who were chosen to work in the camps received a tattoo. But you never had one because you were hidden during the war on the mainland."

"I was never hidden, Jimmy," Yiayia said. "I've never been to the mainland. I escaped with my mama's younger brother and sister to Egypt. The plan was originally to go to Palestine. But the British still controlled it then and they made it almost impossible to enter legally. Most of the ships that set out from Rhodes and other European ports were stopped by British patrols, the detained sent to internment camps. So Uncle Kostas, he found someone that would take us to Egypt. And mama begged him to take me even though neither of them wanted to, they didn't want to be burdened with a child. But you see, I was the oldest child, she thought I had the greatest chance of survival."

Jimmy stared at her, his mouth agape. "What? Why'd you never say anything?"

Ignoring his question, she continued the story. "Kostas you see, he drowned. It was a perilous journey, it was a miracle we all didn't drown. And when we reached Egypt, Aunt Astraia and I were sent to a refugee camp in the desert, Moses Wells it was called. There was no town nearby, nothing but desert. I had escaped Hitler's camps only to be imprisoned in a British one."

Seeing Jimmy's shocked face, she clarified. "No, they were not killing centers, they did not force us to work until we died, but they were a prison all the same. Not enough food, too many people, disease still ran rampant because of the overcrowding. Aunt Astraia, she died a week before Germany surrendered. She'd had appendicitis, but it burst," Yiayia said, wiping a tear from her frail, papery cheek. "Perhaps if she'd been in a proper hospital, in a city, not a medical tent in the desert, she might have lived. But it was war and we were Jewish and our fate was sealed."

"And mom and Uncle Adonis never knew this?" Jimmy asked, incredulous over what he'd just heard.

"No," she said. "Just you. You remind me so much of Kostas. He was only a little older than you are now when we left… when he died," her voice trailed off. "I've harbored this guilt my entire life, that were it not for Astraia and Kostas, I would have died at Auschwitz with my mama and papa and little brother and sisters, and yet neither of them lived."

"But Yiayia," Jimmy said, taking her hand in his again. "You didn't cause either of their deaths. Unfortunate, heartbreaking, but you weren't in any way responsible."

"But why did God choose me to live?" Yiayia asked him, as if he were the wise teacher, and she the unknowing pupil.

"I can't answer that," he replied although he wanted to add that no one can. "So what happened after the war? Did you ever go back to Rhodes? How did you learn about what happened to your family? And how did you get to America when you were in Egypt and orphaned by then?" He peppered her with a gauntlet of questions.

"I've written everything out for you. My entire family's story. But I'm leaving it to you to tell my family's story so that they're never forgotten. I know you'll keep them alive, Jimmy, and Aunt Astraia and Uncle Kostas too, now," she said. *"And the reason I lived, the reason I survived, married, had a family, was because of Egypt. And that's why I want you to go there one day. I want you to make this journey, because I never could. And now I certainly can't,"* she added with a slight laugh. *"You and your brother, and my children, you are a living testament that I survived. And in each of you, I see my parts of my family. Egypt is why I lived."*

By nature, Jimmy was not a patient person. Whatever amount of Greek blood he had in him, it didn't contain the whole relaxed, Greek island life mentality. And so that morning at the Temple of Hatshepsut, he wasn't sure how much time had gone by from when the shooting first started, but it felt like forever, tinged with constant sounds of gunfire and bloodcurdling screams. He wondered that if he were to survive this, would he ever be able to get those horrible sounds out of his head?

He closed his eyes and thought of his *yiayia's* family, trying to imagine the horror they must have felt on the horrific journey from Rhodes to Auschwitz. Of what they must have thought about arriving at Auschwitz in the darkened night, the sobs of families as they were torn apart, the cruelty of the SS guards as they looked on in blatant indifference to the physical and emotional anguish they were causing. He wondered if his *yiayia's* family believed the lies they were told when they were sent to the gas chambers, that they were just going to have a shower.

He told himself this then- that if he were to survive today, he would go to Auschwitz. He would do what perhaps his *yiayia* had never had the mental courage to be able to, even though he'd read that many survivors had gone back to the camps, taking their families with them. He knew she had always wanted to come back to Egypt to thank its people for having saved her as a child during the war. He had done that for her because she'd never had the chance. But he would also do that, go to Auschwitz one day. He knew his *yiayia*. She was so different from his mom in every way even though they had been mother and daughter. His *yiayia* coming to terms with the past, coming full circle she'd like to say in her heavily accented English. Saying a proper goodbye to all of his *yiayia's* murdered family would do that, he thought.

And then Jimmy wasn't quite sure what had happened. Was it what people called an 'out-of-body experience?' When he opened his eyes again, he wasn't at the Temple anymore, Lux and Eleanor weren't crouched down beside him. He no longer heard the sound of gunfire. He was, wait; where was he?

Lux knew one thing. She didn't want to die here, not here, not today. But in the end when it was all said and done, would she really have a choice in the matter? The shooters had come here today with one thing in mind- to kill as many tourists as they could. And from the barrage of gunfire that seemed to never end, it appeared as if they were going to succeed.

She reached down and grabbed each of Jimmy's and Eleanor's hands, placing them within hers. She also knew this- if she was to die today, she wasn't going to die alone. She would die amongst friends, all of whom shared their own personal connection to the country.

"Excuse me, are you Lux?"

Lux stared at the smartly dressed man who looked like something out of a F. Scott Fitzgerald novel. "Yes, do I know you?" she asked, confused as to why this man who appeared from long ago was asking about her.

"Why I'm your father."

"My father?" Lux sputtered. "You're not my father. He died before I was born."

"But I am. I'm Alexander Clarkson. Your mother, Alexandra, was my wife."

"But you're dead," Lux responded, still in disbelief, still not understanding how any of this was happening. "I mean, you died! More than half a century ago. From a scorpion bite of all things! This isn't real," she said, and then kept uttering those words over and over as if they were an incantation.

"But it's real to you, right now in this moment," he calmly replied.

"How come I've never seen you before, never had you come before as you are now?" she asked, her voice now akin to that of a petulant child.

"Because you've never needed me before as you do now, as you do at this very moment."

"So I'm seeing you now because you're telling me I'm going to die? Or you mean I'm already dead?" Lux asked. "And that's why I'm finally seeing the ghost of my father."

Even though Lux was a middle-aged woman, her father looked at her as if she were a ten-year old child. "You're not dead, Lux. It's not your time to leave this life. You must believe that."

"Why should I believe you?" she asked. "And besides, I don't believe in apparitions."

"I'm not an apparition, Lux," her father said patiently. "But my soul is inextricably tied to this place. Just as yours has always been even though you had never been here before. And that's why you're seeing me now at this very moment." He paused then before adding- "Egypt has always

coursed through your blood. She's the reason you're here now, but she won't be the reason you die."

Considering that innocent people were being massacred right before her eyes, Eleanor felt a strange sense of calmness befall her. She glanced first at Jimmy, who appeared stricken, then Lux, whose skin had taken on a ghostly white pallor, tears streaming down her cheeks, but she felt none of those things. Of course, she didn't want to die at the hands of a crazed terrorist, but she reasoned that she had lived a long life, thinking then of all the people she had outlived, all the people she knew who had died well before their time- her mum, her sisters, her brothers, Antony. And then she thought of Eleni, the little Greek refugee girl who had saved her in both body and spirit, saved her from taking her own life prematurely after learning of Antony's death and thus ensured she kept on living. She thought of the talk she and Jimmy had just had, when was that? Yesterday? Heavens, could that really have just been yesterday when everything was fine and normal and she wasn't on the brink between life and death as she was at this very moment?

She had come back to Egypt to say a proper goodbye to the country that had made her a new person, the land that had allowed her to be reinvented, the posh sophisticate, not the girl who had grown up in the slums of the East End. But she had hurriedly left the country, left her adopted land, after Shepheard's and countless other Western businesses in Cairo had been destroyed by the looters in '52, once it was clear that Egypt and the rest of the colonised world wanted their countries for themselves, not only to have but to fully govern. She had been forced to sell her beloved home, Lady Stratton's home, at a loss, something she had resented for years after. So she had come back after all these years at nearly 80 to make things right in her heart, to fully come to peace with it all.

She said to herself then that if she were to make it out of this, she would take Jimmy up on his offer to locate Eleni, whether she was still alive (well, she hoped she was, she'd be what, only a little older than Lux?), how her life had gone. She'd find out. She didn't care what it would cost. She simply wanted to know.

She just never imagined that this would be the fate that would befall her now, here of all places.

"Come on dear girl, or you're going to miss it!" Antony said in a scolding but playful manner as he took Eleanor's hand in his and almost dragged her from their table. They were at Shepheard's, enjoying a night out of dinner and dancing. As he twirled her endlessly around to the big band sounds of Glenn Miller's "In the Mood," Eleanor felt ebullient then, wishing it would never end.

"I have a crazy idea," she said, almost shouting into his ear.

"What's that?" he asked, dipping her backwards so precariously low that she almost bumped heads with another dancing couple doing the same exact thing.

"We should open a dinner and dancing club just like Shepheard's only back in London."

"Straight from the horse's mouth," he said, smiling adoringly at her.

"Or maybe we WORK with Shepheard's, make it all the more official and such," she said, her voice sounding the least bit tipsy.

"Like a colonial outpost, just of the boogie woogie bugle boy variety?"

"Exactly!" Eleanor said excitedly, feeling absolutely alive just then. She glanced up at the clock, dismayed to see the late hour. "Oh, I don't wish the night to end," Eleanor said, her voice no longer carrying the

light, playful banter from just a moment ago but now rather one akin to a child refusing to go to bed.

"Last call, Cairo," he said, whispering into her ear, his breath warm on her skin. "But there's no last call for us. We'll always just be forever."

Eleanor opened her eyes, unsure of where she was. Oh good, she thought. That had all been a dream, the shooting at the Temple. She had dreamt it, nothing more. But then she sat up with a start, realizing that she had absolutely no idea where she was. She looked around and saw nothing but blankness on either side of her- it appeared that she was outside for there were no walls and yet the landscape didn't look real. It was, what did people call hospitals today? Sterile environments? Yes, that's it. It looked like a sterile environment, seeing not an ounce of colour, or anything for that matter.

She could see a man and a child off in the distance, but they were coming towards her. When they appeared closer, she saw the man was dressed in an army uniform, the child, a girl in a dress. But they both looked so peculiarly out of place, their clothing like it was from the past, from another time. They kept coming closer until Eleanor realized she recognized the man, recognized them both. And she stared dumbfounded at them. It was Antony and Eleni. But how was it that they were here together? They had never met. Eleni had come into her life after Antony's death.

And then it dawned on her. She must be dead herself. The shooting at the Temple wasn't a horrible dream, it really happened. Is that why I'm seeing them now? That since I'm dead now, I can see them too since they've already dead? But why is it that Eleni's still a child? She should be an old woman now, like herself. Well, not AS old she thought, but certainly not the girl she knew back in Cairo. But would she have recognized Eleni as an adult? She wasn't entirely sure. And a fresh wave of horror washed over her when she wondered had something happened to Eleni as a child? After her father took her? And that's why she's here in 1997, still a child?

But then the strangest thing happened. The man, Antony, her Antony, walked right through her, as if she hadn't been standing right there, and kept going. She remained motionless, stunned over what just happened as she stared after his retreating figure. But Eleni had stopped, she hadn't kept going with Antony. Eleni was still there with her now. She was holding her hand and Eleanor realized with a start that she could feel it, feel the child's hand, her touch in hers.

"It's not your time yet," Eleni said. "I'm still here with you."

CHAPTER 28

In the days and months that followed, none of them would understand why they ended up being the 'lucky ones.' Why they survived when 58 tourists and four Egyptians were brutally murdered, 12 people from their own tour group. They were not the only ones to make it out of the 'Luxor Massacre' alive, as news reports around the world were calling it, but still, Jimmy, Eleanor, and Lux couldn't help but ask themselves, "why me?"

Only after the attack had ended, when there was nothing but a period of deafening silence, a frightening stark contrast to the previous 45 minutes, did it dawn on Jimmy that never once had he heard someone firing back at the assailants. That the sound of the automatic gunfire had been one-sided the entire duration of the attack. It was only later after talking with Egyptian officials did he learn that by the assailants killing the two police guards who were posted 400 yards from the start of the assault, they completely removed any path to resistance as those two guards were the only armed security at the Temple. And reinforcements did not arrive until after the attackers had fled, after 62 people had been murdered.

They had remained hidden in their hiding place long after the attack ended, so stricken were they with the sickening fear that perhaps the assailants were still lying in wait to murder more of them, once they thought it was safe to emerge. But Jimmy had reasoned he had to determine what was going on, if anyone was coming to their rescue.

And then he saw them, Egyptian police running towards the Temple, guns at the ready, followed by a slew of what appeared to be both civilians and tour guides.

"It's over," Jimmy had said hoarsely over his shoulder to Lux and Eleanor, who were still cowering in fright. "It's over," he repeated the words and then fell to his knees, his legs giving out from under him. And for the first time in his life, he fainted.

It sounded like something out of a old Western, the reports that came out about the pursuit of the assailants. That although the attack had begun about 8:45 in the morning, it wasn't until noon that the police finally cornered the last five of the gunmen after chasing them for more than two hours through desolate desert hills and killing them all near the Valley of the Queens.

Growing up, Jimmy had loved watching old western films like *The Gunfighter* and *The Searchers* with his grandfather. He had always idolized John Wayne, often pretending to be the 'Ethan Edwards' amongst his friends, using his toy guns to take out all the 'bad guys.' Jimmy saw the 'bad guys' that day in Deir el-Bahari and he knew one thing, he never wanted to see any again, pretend or otherwise.

"Can we talk about the elephant in the room? Or maybe I should say camel since we are in Egypt after all."

The three of them had been taken to a local hospital after the attack to be checked out, but only Eleanor had been admitted on account of her blood pressure spiking and her advanced years. She was resting comfortably in her hospital bed but how small and frail she looked just then, Lux thought. How easily it could have all turned out differently, not just for Eleanor but all of them.

"What do you mean?" Lux asked, not sure where Eleanor was going with this.

"When the attack was happening, I don't know if you would call it 'blacking out' but something happened to me at the Temple. I feel like I was starting to cross over."

"Cross over?" Jimmy asked, total confusion on his face.

"To the other side," Eleanor answered. "To death." A pause then before she added, "I saw Antony. He was as fresh and vivid in my mind as if it were 1942 all over again." Then taking a deep breath she added, "I know you're going to think the next thing I say is complete stuff and nonsense but it's not. When I saw him, he started walking towards me and then he walked **through** me."

Both Jimmy and Lux regarded Eleanor as if she had completely lost it, chalking it up to the intense trauma they had just survived.

Jimmy went first. "As in, he wasn't real, just a figment of your imagination?"

Then Lux. "As in, he was a ghost?"

Ignoring both of them, Eleanor continued. "He was there with Eleni, holding her hand. Eleni stopped but he kept going. I think she's still alive. I could feel her touch."

Jimmy looked dumbfounded at Eleanor then.

"Eleni?" Lux broke in, completely confused as she hadn't been privy to the backstory of the little Greek refugee girl as Jimmy had.

Jimmy didn't believe in ghosts, he never had. Until today. Until his own out of body experience which had been what, barely 12 hours ago?

Then looking directly into the older woman's eyes, he said, "I believe you." And then in almost a whisper he added, "I saw my *yiayia* during the attack. It wasn't just me imagining her in my mind. I **SAW** her, she was right there with me."

Eleanor squeezed Jimmy's hand to let him know, she too believed him. Believed what he knew he experienced.

And then Lux completely surprised them all by proclaiming, "My father was there with me today. I saw a man I had never met, never had any memories of, only ever seen a few photographs of. He was with me, talking to me."

Her words sunk in then, the enormity of what she had just said overwhelmed her. Her father, a mythical figure who she had never met before, had come to her. And then in an almost strangled voice she said, "I finally got to meet my father," breaking down in deep sobs.

CHAPTER 29

Pittsburgh, Pennsylvania
June 2001

"Excuse me, but are you Eleni?"

The elderly woman stared back at Jimmy suspiciously, regarding his threat level, mentally determining what course of action she could take upon this stranger who'd shown at her door. But all she said was, "No one's called me that in a very long time. I'm known as Eleanor." And then looking at him quizzically she asked, "Do I know you,?" as if saying to him, how in the world did you know that?

And that's all the confirmation Jimmy needed to continue. "I think we had a mutual friend. Eleanor. Eleanor Greaves."

Eleni put her hand to her mouth and audibly gasped. "How do you...," her voice trailed her hesitantly, unsure how to continue, what to say.

"May I come in?" Jimmy asked politely, his heart nearly bursting knowing he'd finally found her, he'd finally found Eleanor's Eleni.

Eleni ushered him inside, softly closing the door behind him. "Please," she said, indicating a brown recliner for him to sit. "Can I get you anything to drink? Water? Tea? Coffee?"

He wanted to joke and say he wouldn't mind a shot of ouzo but he wasn't there yet, and Jimmy knew Eleni was not remotely there either.

"I'm good, thank you though."

They both sat silent for what seemed like an eternity but in reality Jimmy knew it couldn't have been more than a minute. It was Eleni who finally broke the ice.

"Are you Eleanor's grandson?"

Jimmy started to laugh but stopped, chiding himself because in all actuality, it was a perfectly legitimate question. He could technically have been her grandson had she had children.

"Oh, no. I met Eleanor a few years ago on a trip. To Egypt."

Eleni's eyes widened at this, at the mention of her long-ago temporary home. At the connection she had to her long-ago temporary mother.

"We were complete strangers when we met but became quite close on the tour."

"And she talked about me?" Eleni asked in an unsure voice, sounding almost like a child's.

"Not at first. You see, early on I mentioned that my grandmother had been a young girl during the war and had fled to Egypt. She was a Greek Jew."

Eleni's eyes widened once more at the mention of his *yiayia's* heritage. "She lived in Cairo?" Eleni asked incredulously. "She knew Eleanor?"

"No, I'm pretty certain my *yiayia* and Eleanor,"- Jimmy wanted to say, 'your Eleanor' but didn't- "never met. But I think initially, Eleanor deep down wondered if my *yiayia* had perhaps been-" and now he said it, "**her** Eleni."

He stayed silent for another moment, letting Eleni process it all or try to. Continuing on, "She was quite despondent when I told her what my *yiayia's* given name was, that she wasn't Eleanor."

Eleni smiled wanly then. "You keep talking in the past. Is she...gone?"

"She passed last year."

Eleni sat back in her chair, almost in a state of collapse. "I never forgot her. Never," she said this last word with her voice breaking. "My papa, he was a good man, lost so much during the war. All he wanted to do was protect me. But he never liked me talking about Eleanor, talking about Egypt, the time I was not with him."

"But why?" Jimmy asked, not understanding how a father wouldn't have encouraged his only surviving child to talk about the woman who had saved her, who had kept her safe, provided for her, loved her like she was her own.

"I suppose," Eleni began, her voice tired and weary sounding now. "He failed in his job as a father and husband by not protecting his family. That Eleanor did something he couldn't."

"But it was war, it was the Holocaust for Christ's sake!" Jimmy sputtered almost indignantly.

"I know," Eleni said, reaching out to place her gnarled hand over his. "I'm not saying I agree with it, I'm saying what was perhaps his reasoning, his rationale. Survivor's guilt, isn't that what they call it today?" Silence again. "I think for my papa, if he couldn't go back to the life he had on Corfu with mama and my little sisters, then he was going to start completely new, where there was no 'in-between.' And to him, Egypt, my years spent there, the time I was with Eleanor, that was the in-between."

"She never got over you," Jimmy said, slightly regretting uttering this because he knew it undoubtedly would hurt her and that was not his intention. But it was true. "She stayed in Egypt as long as she did because deep down a small part of her always thought you would come back, that you'd write to her, tell her how you were doing, tell her your accomplishments as you grew from a child into a young woman. Even when the anti-British sentiment in Cairo started to get bad, she stayed. She said she'd say to herself, "if I leave, little Eleni will never be able to find me again."

Now he'd done it, Eleni's eyes were brimming with tears, her cheeks already wet with those that had fallen.

"But she ultimately left?" Eleni asked in almost a whisper.

"Yes," he answered. "After the riots and total destruction of British hotels and businesses in '52."

Jimmy was anxious to change topics, change the mood of the room. He had come here for Eleanor, to do this for her, not bring to tears to an elderly woman who hadn't done anything wrong. He stood up and walked over to the bookshelf where there were a series of antique picture frames on display.

The first one was a black and white photograph of two small children, a boy and girl, twins perhaps judging by the fact that they looked identical in size. Eleni came over to stand next to him. Taking the frame in her hands, she said pointing to the figures in the picture, "My children. Antony and Eleanor," smiling at him, her tears having somewhat dried now as she looked proudly at the photograph.

"She would have loved that," Jimmy said.

"Tell me about your *yiayia*," Eleni said. "Did she ever return to Rhodes to visit?"

"No," Jimmy answered. "She'd always say Rhodes was dead to her, that her birthplace too died in the war."

They'd just finished lunch, Eleni cooking up an impromptu meal of *bourdeto* which she told him was one of Corfu's most famous dishes, a hearty and comforting stew made with all different sorts of fish that's cooked in a spicy tomato sauce. To cook an entire meal from scratch for a complete stranger, it's exactly something his *yiayia* would have done.

"It's sad isn't it," Eleni began, staring pensively into the cup of tea she held between her hands. "People always equate war with the loss of life, but it's so much more than that, it's always so much more complicated and involved."

"Never just black and white," Jimmy added.

"Americans and their idioms," Eleni said, smiling. "Although that is one I do like, I must say."

"What about you?" Jimmy asked Eleni. "Did you ever return to Corfu?"

She regarded him almost sorrowfully before saying, "No, I never had the courage." She sighed before continuing. "I think when I was still just a child, right after the war I mean, I think a small part of me felt that Nazis would still be there. Fellow Corfiots would still be there, those who had betrayed my mama and little sisters to the Nazis…" She broke off then, as if she were someplace else. "You see, when rumors got out that the Jews of the island would be arrested, sent to camps in the East, this is in 1944, when it was apparent that the Germans were indeed losing the war, especially after the D-Day, Mama paid a neighbor, someone she had known for years, to hide them. So he hid them, only to tip off the Germans ahead of time that they were there, hiding in a secret chamber in his barn. He got a reward, they were immediately arrested and imprisoned in the castle before they were deported."

"What about your father? Did he ever go back in later years?"

"Never. What's funny is that here in America, we settled in Chicago's Greektown, where he spoke Greek all the time even though he knew other languages, including some English, did the accounting books for different Greek-owned businesses, ate nothing but Greek food. Said I could only marry a Greek-American boy, someone whose family had already been in this country. I never asked why but I think he thought I'd somehow marry someone whose third cousin had deported Mama and my sisters. I know, crazy thought," Eleni said looking at him, a tired smile on her face. "But I know, deep down inside him, he hated Greece the country for ruining his life."

She stood up now and went to the shelf, where she returned with another framed picture. The man in the image had a full head of black hair and had his hands on the shoulders of a teenage girl who Jimmy assumed to be Eleni. But it was his eyes that gave Jimmy pause- they had such a look of deep haunting to them, a man who looked as if he'd been to hell and back. But Jimmy knew in a way he had been. He may not have experienced the horrors of deportations and the camps, but he was horribly affected by them all the same.

"I don't remember my papa ever truly laughing after the war," Eleni quietly said. "He would sometimes smile at things- something I'd say, something funny on the television, but it was never like before the war." Taking a deep breath, she added, "He died quite young, he wasn't even fifty when he suffered a fatal heart attack. He never saw me get married, never got to hold his grandchildren. Quite sad, really," Eleni said, dabbing at her eye with a tissue.

"Is that when you became Eleanor?" Jimmy asked.

"How well you already know me," Eleni said with a mischievous look. "But yes, he had forbidden me from talking about Eleanor, so as both my tribute and love for the woman who had saved me, I became her by taking her name after his passing. I told people I wanted to be more American, that Eleni was too foreign."

"But now I must ask. How on earth did you ever find me?"

CHAPTER 30

24 November 1997
Cairo, Egypt

"Well, I can say with the utmost certainty that when I get on that plane tomorrow, I will not be coming back here. Unlike all those years ago."

Eleanor and Jimmy were sitting outside on the terrace at the Mena House, the striking view of the pyramids directly in front of them, as they drank glasses of cold hibiscus tea. After being discharged from the hospital in Luxor, they had been taken on a private plane back to Cairo where their respective embassies and medical personnel further examined them. That was now two days ago. They would both be leaving Egypt tomorrow; Lux having already departed for Istanbul that morning.

The three of them had asked the Egyptian government staff if they could all share a room, none of them wanting to be alone. A cot had been wheeled in for Jimmy while the women took the two beds. It seemed ludicrous, the three of them crowded into one room and yet not any of them slept at night; none of them had really slept at all since before the massacre and only then when the doctors on the first day had given sedatives to both Jimmy and Lux.

Jimmy didn't say it out loud but he was undoubtedly thinking the same thing. He didn't blame Egypt or its people. As the grandson of a Holocaust survivor, he knew more than anyone how the actions of just a small few can inflict so much horror and evil upon the world. That's how he thought of the Islamic terrorists. But for Eleanor, he knew it was different. She was nearing the end of her life but she'd finally come full circle for something she had always wanted to do-say a proper goodbye to both Egypt and her memories.

"Have you spoken to your parents and your girlfriend since that first time a couple of days ago?" Eleanor asked.

"My parents, yes," Jimmy said. "My mom thinks I'm nuts for still being here." He paused then, remembering his dad's voice breaking and him breaking down into heart-wracking sobs when he called them from the hospital letting them know he was okay. His dad, who was the very definition of a man's man, had displayed emotion in a way Jimmy had never seen before. As for Kathy, his girlfriend of only five months, that was something he wasn't sure about. Before hanging up with her, her last words had been "I told you not to go." He felt doubly bad because there had been no one for Eleanor to call and check in with.

And then he voiced out loud what had been bothering him for days. "How do you just go on like nothing's happened?"

"I think," Eleanor began, "that's why they say tragedy forms bonds like nothing else."

"Yeah, but it's not as if the three of us will be able to meet once a week for dinner and drinks."

"No, but there's always the telephone and while I know many consider letter writing to be a lost art, I still thoroughly enjoy both writing AND receiving letters." Then, placing her hand on top of his, she added, "You will never be alone, Jimmy."

At this, Jimmy felt a tear roll down his cheek. Since the attack, he would feel fine, almost normal even, and then he'd feel like he could burst into tears, like he was a little boy who'd just fallen off his bike and skinned his knee.

"I've been thinking though," Eleanor began, picking at an imaginary piece of fuzz on her white capris. "I want to find Eleni."

Jimmy was taken aback, unsure how to answer.

"I know what you're thinking," taking Jimmy's silence as reason to go on. "That it's pure lunacy."

"I wasn't going to say that," Jimmy quickly added although he was sure as heck thinking it.

"That there are countless hindrances standing in my way, especially the fact that she may not even be alive. But if one thing came out of surviving Luxor, it's that I saw her. I saw her there with Antony but I also saw her not go with him. And to me, I take that as a sign she's still alive. And if she is, I would very much like to see her one more time before I pass."

"But the cost alone, Eleanor, for such an undertaking," Jimmy responded. He didn't say the other thing that was at the top of his mind-he didn't want her to be utterly heartbroken by disappointment.

"I have more money than I could ever possibly spend at this stage in my life," she said smugly. "And I can't think of a better way to spend it than finding out about the little girl I thought of as my own daughter who I've never forgotten."

"It wasn't, not at first. Well, if I'm being honest, it wasn't easy for the first year, year and half," Jimmy said. "Once I returned home to the States, I started researching areas that had large Greek immigrant populations, or at least had at one time."

"But how on earth did you think to try America?" Eleni asked, doubt appearing on her face.

"Eleanor was adamant that that's where Eleni's father," he blushed then before correcting himself, "your father would have gone. That even a place like London, more than a thousand miles from Corfu, that it was still Europe. That in its own way still bore the ashes of the war, ashes of its victims."

"Did you know that 'Holocaust' is a Greek word?" Eleni asked. She looked to the side now, to the shelf with all the picture frames. Jimmy didn't answer so she continued. "Yes, it's a word of Greek origin meaning 'sacrifice by fire.' More involuntary, I'd say, in the case of my Mama and sisters, and the six million others."

"I'm sorry, my dear. Please continue," Eleni said readjusting herself to face him again.

"Well, there's a lot of Greek communities in the States," Jimmy said, half-smiling. "But I narrowed it down to the Astoria section of Queens in New York, Boston, and Chicago. And at that point on Eleanor's behalf, I hired a private detective. And for more than a year, I felt that Eleanor was throwing her money away on this P.I. But she was adamant he not stop until all possibilities were checked and ruled out. Chicago ended up being the last place he tried."

Eleni was listening in rapt attention now, as if Jimmy were telling the most wonderful tale.

"He struck out when asking for information on your father's name or your name. Apparently, there were more Spiro Algazis and Eleni Algazis than one would have thought in Chicago's Greektown." Eleni smiled at this. "And we all surmised that by now, you'd be married and have a different last name and well, that could be anything."

"Then how?" Eleni kindly demanded.

"I had traveled to Chicago the weekend we found you, well, found a trace of you I should say. I knew enough Greek to come in handy when visiting some of the businesses that had elderly owners who hadn't really assimilated into American society, at least language wise that is. I ended up showing a picture of child Eleni to an elderly man who owned a little grocery. He said he didn't recognize the girl, but the woman there, his wife I presume, she popped out of the chair she was sitting in as if she were about to run in a race and the starter pistol had just fired. And she said, 'That's Eleni! Eleni Algazi!' And I'm not joking when I say that the three of us- me, the private detective, and her husband's jaws all dropped. This was almost a half a century ago, the woman ancient, had to be in her late 80s, early 90s even, and she recognized a picture of you from childhood as if it were just yesterday and you had just come in to buy some pasteli."

And then Jimmy was further blown away when with the utmost clarity, Eleni whispered, "Mrs. Halikiopoulos," a name she hadn't spoken since childhood.

"She couldn't remember where you had moved after getting married, she thought maybe it was Cleveland or Pittsburgh. But she remembered your husband's name and said how beautiful a bride you were on your wedding day, and how bad she felt for you having no family, well, no blood family there on your side." Eleni's father had died three months before the wedding. "But we finally had a concrete lead to go on."

And then Jimmy mentioned the elephant in the room.

"Eleanor passed away last year. She knew the trail was no longer cold when she died, but she didn't know I had found you, well, an address that is."

Eleni was overcome with a profound sense of sadness then, as if she were personally responsible for an old woman not having her end of life wish come true, by being too hard to find, by not leaving a better set of breadcrumbs in her wake.

"I told her I would keep looking for you," Jimmy said, "no matter what."

"And you did," Eleni said, incredulous to think that an old woman like her seemed so important to others, that it was worth all the time and money spent to locate her.

"Eleanor never wanted me to tell you this part, what happened to us in Egypt." Eleni didn't say anything but a look of concern passed across her face. "I'm not sure if you remember reading a couple of years ago about a terrorist massacre there at a famous tourist site."

"Not really," Eleni admitted, "but my mind isn't always the freshest." Jimmy silently laughed at this, thinking how she so quickly remembered the name of the grocer's wife from her childhood.

"We survived it, when dozens who were brutally murdered in front of us didn't. Well, me, Eleanor and another woman we had become friends with, another woman who also had a connection to Egypt like we did. There were other survivors too but that day at the Temple, the three of us all had an out of body experience you could say." He paused then to let the enormity of his words sink in. "I saw my *yiayia*, Lux, our friend, she saw her father who she'd never met but had lived in Egypt, and Eleanor saw Antony and you. She said Antony and you, well, child you that is, walked together towards her. She said Antony passed right through her as if she were a ghost, but you stopped, and she said she could tangibly feel your hand in hers. That's the sign she took that you were still alive, somewhere."

Eleni remained silent, but put her hand to her mouth.

"And here you are."

They stared at each other, each in amazement at the person before them. And then Eleni darted up and rushed into the kitchen, only to reappear a moment later with a bottle Jimmy personally knew to be ouzo and two shot glasses. Pouring each glass with a quick and skilled hand, she raised her glass to his.

"*Yiamas!*"

"*Yiamas!*"

"To Eleanor!"

"L'chaim!"

To life.

EPILOGUE

Corfu
June 2004

When Jimmy had told Lux months ago that he and Eleni were traveling to Europe together to visit Corfu and Rhodes, while on their monthly phone call, she had surprised Jimmy when she asked if she could join them. Lux, of course, had never met Eleni but just like Jimmy, felt a bond with her all the same because of Eleanor. She'd also joked that she was too close not to visit. Jimmy had immediately said yes and Eleni agreed when asked, having heard so much about Lux by then.

On the ride from the airport to Corfu Town where they would be staying, Eleni had constantly shifted in her seat, craning her neck this way and that for a better view of the surroundings. Jimmy and Lux had silently smiled at each other, both of them so happy that Eleni in her twilight years was getting this. Eleni had said more than once during the ride that it all "looked so different, so much development." Corfu had always attracted the foreigner, being controlled by many different countries and governments throughout its history- the Venetians, British, Greeks, even the French for a short time- but today, one also heard other foreign tongues being spoken. Not surprising at all, Jimmy thought. It was truly one of the most beautiful places he had ever visited.

When they walked the narrow, hilly streets of the old town, Jimmy worried it would be too much for Eleni, but the opposite was true. Being there on the island seemed to rejuvenate her, make her younger.

"It's cathartic in a way, being here," Lux said to Jimmy when Eleni had started talking animatedly to a shopkeeper who had immediately recognized Eleni's Corfiot accent, which she'd apparently never lost.

"And tomorrow?" Jimmy asked. Tomorrow would be hard, he knew. Tomorrow they'd be stepping back into the past, Eleni's past. They would be seeing her childhood home, the synagogue where she'd once worshiped with her family, and the Fortress, where her mother and sisters and the other rounded up Jews of Corfu had spent their final hours on the island before they were sent to the camps.

"She needs a proper goodbye, to both their memories and their ghosts," Lux said firmly. "I more than anyone know how important that is," alluding to her own past.

The next day early in the morning before the heat of the day got to be too much, Eleni knocked on the door of the home where she had spent the first ten years of her life. No one answered and Jimmy thought he heard her mutter to herself, "it's probably for the best" but he wasn't entirely sure. She touched the door, her hand lingering on it, as if she were taking in all of the memories from more than 70 years ago, her hand connecting to the door allowing its former inhabitants to go with her.

When they stood in the middle of the Kato Platia, the main square of the old town where the island's Jewish inhabitants were ordered to meet on 9 June 1944 before they were taken to the old Venetian fortress nearby, Eleni's eyes brimmed with tears.

At the Holocaust Memorial for the 2000 Jewish citizens of Corfu who'd perished in the far-off camps of Auschwitz and Birkenau, Eleni looked grimly at it, the bronze sculpture depicting a naked family of four, the text on its plaque reading, "Never again for any nation."

"I think my biggest problem with memorials such as these," Eleni said, still staring at it, "is that they don't remember the individual victim. They're all just lumped together as if it's the ingredients you add to a mixing bowl when baking."

It was at the fort where Eleni's steel resolve finally gave way to the overwhelming emotions she felt then, the enormity of where they were standing.

"They make what happened in the Holocaust all about the numbers- this many people killed, this many victims from here, from there," Eleni trailed off, staring out into the open water that surrounded the fortress' walls. "Did you know that over a million of the six million victims of the Holocaust were children?" Eleni stated, neither Jimmy nor Lux knowing if she meant this to be a rhetorical question. "Children who never got to grow up. Who weren't just 'lost boys,' but permanent lost souls. Like my little sisters, Erini and Areti," Eleni said, tears streaming down her cheeks. "I've spent my whole life wondering what type of people they would have become, would they have remained my annoying little sisters as grown women or been best friends to me? Even something as simple as what they'd look like at 20, 50, old women like me now?" she added, smiling faintly now.

Lux then pulled three small stones out of her tote bag and Jimmy could see there was writing, Greek characters on them. She turned to Eleni and said, "Although I'm not Jewish, I have a good Jewish friend who told me about the custom of placing small stones on Jewish graves in an act of remembrance for the dead. I had your mama's and sisters' names inscribed on each one."

Eleni gasped, putting her hand to her mouth, as she took the stones from Lux, carefully studying each one.

"I know they have no gravesite, but I know that here, where we're standing now were their last moments on Corfu," Lux continued. "I thought that maybe here we can place them in a spot where perhaps they wouldn't be disturbed or moved like they would be at your childhood home or even the other Holocaust Memorial in the old town."

Eleni was shaking now, Jimmy could see, but she drew in a deep breath and said, "Thank you," taking Lux's hand and squeezing it and then Jimmy's too.

"She would love this," Jimmy said, sitting back in his seat, completely stuffed from all the food he'd just eaten. They'd all ordered different dishes so they could all try each other's- Eleni had ordered the sofrito, a traditional Corfiot beef stew that had a sauce made from parsley and spices that are used to marinate the veal; Jimmy, the pastitsada, a pasta dish topped with meat braised in a spicy tomato-based sauce; and Lux, the kleftiko, slow-roasted lamb that's cooked in parchment with potatoes and vegetables. And now, the three of them had split a slice of sykomaida, a dried fig cake made with wine and ouzo. It was not at all the type of dessert that Jimmy was expecting or preferred but Eleni had just said as she almost lovingly stared at it, "my mama would make this for us for our birthdays."

They'd come to the village of Pelekas in the early afternoon, at first wandering its streets that were dotted with bougainvillea-covered stone houses that sat amongst olive groves and vineyards. Just below were some of the prettiest, unspoiled, sandy beaches and then the endless turquoise waters of the Ionian Sea. They'd come later in the day to take in the sunset as everyone on the island had told them it was the best spot to watch it as the village overlooked the island's western coastline.

Hours later when they stood at Kaiser's Throne, a former observatory that offered panoramic views of the whole island, they all watched in silent awe as the sky put on a most dazzling show for them, turning it into an artist's canvas above them with colors of gold and orange and purple and pink on display.

"I may not get back up," Eleni said as she lowered herself to the ground, "but I can't think of a better place to go if that is indeed the case."

They laughed, sitting down on either side of her, continuing to watch the show in silent, amazed wonderment.

"I didn't make the connection at the time," Lux said, pulling a worn-looking leather journal from her tote. "But I think I was indirectly tied to Eleanor. I think my parents were friends with Eleanor's husband's parents. The Sir Robert and Eliza my mother references, I think that was Antony's parents." Flipping to a page, she handed Eleni the book, pointing to a paragraph. Eleni read it, smiling, then handed it to Jimmy.

He stared, amazed at the words that were written nearly a century ago.

I consider Sir Robert and Eliza to be my dearest friends and was so honored to be asked to be baby Antony's godparent.

"It's like we, all of us, we were always destined to meet," he said. "And Egypt would have it no other way."

AUTHOR'S NOTE

When I told people I would be traveling to Egypt, most responses were, "aren't you scared?" After my successful and I might mention, completely uneventful trip there, people's first questions were, "weren't you scared?" And for each question, I'd say no.

I think for many avid world travelers like myself, traveling to Egypt is akin (in a decidedly less dangerous, physically taxing, mentally grueling, and less costly way) to reaching the top of Mt. Everest in the sense that seeing the pyramids IS the pinnacle of travel. Especially when you consider the fact that the Great Pyramid of Giza is the only ancient Wonder of the World still standing. And when you see it up close for the first time and know that it's thousands of years old, well, wonders (ancient or not) will never cease to amaze you.

Although I've talked to many people who had been to Cairo, seen the pyramids of Giza (there are three in total at that site, although the name 'Great' only applies to the largest one), many never saw more than the Egyptian capital and its environs. For me, traveling all that way, I couldn't come and stop there. So I booked a Nile River cruise which would have me sailing "up." (Elementary school geography lessons, remember folks, the Nile River flows from south to north, so traveling south in the country actually means you are sailing "up" the longest river in the world.) I also likened Egypt to Peru- a country most well-known for its own wonder of the world, the Inca city high in the Andes, yet is home to other incredible and breathtaking pre-Colombian sites. Sure, there's (hopefully) not a single person who couldn't recognize the Great Pyramid of Giza. But what about Saqqara, home to Egypt's oldest pyramid, or Karnak, home to the second largest temple in the world (following only after Angkor Wat in Cambodia which I've also seen), or Kom Ombo, a name I had never heard prior to booking my trip. Yet I would learn (and see) this beautiful double-temple which was dedicated to not one, but two gods, one of which was a crocodile god and the temple actually had on display mummified crocodiles from ancient times. Yes, this was entirely ghoulish and bone-chilling creepy to me; mummified humans I'm okay with, mummified crocs, not so much. For almost any country, there's so much more to it than just the number one most globally recognized site.

Sadly, my sailing vessel was not as lovely or Old World feeling as the SS Sudan, the historic steamboat featured in Agatha Christie's beloved work, *Death on the Nile*. But there were also no deaths taking place on board, so that was entirely a good thing. But I got to spend one of the most incredible 10 days in one of the most amazing countries from a tourist sight perspective on this earth.

Earlier that year I had visited Budapest, Hungary, a city I had long wanted to see. And as was the case with *The Auschwitz Photograph* (previously published as *The Dead Are Resting)* after visiting Berlin, Germany, and *Red Clay Ashes* after visiting Vietnam, I returned from Hungary thinking I would set my next book there, a story set after World War II when the country was under brutal Soviet rule and would of course, culminate in the events of the Hungarian Uprising in 1956. But then I went to Egypt and everything changed, at least in terms of where I wanted to set my next book.

When I was in elementary school in the 90s, I remember there were constantly news reports about a terrorist attack in Egypt. And I vaguely remembered there being a particularly heinous one in the late 1990s. But then the events of September 11 happened only a couple of years later and terrorism carried out by Islamic fundamentalists was no longer confined to the "dangerous" Middle East but was now happening in America and countless European countries (France, Spain, England, Belgium).

I go to Europe frequently enough where the sight of police officers brandishing huge weapons on the streets or in train stations as they're patrolling doesn't faze me. It was the same in Egypt, just more so. Every time our motor coach arrived back at our hotel in Cairo, it had to stop for a bomb sweep. And while the hotel had metal detectors that guests were supposed to use, we were frequently waved through. But on the first day of touring in Cairo, a man in a suit and tie came aboard and our tour director told us the man's name and explained that in Egypt, as part of the government's efforts to protect its tourists, tourism being its most lucrative enterprise, all groups were assigned an armed escort. More often than not, the escorts brought up the rear with those who had ambulatory issues and couldn't walk as fast as the rest of the group. Most of the time they were middle-aged men but our day in the Valley of the Kings, our escort was actually young and particularly good-looking (to me he resembled Cristiano Ronaldo, and he even told me I was beautiful- I should add that even in my mid-30s, I was the youngest person in the group by far). But Egyptian men were constantly telling me this as I looked straight ahead, walking as fast as I could (oh, and a couple also called me Shakira which I never quite got since I don't really feel we share much of a resemblance outside of having long hair?).

But the further south we went in the country (or the more we ventured into Upper Egypt) the broader the security measures seemed. At the Aswan Airport, there were multiple metal detectors to pass through and in the village of Abu Simbel (more on the famous temple in a little bit), there were Humvees at various areas on the streets, soldiers sitting in the machine gun mount at the ready. This was the only time I felt a bit disconcerted since this seemed more of a sight you'd see on the streets of Basra and Kabul, cities in war-torn nations. Although Egypt has done a very good job at battling insurgents, in the south (or Upper Egypt), the dangerous threat still persists.

It was only after I returned home, did the sheer enormity of where I had been truly sink in, especially after reading up on the Luxor Massacre that happened in 1997. On 17 November, 62 people, the majority of whom were tourists, were brutally killed at Dayr al-Bahri, a famous archaeological site located across the Nile from the city of Luxor. It was carried out by members of al-Jama'a al-Islamiyya, an Egyptian Sunni Islamist movement, and considered a terrorist organization by multiple Western nations. Dayr al-Bahri is home to the Mortuary Temple of Hatshepsut, a truly sublime masterpiece of ancient architecture that was built into the cliffs there. If you've ever been to Dayr al-Bahri or seen in-depth pictures of it, you'll know or realize that there's not really any place you can hide. And you can see how so many people ended up being killed. When you visit a place like a concentration camp or a plantation in America's South and tour the former slave quarters, these were places that were constructed for completely evil and heinous intentions. A place like the Mortuary Temple of Hatshepsut, a tourist site that, once it was "rediscovered" by Western archeologists, was meant to exemplify a marvel of the ancient past. But realizing I had stood where people in modern times were gunned down, shook me in a way. So it was at that time I ended up going down a rabbit hole of Egypt's modern past in regards to its incidents of terrorism from a tourist perspective.

I discovered that the reason Nile River cruises don't start in Cairo is due to the threat of terrorism that still exists in the area between Cairo and Luxor (one takes a quick flight between the two cities where you then board your ship). This practice ceased in the 1970s/1980s timeframe (if you ever did read *Death on the Nile,* the journey on board the SS Sudan began in Cairo). I also learned that at one time, tourists could traverse the areas between Dayr al-Bahri and the Valley of the Kings/Valley of the Queens (where the pharaohs and queens were once buried). This also ceased due to the danger threat that emanated from terrorists hiding out (and it was in these hills where the assailants from the Luxor Massacre were ultimately apprehended and killed). The landscape is very reminiscent of America's Old West, a la Butch Cassidy and the Sundance Kid and other infamous outlaws.

But let me backtrack a tiny bit and let you know how I ended up writing a novel set in Egypt.

Although I absolutely adored seeing the myriad of sites that comprise ancient Egypt, I don't have much interest in reading historical fiction about it, namely because it's so interpretative. Obviously, we have no idea how the people of ancient Egypt talked or things they talked about beyond what is recorded in hieroglyphics. And I've also always been an individual more interested in modern history and by modern I mean roughly the last 150 years. I've always been interested in the famed Golden Age of travel, colonial empire outposts, and of course, anything having to do with World War II. Even the beloved British television series *Downton Abbey* has its own Egypt connections- the real life earl of Highclere Castle (the name of the real-life estate), the 5th Earl of Carnarvon, was obsessed with ancient Egypt. Although he had initially traveled there for health reasons with its warm, dry climate, the Earl soon began to fund archaeological digs in Egypt, including the most famous one of all when in 1922, Howard Carter discovered the never before seen/completely sealed tomb of King Tutankhamun in the Valley of the Kings. Tragically, just like the character of Alexander who suffers a fatal scorpion bite, Lord Carnarvon suffered a severe mosquito bite, which became infected after a razor cut, resulting in blood poisoning that progressed to pneumonia. And there are those who believed at the time (and some who still do) that those who had a hand in discovering and unsealing the Boy King's tomb were forever cursed. Arthur Conan Doyle even told the American press that 'an evil elemental' spirit created by priests in ancient Egypt to protect the mummy could have caused Carnarvon's death. Is there any truth or validity to those claims? No one will ever know, although in succeeding years there were a series of deaths of various members of Carter's team and visitors to the unearthed tomb who died in violent or under unusual circumstances.

While utterly cheesy (and somewhat outdated when you compare its special effects with those of today), *The Mummy* movie starring Brendan Fraser and my favorite, Rachel Weisz, is one of my favorites (especially since Weisz's character just happens to be a nerdy bookworm who catalogs books and other artifacts). But I really love the time period that it's set in right around the King Tut mania that took the world by storm. During the Second World War, my paternal grandfather served in the United States Army Air Corps, fighting in the North Africa campaign. Tunisia was as far east as he went, but Egypt (from a British perspective), was a major player in the war. Cairo, the hotbed of it all, was the ultimate victor's coup, although Hitler's commander, the Desert Fox, never quite made it there.

And then of there is the matter of the Greek Jews during the Holocaust. Although much has been written on the fate of the Hungarian Jews and how their mass deportations happened in the waning months of the war, when it was clear that Germany was not going to win, little is said on the fate of the Greek Jewish populations, specifically those from the islands of Rhodes and Corfu. They too had stayed relatively safe during the early years of the war since it was Italy and its Fascists who governed the island, not the Germans. But once Italy surrendered to the Allies in 1943, situations on the islands for the Greek Jews became much more dire and many fled- to places like Turkey and Syria and many south to Egypt. As a huge fan of the television series *The Durrells in Corfu,* I loved the idea of having a connection to Corfu, even if it was a tragic one. But a sobering and heartbreaking fact- on the eve of the Second World War, the Jewish community of Corfu had 2000 members (small compared to that of Hungary's but within a far smaller overall population too). After the war, fewer than 200 had survived. Today, there are only around 60.

But what I loved even more was the idea of tying these times and storylines all together with characters who overlapped, either directly or indirectly. And while some may think it all fits together a little too perfectly or it's all too "Dickensian" that is where the beauty of historical fiction lies. Although I pride myself on the level of historical accuracy in my books with the extensive research I do prior to writing, I allow myself some of those "what are the odds" because I can, because it's fiction (i.e. Eleanor happening to meet and fall in love with the son of Eliza who happened to have been good friends once with Alexandra and Alexander).

As someone who's been to 40 countries, I consider myself an intrepid traveler and explorer. But I'm doing my travels in the 21st century where I have the added benefit of countless modern innovations that make travel so infinitely easy, effortless even- smart phones... Google maps that have GPS... high speed travel... and of course, air-conditioning. But when I first started doing my research, I came across the names of unknown but amazing female figures who, considering the time in history in which they were traveling and exploring Egypt, were truly intrepid explorers. Lady Duff-Gordon, who I reference in *Last Call, Cairo* because she was so well-known amongst the 19th/early 20 century globetrotting set, perhaps started the romantic obsession with travel to the once ancient Egypt. Although she left the damp streets of London to spend the final years of her life in the desert climate of Egypt in an attempt to contain her tuberculosis, she ended up falling madly in love with both the country and its people, a rarity in the 19th century when the "other" was hardly considered equal to the white race. Although famous for her work in the Crimean Peninsula where she served as a nurse during the Crimean War, Florence Nightingale actually traveled up the Nile on a *dahabiya* in 1849-50. And then there's Amelia Edwards, who toured Egypt in the winter of 1873-74 and upon her return to her native England, wrote a vivid account of her journey, *A Thousand Miles up the Nile* which was published in 1877. She would go on to become a staunch advocate for the preservation and research of ancient monuments in Egypt. For all the names we do know of the female explorers, there are many more we don't remember but who traveled there, blazing the way for travelers like myself more than one hundred years later.

If there's one book I absolutely recommend you read that will make the "modern-day" past of Egypt come alive, it's *Empress of the Nile: The Daredevil Archaeologist Who Saved Egypt's Ancient Temples from Destruction* by Lynne Olson. Another forgotten name in women's history is Christiane Desroches-Noblecourt. A Frenchwoman, she entered the field of archaeology in the 1920s when it was still very much a man's game. But she didn't let gender bias or discrimination deter her from doing what she loved the most-studying ancient Egypt. She participated on countless digs, never once letting her gender define what she was capable of doing, truly a real-life Indiana Jones. And with the outbreak of war, she also became a member of the French Resistance, risking her life and surviving imprisonment by the Nazis. She led the efforts to save Abu Simbel and other ancient Egyptian temples from the floodwaters of the Aswan Dam in the 1960s. Although Abu Simbel, Ramses II's epic he built to honor himself and his wife had survived thousands of years, it was the threat of modernity that almost caused its permanent demise. A new dam was being constructed along the Nile River and while it would improve irrigation throughout the valley as well as significantly increase Egypt's hydroelectric output, in just a few years its swelling waters would also completely submerge Abu Simbel's magnificent temples and other prized sites in the former Nubian Kingdom. (For reference, this is in southern Egypt, or Upper Egypt, near to the border of modern-day Sudan.)

Well, Desroches-Noblecourt would have none of it, not taking no for an answer. She galvanized a world-wide campaign to save the temples, a project that would take years and millions of dollars, one in which the several thousand year-old fragile sandstone temples were dismantled piece by piece and rebuilt on higher ground.

Originally, I wasn't planning on visiting Abu Simbel as it was an extra cost, would require another plane ride from Aswan (along with a 3AM wakeup), and result in a terribly long day. I likened it to the adage, "you've seen one, you've seen them all." But there's nothing else like it. And when you know the full history behind it, its modern-day history, it will leave you all the more speechless, especially when you consider that it could be underwater now were it not for a very brave French woman.

My only disappointment in Abu Simbel? Well, unlike in *Death on the Nile* or any number of the beautiful watercolor paintings and illustrations you see from Egypt's Golden Age of Travel, where travelers disembark right at the shore's edge and voila, there are the temples, today it's decidedly less romantic. You'll be dropped off in a parking lot along with hundreds of other visitors and then feel like sardines in a can when you step inside the temples themselves. That's probably why I enjoyed my visit to Kom Ombo Temple so much; it's the only ancient Egyptian temple today where you disembark from your vessel right at the temple.

But I digress. Back to the story. Although some may think it morbid to include a horrific event like the Luxor Massacre in the book, it was the circumstances of the event that had the characters and each of their personal connections to Egypt that saved them. I'm not a religious person but I am a spiritual one and while I've never had an out of body experience, I do believe in them. I also believe in the concept of having people, loved ones who've passed, watch over us. And that is how I thought of the characters of Alexander, Antony, and Jimmy's *yiayia* during the scene in Deir el-Bahari.

Egypt has enchanted visitors with both its storied ancient history and its awe-inspiring sites for hundreds of years. And a trip there makes it easy to see why. But for now, I hope that by reading *Last Call, Cairo* you were able to be transported there too, at least until you book that trip.

REFERENCES

Cooper, Artemis. *Cairo in the War: 1939-45.* John Murray Press, 2013.

Cowell, Malcolm, et al. "Luxor Survivors Say Killers Fired Methodically." *New York Times,* 24 Nov. 1997, https://www.nytimes.com/1997/11/24/world/luxor-survivors-say-killers-fired-methodically.html. Accessed 9 Apr. 2024.

Frank, Michael. *One Hundred Saturdays: Stella Levi and the Search for a Lost World.* Avid Reader Press/Simon & Schuster, 2022.

Humphreys, Andrew. *Grand Hotels of Egypt: In the Golden Age of Travel.* The American University in Cairo Press, 2015.

Humphreys, Andrew. *On the Nile in the Golden Age of Travel.* The American University in Cairo Press, 2021.

Naunton, Chris. *Egyptologists' Notebooks: The Golden Age of Nile Exploration in Words, Pictures, Plans, and Letters.* Getty Publications, 2020.

Olson, Lynne. *Empress of the Nile: The Daredevil Archaeologist Who Saved Egypt's Ancient Temples from Destruction.* Random House, 2023.

Pasquet, Yannick. "How the Few Jews Left on the Greek Island of Corfu hold onto their history." *The Forward,* 19 Feb. 2022, https://forward.com/news/482721/corfu-jews-greece/. Accessed 20 Mar. 2024.

Wilkinson, Toby. *The Nile: Travelling Downriver Through Egypt's Past and Present.* Vintage; Reprint edition, 2015.

Wilkinson, Toby. *A World Beneath the Sands: The Golden Age of Egyptology.* W.W. Norton & Company, 2022.

BOOK CLUB
DISCUSSION QUESTIONS

1. Has reading *Last Call, Cairo* made you want to travel to Egypt and sail up the Nile? What ancient Egyptian site would you like to see the most?

2. What do you think it is about Egypt that has intrigued and captivated travelers for centuries?

3. Do you think Alexandra should have gone against her father's wishes and run off with Alexander when he asked her to? Break the heart of a dying man or the man she truly loved?

4. The fact that Alexandra and Alexander were able to find each other again after all those years apart and with Alexander surviving the horrors of the Great War, do you think it was a case of pure kismet or Alexandra's father looking out for his daughter from the other side? Putting to right the mistakes of the past?

5. Were you surprised to learn that in the golden age of Egyptology it was quite easy to be an "amateur" archaeologist and as the saying

goes, "start digging?" That is, provided you had the financial backing of a wealthy benefactor like Howard Carter had with the 5th Earl of Carnarvon when he made the discovery of a lifetime with the 'Boy King's tomb being found (King Tutankhamun).

6. If you had suffered a heartbreaking tragedy like Alexandra had after her husband died from the scorpion bite, would you too have never returned to Egypt, even if it meant your own child never knowing fully where she came from or learning about the place that her father had loved so?

7. Do you think Eleanor genuinely loved Egypt or would have loved any country or place that gave her a fresh start, a chance to reinvent herself, become someone other than the girl from the slums of East London?

8. Did you have a sense that Eleanor and Antony's love affair would never be able to be more than a "wartime romance?" Do you think his death is the reason why Eleni showed up on her doorstep when she was at her lowest point emotionally?

9. If you were Eleanor, would you have taken Eleni in and treated her like she was your own child? Or would you have turned her over to the authorities?

10. Do you think Eleni's father was right to permanently sever contact with Eleanor after he came for his daughter?

11. Were you shocked to learn about what had happened to the Greek Jews during the Holocaust? Do you think this is a period of history not many people are aware of, especially since when

one thinks of the Holocaust and its victims, they don't usually think of Greece?

12. As you were reading Part III, did you initially think that Eleni was Jimmy's grandmother, especially after discovering she too was a Greek Jew who had fled to Egypt during the war? Were you disappointed to learn she wasn't?

13. Do you think the characters of Lux, Eleanor, and Jimmy were brought together for a reason? That they traveled to Egypt, booked the same tour at the same time because they were meant to?

14. Throughout *Last Call, Cairo,* all of the main characters seem to have their guardian angels watching out for them, making sure they not only survive but in the case of Alexandra learning she was pregnant after Alexander's tragic and sudden death, so she was never truly without him, she had a living legacy with her. Do you believe all of us have our own guardian angels whose "metaphorical glass is broken in the case of an emergency?"

15. A quote by the author of *Peter and Wendy* (more popularly known today as *Peter Pan*)- "Never say goodbye because goodbye means going away and going away means forgetting"- is referenced throughout *Last Call, Cairo.* Do you think this is something the characters subscribe to? Is it something you will or do subscribe to?

Pyramids of Giza- Egypt
December 2022

Julie Tulba is the author of the historical fiction books, *Red Clay Ashes*, *The Auschwitz Photograph* (originally published as *The Dead Are Resting*) and *The Tears of Yesteryear*. It was series like Dear America, Little House on the Prairie, and American Girl that instilled in Julie at a young age her lifelong love and fascination with history. And a childhood spent growing up in Philadelphia, colonial America's foremost metropolis, further cemented this love affair. She lives in the Pittsburgh area, passport always at the ready for her next international adventure, but also brainstorming ideas for her next novel. For more information, please visit her website, www.julietulba.com.